SEETEE SHIP

SEETEE SHIP

JACK WILLIAMSON

BART

NEW YORK

Reprinted by arrangement with the author

ISBN: 1-55785-110-7

First Bart Books edition: June 1989

Bart Books
155 E. 34th Street
New York, New York 10016

Manufactured in the United States of America

SEETEE (from **CONTRATERRENE, CT; ANTI-MATTER**). *An inverted type of matter, foreign to the Earth but forming many meteors, comets, and asteroids. Seetee atoms are inside out, electrically, with negative nuclei and positive electrons. An invisible difference—but deadly. Seetee looks like the common terrene stuff of Earth and men—until they touch. But then unlike charges cancel out. Unlike particles explode into free energy, at the rate stated in the famous Einstein equation. That ultimate reaction makes uranium fission seem feeble as a safety match, yet there are men who talk of taming it. Spatial engineers, dreamers like Brand and Drake, who talk of seetee machines, run by remote control, to mine and refine contraterrene ores and feed contraterrene power plants. They are fools. Seetee is untouchable. A safe bedplate, to support contraterrene tools on terrene foundations, is impossible by definition. For all such reckless talk, the seetee drift seems certain to remain importantly only as the supreme hazard to interplanetary navigation.*

—SPACEMAN'S HANDBOOK
By Captain Paul Anders, HSG

For Larry, Don and Neil,
who are sturdily striving
to reach the untouchable

Chapter 1
The High Frontier

PALLASPORT WAS a fleck of life on dead Pallas. A raw frontier town, on a mountain peak that the spatial engineers had drilled for paragravity and wrapped in a thin wisp of synthetic air. A new, gaudy, flimsy, brawling town of rootless adventurers, yet it was the capital of all the far-flung asteroids of the High Space Mandate.

Rick Drake got back there from Earth, on a March morning of 2190, aboard the *Planetania*. He had spent four years at Solar City earning his degree in spatial engineering, and now he had come back to the Mandate, with his new degree and his daring dreams and not much else, to build a seetee bedplate.

He was a long time getting off the liner, because he had worked his way out, standing dangerous watches with the collision crew. He had to make his reports and check in his repair tools and dirigible armor, and wait aboard until the paying passengers were off.

He came out on the long gangway at last, a lean young giant with bright blue eyes and bronze-red hair, tramping restlessly after a long line of bonded laborers shuffling down toward the customs and immigration men.

He looked hopefully around for someone he knew. His home on the little asteroid Obania was still twenty million kilometers away, but few ships ever called there in these hard times. He was hoping that his father would be here to meet him, or at least old Rob McGee.

Ships like silver spires stood crowded on the rounded mountain top, but none of them was McGee's battered tug, the *Good-by Jane*. Men of all the planets swarmed

7

over the ramps and ways around them. A furious Venusian-Cantonese importer shrilly pursued a ragged urchin, running away with a stolen orange. A stern Martian-German officer in the neat black of the High Space Guard snarled harsh gutturals at a quivering young recruit, still pink-cheeked from Earth, who must have failed to salute. A huge, black-bearded Callistonian stood silently overseeing a gang of tired asterite stevedores transferring heavy crates stenciled MINING MACHINERY from the *Planetania* to the holds of the freighter *Ivanov*, smiling as serenely as if each long crate held an illicit spatial rifle for the Jovian Soviet. A soft-fleshed, hard-eyed Interplanet buyer haggled in clipped Earth-English with two lean rock rats for a few heavy bags of thorium ore. Men of every planet that schemed and strove for the shrinking wealth of the Mandate—but none of them was gaunt old Jim Drake, or his gnarled little asterite partner.

Disappointment erased Rick's eager smile, and cold worry pinched his rawboned face. Private contraterrene research was frowned upon by Mandate officials afraid of seetee bombs. Though Drake and McGee had never planned to mount any sort of weapon on the seetee bedplate, Rick flinched from a sudden pang of fear that something had got them into trouble.

Frowning uneasily, he decided to call his father's office on Obania. He was afraid to make any open reference to seetee—too many power-hungry planets had too many secret agents tapping the photophone beams. But he had to find out whether anything was wrong. Restlessly, he hitched his space bag higher on his shoulder, and inched impatiently on down the gangway behind the line of overalled bondsmen.

"Miss Karen Hood!" A steward in line behind him reached appreciatively to nudge his arm and turned to stare again. "The High Commissioner's niece, you know. With twenty-seven pieces of that monogrammed luggage, and never mind the excess weight. Look at her! Something, huh? And her uncle up to meet her, in that official car."

8

Rick looked. Although they had come all the way from Earth on the *Planetania*, he hadn't met Karen Hood on board. They couldn't meet, because they belonged to different worlds. She owned Interplanet shares. That made her a princess of her own proud world, for Interplanet ruled the Earth and once had owned all the rocks of the Mandate.

Yet Rick could look, and he liked what he saw. A trim redhead, so straight she seemed tall, laughing with the eager men around her on the ramp below—the young Guard officers and the junior Interplanet executives who must have dined and danced and flirted with her on the first class decks. He liked the slim shape of her in the tailored jacket and slacks, and the way she moved, lightly evading her admirers. Her smile caught his breath, when she turned to meet the fat High Commissioner.

"Something, huh?" the awed steward murmured.

But Rick shook his head, because she annoyed him. She was too beautiful for the ugly narrow streets of this cheap sheet iron town. Her place was in a penthouse, he thought, on some tall white tower back in Solar City. All she needed from these rocks was their rich metal, shipped home for her and her pampered sort to squander. He wondered for a moment why she wanted to risk her expensive neck off the Earth. Boredom, maybe. Maybe she had got tired of yachts and night spots and villas by the sea.

He nodded, in absent understanding. His own four hard years on Earth had seemed too long to him. The dull skies and the close horizons and the suffocating weight of air had made him homesick for his native rocks; for the frosty splendor of stars and darkness, for the clean freedom, the savage sun, the soundless peace and boundless space.

But she was an earthling, born to the dull security and all the smothering comforts of the mother world. He thought she wouldn't like it here, not even with the costly contents of all that monogrammed baggage to keep her lovely and all those lonely men begging her to stay. She would look at Pallasport and lift her charming nose and probably take the same ship home.

A sudden envy stabbed him, as he watched the eligible Earthmen swarming around the flame of her hair. He tried to guard himself. For she was untouchable. No asterite could hope to reach her exclusive world, any more than terrene men could grasp seetee. But Rick wasn't all asterite—she reminded him painfully of that.

Though his father's people had lived three generations on this new frontier of high space, defying the meteor swarms and the seetee drift to explore and terraform and mine the terrene rocks like Obania, his mother came from Earth. She had run away to space from an Interplanet family as old and rich and proud as Karen Hood's, to marry a rock rat named Jim Drake.

He scowled and set his jaw and shuffled down the ramp in line again, crushing out that wistful recollection. Unaware of him, the redhead slid into her uncle's long car and turned in the seat as it glided away, to wave gayly at the men she left behind.

Glad when she was gone, Rick filled his lungs with the thin, clean air and looked around him eagerly. The standing ships were a forest of tapered silver trunks, and they seemed to lean crazily apart, with those at the edge of the field jutting out insanely toward the stark desolation of Pallas, toward the wild crags of broken stone and black pits of airless shadow—because only this mountain and not the whole planetoid had been drilled for paragravity, one speck of life on a world still dead.

His blue eyes smiled at that cruel landscape, and his lean shoulders lifted the space bag lightly. The old world of Karen Hood and Interplanet had reached this far, with fission power, to plunder all the planetoids of their uranium and thorium, but now the ores were running out. The colonized planets had fought the Spatial War for those precious power metals before Rick was born, and they still fought covertly for the vanishing reserves, beneath the uneasy truce of the Mandate. But the fissionable ores would soon be gone, and her world with them.

Rick's eager eyes scarcely saw that deadly desert of naked rock and savage cold and deadly nothingness that the dying power of fission had failed to tame, for in his mind it had already been transformed with the might of reacting seetee. In the hands of the spatial engineers, that unlimited energy could clothe all the broken stone of Pallas in air and warmth and transplanted life.

All the asteroids could be tamed with contraterrene power, terraformed and reshaped into human homes. That was the dream and the driving purpose that Rick had caught from his father. He lived for that magnificent new world, which must stand—if ever it stood at all—upon a successful seetee bedplate.

Cautious Earthmen had always called that device impossible, but he was not an Earthman. These rocks were his world, and he was home again. Even though the drift was still untouchable as Karen Hood's bright hair, there had to be a way. Fissioning uranium had once seemed equally intractable, before paragravity harnessed it to conquer space. He was now a spatial engineer. With his eager pride in that, and his lean fitness, he felt competent for anything.

Worry began nibbling away his first joy at getting home, however, as the line of patient men ahead of him crawled on down toward the gates. His father should have been here, or at least McGee. When at last the slow inspectors had searched his bag and stamped his passport, he hurried to a telephone booth in the Interplanet terminal, and called Obania.

"The office of Drake and McGee," he told the operator. "I'll talk to whoever answers."

"Deposit ten dollars for ten minutes, please," the operator said, and his eagle rang in the receiver. "Hold your line for the return beam, please." He had to wait three minutes, while one thin ray of modulated light went out to find that far-off rock and another came back. "Your Obania call, sir. A Miss Ann O'Banion answers. Go ahead, please."

Ann O'Banion. . . . For a moment he couldn't go

11

ahead. Ann was the brown-eyed asterite girl who had played spaceman-and-pirates with him in the abandoned mine pits on Obania when they were young, and helped with his problems in astrogation when they were in school. She had cried a little when he left for Earth, and stayed on the rock to keep her father's house. He stood for a moment wondering what four years had done to her.

"Go ahead, sir."

"Ann, I'm coming home to—to go to work." He caught his breath, and reminded himself not to speak about seetee. "I wrote my father I wanted a job, and I was expecting him to meet me. Or Rob McGee. But the *Jane* isn't here. I wonder—I hope nothing's wrong."

He had to wait again, while the narrow beam crossed those empty millions of kilometers and brought back her voice.

"Hello, Rick. I'm so glad you're back."

Thinned to a whisper with the distance, it was still the lively voice he remembered, and it recalled the lean vividness of her brown face and the boyish cut of her dark hair—but of course she would wear it longer, now that she was grown.

"You seem surprised," she said. "I guess you hadn't heard I'm working for the firm. I know your father doesn't write, but he got your letter. He meant to go with Cap'n Rob to meet you, until—until this came up."

He heard her hesitate, and knew she was afraid to say too much.

"But don't you worry, Rick," she went on hastily—he thought too hastily. "They're both all right. They're just out at work on this new project. Your father was expecting you to call, and he told me to tell you all about it."

Yet he knew she couldn't tell him all about it. Not if it involved seetee, and her worried tone made him sure it did. Legally, as well as actually, seetee was untouchable. The laws of the Mandate required an official research and exploration license for any approach closer than one hundred kilometers to known bodies of seetee.

Drake's little firm had been granted such a license once, when he and McGee held their contract to mark the most dangerous drift with the blinkers Drake invented—colored mirrors mounted on heavy iron wheels, set to spinning like tiny satellites around the deadly rocks. The markers still flashed their warnings, all around the sun, but the commissioners had canceled Drake's survey license when they set up the Seetee Patrol.

The asterites had no member on the Commission, and Drake and McGee were just rock rats. Even though they had explored and marked so much of the drift, they were still friends of Bruce O'Banion—that tired and hopeless old agitator for the freedom of the rocks. The shrewd men of Earth and Mars and Venus and the Jovian Soviet were still a little afraid of the tough pioneers they had come to rule and bleed, Rick thought, and desperately afraid of seetee.

Ann had paused, as if she really couldn't tell him anything at all about that engineering job, but he said nothing. Too many spies might be listening in, and besides the beam would be too long taking his questions to her.

"There's a rock, four million kilometers on beyond Obania," she went on suddenly, and he thought he heard a breathless strain in her thinned and flattened voice. "A little iron asteroid, just like your father wants for a—a metallurgy lab."

He heard her faint hesitation, and knew she meant a seetee lab.

"He's working now for a legal title to it. You see, Cap'n Rob found that it's on a collision orbit—moving toward one of the little seetee planetoids they marked years ago. And they've found an old Mandate law, that anybody can claim any uninhabited rock that he finds in danger of collision with seetee, in reward for changing the orbit."

Rick nodded uneasily in the gloomy little booth. He knew about that law—passed to help prevent the blow-ups that cluttered the space lanes with new clouds of

13

deadly meteoric drift, both terrene and seetee. But how could Drake and McGee change an orbit?

"Isn't it wonderful?" the thin thread of her voice ran on. "A new asteroid of our own, for the shops and plants your father wants to build. He let me name it, when he filed the notice of danger and intention. We're going to call it Freedonia."

She didn't say why, but Rick understood. He had read Brand's book and heard his father's hopeful talk of the "fifth freedom"—of an enormous transmitter to revive all the power-starved planets with the boundless energy of seetee, broadcast free.

"Of course they haven't changed the orbit, yet," she said. "I don't even know how they hope to do it, because Freedonia weighs too many billion tons for the little *Jane* to move, and I don't think they have equipment to terraform it now. But they filed the notice, and they're trying to do it. Somehow!"

Cramped in the booth, Rick shrugged uncomfortably. A terraformed asteroid was protected from collision by the same selective paragravity field that held its artificial atmosphere, but to terraform even the smallest rock took a million dollars worth of fission reactors and tuning diamonds and condulloy cables and castings—that Drake and McGee had no million to buy.

"They're out there now, on the *Jane*." Anxiety edged her tone. "I'm not sure they have time enough—both rocks are so near the collision point that the Seetee Patrol has already diverted all shipping beyond Obania. But your father said they could do it, and McGee didn't seem afraid."

She paused uncertainly, and again he felt her worry.

"Anyhow, we'll soon know," she finished hastily, as if she had remembered all the agents who might be listening in. "I'm glad, Rick, you're coming home. But I guess you'll have to find yourself a room, and wait at Pallasport till Cap'n Rob can get there with the *Jane*."

She hung up then, with an abruptness that disturbed him.

He extracted his rawboned frame from the cramping booth, and stalked restlessly out of the terminal building with his bag on his shoulder. Out on the street, he paused to frown up at the sky southwestward, beyond the leaning ships and the thin crown of air, wondering how his father hoped to change an orbit.

All he could see was blue darkness, however, and a few steady stars creeping into view when he turned away from the purple circle around the naked glare of the dwarfed but savage sun. Those masses of terrene iron and contraterrene stuff sweeping toward collision were too far off for him to find, and he knew no way for his father and McGee to halt that cataclysm. Not unless they meant to use seetee!

He shook his head apprehensively at that, because they weren't prepared to work seetee. Nobody was. Rob McGee was almost illiterate, though that odd little asterite did have an uncanny sense of time and distance and mass and motion. The intricate science of spatial engineering had moved a long way forward, in all the years since old Jim Drake left school. Rick knew they had no safe seetee bedplate.

Yet their scheme involved seetee. That was what Ann had meant to say, with her hesitant and apprehensive mention of a metallurgy lab. The want of means and the frown of the law had forced them to gamble their lives on some untried device, in hope of winning a site for their dreamed-of laboratory—that stark conviction stiffened his big fingers on the strap of his bag.

They should have waited for him—but of course they couldn't wait, with the rocks about to collide. Space was vast, and collisions rare events; such a chance to claim an asteroid might never come their way again. But he was too late, and still too far away to offer any help. He shrugged at the somber sky and walked off the field to look for a room.

Chapter II
Fire in the Sky

HE SAW Karen Hood again on the street beside the space port—it was a noisy, dirty street of repair shops and freight warehouses, of lumbering trucks and swinging cranes and greasy mechanics and shouting stevedores. He turned unbelievingly, to look at her proud head and cataclysmic hair, because she was out of place.

If she wanted to walk about Pallasport at all, her place was on the clean avenues of expensive shops and exclusive restaurants and guarded official residences that belonged to the masters of the Mandate. Men were working here, moving cargo and overhauling ships: sweaty, grimy, common, useful men.

Yet she seemed to feel at home. Her small boots came firmly down on the trash-cluttered pavement, unafraid of honest dirt. Her blue eyes, lifted to the leaning ships and swinging booms and snake-like cargo-tubes, were bright with an interest as eager as his own.

She turned, as a writhing conveyor looped above them began spitting heavy crates into a waiting truck, and saw his admiring smile. She glanced at him curiously, at his awkward, rawboned height and his stiff bronze hair and the worn bag he carried, as if puzzled by his look of recognition.

He froze his smile, and swung hastily away. She didn't know him. She never would. She didn't belong to this busy street—but it belonged to her. She owned Interplanet shares. She had right enough to inspect these men sweating to collect the raw wealth of the rocks, because most of them were Interplanet bondsmen, still working out their passage. Except in name, they were her slaves.

He was three steps from her when it happened. A sudden glare of blinding light, silent, yet startling as a scream. It burned all the color from the glass fronts of the warehouses, and splashed the leaning ships with hot blue fire, and cast shadows like frozen ink. He didn't look toward it, but he knew what it was.

Seetee—reacting with something terrene. Attracted atoms crashing into unlike atoms and ceasing to be atoms. Mass shattered into untamed and pitiless energy, with a thousand times the fury of fissioning plutonium. He ducked his head and ran. He didn't look back, but he saw which way those hard shadows pointed.

They pointed southwestward, to where his father and Rob McGee had tried to keep those unlike asteroids from colliding. That meant they had failed. They had lost the small iron world that Ann O'Banion wanted to call Freedonia, and possibly their lives. He had come too late to help, and now there would be nothing he could do.

Rick had dropped his space bag and darted for shelter, instantly and unthinkingly, because he knew that frightful fire of annihilated matter. He knew how it shone through the body, burning flesh and blood and bones, to cause the radiation sickness spacemen called seetee shock.

The stevedores around him knew it, too. They shouted, profanely afraid. The hum and rumble of machinery was cut off. Running feet clattered on concrete. The street was suddenly drenched in silence, so still that Rick could hear Karen Hood's wondering voice behind him.

"That light—what is it?"

He looked back from the dark shelter of a narrow alley between two Interplanet warehouses, and saw her alone on the street. Standing there, flinching from that savage blaze, but shading her eyes to find its source.

"Don't look!" he gasped. "That's *seetee!*"

That shocking word should have been enough, but she didn't move. He dashed out again into that driving fire, swept her off the pavement, set her down in the alley. She wrenched away from him. Her hard little fist swung

17

at his jaw, and she ran for the street again. He ducked her fist, reaching with a long arm to snatch her bright hair and drag her back into the shadow.

"Let me go." She swung again, and hit him hard under the eye. Her angry voice held no panic. "You could lose your life this way, you know."

So could she, he tried to say, but she had found his midriff with a short punch that took his wind. He caught her elbows and pushed her back against the sheet iron wall and crushed her struggles with his weight, gasping for air enough to speak.

"Brute!" The heel of her boot came down on his instep, savagely. "Better let me go!"

He held her a moment longer, still fighting for his breath, until his narrowed eyes saw that cruel blue light redden and suddenly grow pale. The danger had passed. He released her gingerly, guarding himself.

She ran screaming for the street. Men began to reappear uneasily from the shadows where they had flung themselves, their dazzled eyes still squinted against that dying fire. A tall captain of the High Space Guard came running suddenly toward her through the jam of abandoned trucks, and her screams subsided when she saw him.

"Paul! I'm so glad—" She clung to him, trembling, and turned wrathfully to face Rick, who had started limping back to recover his dropped space bag. "That man assaulted me!" She pointed accusingly. "I had seen him staring. When I turned to look for that light, he grabbed me. Dragged me into that alley. A powerful beast, but I got away."

Rick straightened uneasily with his bag, still breathing heavily. The stevedores began scowling at him, muttering as they heard her accusation, and he remembered uncomfortably that he was just an asterite, with no commissioner to defend him.

The tall Guardsman, however, didn't seem excited. "P'raps he meant no harm, if you were really looking for that flash," he murmured to the girl, in slurred Earth-

18

English. Ignoring Rick, he smiled down at her admiringly. "Looking great, Kay! Wanted to meet your ship, but your uncle keeps me occupied. 'Specting to see you at his reception tonight, but not out here." He shook his head reprovingly. "No place for you."

"I'm all right now," she protested quickly. "Uncle Austin had to go back to a meeting, and I just slipped out to see the port." Her blue eyes flashed wrathfully at Rick. "I didn't expect to be attacked."

"P'raps you weren't." He swung quietly to Rick. "What say, mister?"

"I'm very sorry," Rick muttered awkwardly. "I was expecting a major collision. I saw Miss Hood standing in the open, looking toward the flash. I called to warn her it was seetee. She didn't move, so I carried her out of the radiation. I'm afraid she misunderstood."

" 'Parently." The tall Earthman grinned at Rick's smarting face. "Thanks, anyhow."

Karen stared blankly at Rick.

"Thanks?" she whispered sharply. "What's seetee?"

"Contraterrene matter," the Guardsman told her. "Reacting with a terrene rock. Twenty-five million kilometers away. Too far to be dangerous, you think? Well, remember there's no air in space to stop the radiation, and not much even here over Pallasport."

"You don't mean—" Her red head shook unbelievingly. "Just that light—"

"Gamma rays," he said. "The ones you don't see—and can't detect without a geiger." He touched the little safety device, no larger than his watch, on his other wrist. "But they burn deep. Cause radiation sickness."

"Oh—" She blinked at Rick, and bit her lip. "Then—then he—"

"Prob'ly saved your eyesight," the Earthman told her gently. "Poss'bly saved you from producing a mutant when you marry. Might have saved your life, if that radiation had been a little stronger."

"Oh—" She shrank against him, shuddering. "Of course I've always heard about the contraterrene drift," she

19

whispered huskily. "I even knew the term's abbreviated to seetee, if I'd had time to think. But I never thought of any danger, right here in the capital."

She peered anxiously at the geiger on his wrist.

"Does that show—how much radiation?"

"No dangerous amount—not since he kept you from looking directly at it." The Earthman glanced at Rick, and grinned again. "He seems to be the only one really damaged."

She stepped quickly toward Rick, and turned pink white embarrassment when his hand came up defensively.

"I *did* hurt you!" she gasped. "My ring." She rubbed at the knuckles of her right hand; and sunlight shattered on the immense diamond with the tiny white iridium space ship embedded in the table facet, that identified her as an Interplanet owner. "I'm so terribly sorry," she whispered. "When you were really only trying to save my life—how can I ever repay you?"

"Just forget it." Rick found his handkerchief and dabbed clumsily at the blood where that great stone had cut his cheek. "I'm not really injured."

And he turned away from her to the dark southwestward sky, in time to see the orange spark turn cherry red and disappear, where his father and Rob McGee had tried somehow to move that iron asteroid out of its collision orbit. He wasn't hurt, but they might be dead.

"But I must do something, just to keep from feeling so awful over this." She touched his arm insistently, when he kept looking at the sky. "Anyhow, won't you let me know your name?"

He swung to face her, frowning.

"Richard Drake," he said. "I was on the *Planetania*. Working my way, standing watch with the meteor gang. You were pointed out, as we got off the ship. Forgive me for staring."

Her fair skin flushed again, but she gave him her hand. "Hello, Mr. Drake. I want you to know Captain Paul Anders." She smiled up at the tall Guardsman. "Also from Earth. A spatial engineer, doing his hitch in the service as a special aide to the High Commissioner. An old friend of mine."

"Ever since the time she blacked my eye at somebody's birthday party, back in Solar City when we were about five years old." Anders grinned at her, and reached to shake hands with Rick. "She always was handy with her fists. Good to meet another Earthman, Mr. Drake."

"An asterite, Captain." Rick stepped back. "Just on Earth to study engineering. Nice to know you, but I'm from the rocks and now I'd better be getting along."

"Does it matter where you're from?" Her blue eyes appraised him, as levelly as if it didn't. "If you're a spatial engineer, just coming back from school, don't you need a job?"

"I have one."

"With Interplanet?"

He shook his head.

"Then that's what I can do!" Her eager smile took his breath again. "You see, I came out to work for the company, and Uncle Austin is in charge out here. He can have Max Vickers put you right on the Interplanet engineering staff."

"Thank you," Rick said. "But my father has his own little firm. I'm going to work with him."

Building a seetee bedplate—if Drake and McGee were still alive, and if they could find another site for that perilous project, with Freedonia now lost. But he couldn't speak of that, because it was her Uncle Austin who had suspended their research and exploration license.

"Anyhow, we'll drive you wherever you're going with that." Anders nodded at his heavy bag. "My car's just around the corner."

"Don't bother," Rick protested. "I was only looking for a room. There used to be a reasonably decent place just down the street—"

"Please!" Karen Hood broke in. "Isn't there *something* we can do?"

"Not a thing," Rick said. "But thank you, just the same."

21

" 'Preciate it, Drake," Anders murmured. "Call on me, if you ever need a friend."

Rick had swung the bag to his shoulder and turned to plod away, but a certain honest warmth in the Earthman's voice halted him uncertainly.

"I do need a friend," he blurted impulsively, and then stood awkwardly silent, frightened by what he had said.

"So?" Anders nodded. "And what can I do?"

"My home's out on Obania, you see. Out toward where that collision must have been." He was almost sorry he had spoken, yet he had to know about that flash. "Can you—" He paused to pick his words, afraid of giving anything away. "Can you find out if anybody there was hurt?"

"Just come along." The Earthman nodded readily. "I'll call the Seetee Patrol." He saw Karen's inquiring look. "Part of the Guard. Assigned to watch the drift and maintain the markers. I know the commander of the ship stationed on Obania—a bullet-headed Martian named von Falkenberg."

He caught her arm and nodded for Rick to follow.

"Though I don't think you need to worry over anybody on Obania," he added casually. " 'Cause what collided must have been another rock—a smaller uninhabited asteroid, four million kilometers beyond."

Rick picked up his bag again and followed silently, afraid to say that his father must have been on or near that asteroid when it struck the drift, but Karen Hood whispered sharply:

"You expected *that?*"

"The Seetee Patrol put a warning out last week," he told her. "Von Falkenberg was telling me how some little rock rat engineering firm found that asteroid on a collision orbit, and filed a salvage claim to it. He knew they didn't have a chance."

"Men were out there, you mean?" Karen Hood turned to stare unbelievingly at the empty gloom where that sudden, dreadful blaze had been, and she shivered. "Trying to stop that explosion."

22

"For a lump of next-to-worthless nickel-iron." The Earthman shrugged. "They could have earned a good legal title to the rock, you see, for nudging it off that collision orbit—if they'd had a shipload of terraforming equipment and six months of time. But von Falkenberg said there was no time for anybody to do anything except scoot for cover, or else he'd have moved in with Patrol equipment."

"But they were still trying, in spite of that?"

"S'pose so." Anders swung casually to Rick. "Anyhow, Obania's safe. Von Falkenberg's somewhere out there on the *Perseus*, and he warned everybody. Nobody hurt, I'm sure. Not unless it was those two ambitious rock rats, Drake and—"

He broke off, with a sharp glance at Rick.

Rick looked back at him, and nodded slowly. "My father."

"Oh—" Distress whitened Karen's face. "I'm sorry!"

"So that's what you want to know?" Anders nodded sympathetically. "I'll find out all I can. But don't expect good news. That blast must have killed anybody on the rock—or within half a million kilometers."

They came to his car, parked behind the Guard headquarters building, and Karen waited there with Rick while Anders went inside to make his call. Rick wiped absently again at the scratch below his eye, and then sat slumped down with his feet on his bag, staring moodily at nothing, until Karen started asking questions about seetee.

"Of course I've always heard about the drift," she said. "But when you're on Earth, safe under a hundred miles of terrene air, it doesn't seem so dangerous. Is seetee really so much worse than plutonium?"

He looked up at her, not really seeing the clean planes of her face or the cool blue of her eyes, but yet gratefully aware that she was trying to ease his strain while he waited for news of his father.

"Of course seetee doesn't fission by itself," he said. "You have to touch it with something terrene. But when

23

it does react, all the mass goes into energy. The best fission reactors release about a tenth of one percent. That difference makes seetee about a thousand times as bad—or good, depending on your point of view."

"Good?" She made a startled gesture toward the empty blackness where that savage light had burned and died. "How could those deadly rays be good?"

"They're energy." Rick straightened in the seat. "And energy, if you stop to think about it, is pretty necessary. Our lifeblood, really. Out here fission energy drives our ships and our terraforming installations. It's all that makes life possible on these rocks. But the fissionable matter is just about used up."

She stared at him. "You aren't talking about—seetee power?"

He nodded soberly. "It has to come—soon. We've no coal or oil on Mars or the Jovian moon's or any of these rocks. If we're going to stay, after the uranium and thorium are gone, we'll have to use seetee."

"But how?" She glanced at the black sky uneasily. "If it always explodes like that when you touch it—"

"We can't touch it." He sat silent for a moment, frowning at her thoughtfully. "That's the whole problem—to work the stuff without contact. We've got to find some way to join seetee and terrene matter, and yet keep them from reacting. To put terrene handles on seetee tools, and support seetee machines on terrene foundations."

"That calls for a bold man, Mr. Drake." She turned quickly in the seat to study him, as if she hadn't really seen him before. "Would you try it, yourself?"

"An academic question." He saw now that he had talked too much, but he tried to smile disarmingly. "You'd need a lot of money and a license from the Mandate, neither of which I have."

"Suppose you did?"

"I'd try," he told her soberly. "Because I think we've come to a turning point. We must make seetee bedplates, and build the power plants for a new world on them. Or else just wait for this old world to blow up under us—

when the tensions of the struggle for what is left of the old power metals reach the breaking point of the Mandate."

"Do you mean—war?"

"Fought probably with seetee bombs."

"Bombs?" Her red head shook protestingly. "But can you make seetee bombs without this bedplate?"

"Somebody can and will." He nodded bleakly. "To generate useful seetee power, you'd need a whole chain of seetee machines to mine ore and work metal and build more seetee machines—all untouchable. But any lump of seetee will function as a bomb, if you can just deliver it on anything terrene—and I'd bet that every major planet has engineers at work right now on methods of delivery."

"I did hear war talk, even back on Earth." She nodded reluctantly. "And I can see that Uncle Austin's worried about the situation here. But how do you think seetee power could help?"

"Energy means life," he said. "We're about to fight for the few last deposits of uranium and thorium, just because they aren't rich enough to keep us all alive. But a lump of seetee the size of your fist will yield more energy than a ton of uranium or a million tons of coal. And there are whole planetoids of seetee. More than enough to go around, if we can just develop it."

"I see." She looked hard at him, her blue eyes unsmiling. "Now will you tell me something else?"

Afraid he had already told her too much, he waited silently.

"You're an asterite," she said quietly. "I've heard that most asterites are unhappy under the Mandate. Is that true?"

"We were betrayed." He nodded soberly. "By your company. After we took your side, in the Spatial War. Asterite fighters like old Bruce O'Banion saved Earth and Interplanet from being crushed altogether by the allied planets. We should have had our freedom—but you traded our rights away, and all you had promised us, when you set up the Mandate."

25

"So you're an enemy of Interplanet?"

He shook his head. "Just an engineer."

She frowned at him doubtfully.

"Suppose the company offered you an engineering job —designing this seetee bedplate?"

"You won't." He grinned bleakly. "You have too many hundreds of billions sunk in uranium and thorium mines. You're simply forced to protect those investments, against cheap seetee power."

"That may be true." She nodded unresentfully. "But anyhow, I want you to have a talk with Uncle Austin."

"About seetee?" He shook his head. "Men like my father and Martin Brand have spent their lives trying to interest anybody in seetee power. Nobody's interested."

"I'm interested." She gave him an impulsive little smile. "I'm going to talk to my uncle about it—"

He wasn't listening. He saw Captain Anders come striding from the Guard building, and he turned uneasily to wait for news about his father and that seetee explosion.

Chapter III
Between Worlds

THE EARTHMAN came soberly up to the car, with a look of wonder lingering on his lean-cheeked face. He peered at the sky where that savage blaze had been, and shook his head dazedly.

"The damndest thing!" he said.

"Did you—" Anxiety caught Rick's voice.

"Cheer up, Drake." He grinned suddenly. "I've been talking to our Martian friend, on the *Perseus*, and he says it looks like Drake and McGee have earned their salvage title to that rock. The thing that knocks you over is how they did it."

"But—that flash—" Rick had to gulp. "Wasn't that seetee?"

"A seetee blast." The spare-fleshed Earthman nodded. "But one they set off themselves—'magine that!" Awe still echoed in his voice. "Von Falkenberg says that's the way they averted the collision. Blasted an asteroid off its orbit!"

"Do you know if they were injured?"

"Safe as Earth," Anders said. "I waited for von Falkenberg to call them. They answered from this terrene rock they call Freedonia. All they wanted was him to witness that they had really earned their legal title to it, by keeping it from hitting that seetee asteroid."

"Thanks, captain." Rick grinned feebly. "I thought it had collided, and very likely killed them." He caught his breath. "Do you know how they stopped it?"

The Earthman nodded. "Seems they had to tell von Falkenberg all about it, to get their claim allowed. They had no time or equipment to terraform and move the terrene rock, so what they did was to change the orbit of the seetee body, with the blast we saw."

"But how did they set off a seetee explosion?" Karen Hood broke in. "If men can't touch seetee!"

"That's what knocks you cold." He beamed admiringly at her red hair. "They didn't touch it. Didn't even go inside the legal danger-zone. Von Falkenberg says all they did was nudge a ten-kilogram block of terrene iron into a path that would bring it to meet the seetee asteroid—from twenty thousand kilometers away."

"And that moved the asteroid?"

"Far enough," Anders frowned and looked at Rick. "One funny thing about it. You wouldn't think anybody could hit a moving rock with such a pebble, that far away. But seems Drake and McGee forecast the exact instant of impact, in their filing papers. They even described the new orbit the asteroid would take, safely away from the space lanes and the terrene rocks—and von Falkenberg is already sure they hit it on the nose. B'lieve it?"

"I do," Rick nodded gravely. "Because I know McGee. An odd little elf of a man. He never has much to say, and you might think he isn't quite all there. But he has a sense I don't understand—and he can't explain—for time and space and mass and motion. Just a feeling, he always says. He probably just *felt* that collision about to happen, in the first place."

Karen sat watching Rick, her eyes gravely wide.

"Anyhow," she whispered, "they moved that rock with seetee power."

"Quite a feat," Anders murmured. "Not that it really ushered in the Seetee Era."

And Rick nodded heavily, as his first sense of a dazzling triumph died. Drake and McGee were safe, but all they had done was to claim a barren site for a "metallurgy lab." A stable seetee bedplate was still impossible by definition, and unlicensed seetee research still against the law. He began to regret that he had talked so much about Drake and McGee.

"A perfect sense of time would be a useful gift." Karen gave her watch a faintly startled glance. "Uncle Austin will be out of his meeting by now, and wondering what happened to me. Paul, you must drive me back to the residency. And then won't you help Mr. Drake find a place to stay?"

"Right." Anders nodded. "Nice little hotel on Ceres Street, where I know the manager."

They left her at the impressive pile of colored glass and shining nickel that was the official dwelling of the High Commissioner, and Rick took a room in that hotel on Ceres Street. The telephone rang, before he had unpacked his bag.

"Mr. Drake?" The voice was Karen's. "I've just seen my uncle, and he wants you to have lunch with him."

"High Commissioner Hood?" Astonishment took Rick's breath. "Today?"

"Fourteen o'clock today, at the Mandate House. If you are free?"

"People are always free, when your uncle asks them. Tell him I'll be there."

She hung up, and he turned with a frown to unpack his dress suit. The unexpected invitation worried him, as he began to think about it. Karen Hood might be interested in seetee power, but he knew her uncle wasn't. More likely, he thought, the High Commissioner just wanted to make sure that Drake and McGee weren't at work on a seetee bedplate.

At fourteen o'clock he entered the ornate golden portals of the Mandate House, the expensive restaurant that catered to officialdom. The cost of living was high everywhere in the Mandate, because food production was prohibited—to force the asterites to barter their uranium and thorium for imported food, Rick supposed. And prices at the Mandate House were fantastic.

Rick paused uncertainly at the doorway to the bar. He

29

felt suddenly out of place. Rock rats weren't asked to lunch with the High Commissioner. Even though he couldn't afford to lower his guard, he wanted one drink to smooth his social awkwardness.

The barroom was dimly lighted through a red glass ceiling, and paneled with shining ebonwood shipped all the way from Vesus. The air was thick with smoke and alcohol and guarded talk in four languages. The surface atmosphere seemed friendly, but he could feel veiled undercurrents of harsh conflict.

The blond, sunburned attachés of the Martian commissioner were gathered at the table of a hawk-faced visiting general. Nursing heavy steins, all very stiff and courteous, they seemed withdrawn to themselves. Huge, bearded men from the Jovian moons were industriously drinking vodka, cheerful and noisy but yet alert. The Venusians, at a table of their own, were sipping rice wine and tea with an air of bland secretiveness.

A group of Earthmen were drinking whisky-sodas at the bar and they seemed to Rick a little too confident and loud. One of them, a very junior officer from the *Planetania*, beckoned him to join them. After he had sensed that strain of secret mistrust in the long, smoky room, however, he decided to keep himself alert to deal with High Commissioner Hood.

He gave his name to a waiter and stood in a corner of the noisy lobby, until the great man came in with Max Vickers, who was the Interplanet branch manager, and a group of their aides. Hood was heavy and ruddy, with a fringe of red hair around his balding head. He left the other Earthmen, when the waiter pointed, and came waddling to Rick.

"Glad to know you, Drake." He gripped Rick's hand heartily. "If you don't mind, let's eat alone. We've got business to talk over, but not till after lunch."

A little too determinedly bluff and unassuming, he waved at Vickers and nodded for Rick to follow him into a luxurious private room. His order seemed important as

30

a government decision; he finally selected capon with dry Martian wines.

At first Rick felt stiff and diffident. Perhaps the wine helped melt away his awe; as the meal went on, he began to regard his host with a mixture of admiration, amusement, and unexpected liking. Hood's chief qualification for his difficult position seemed to be an excellent digestion.

"You think I'm a hearty man, Drake?" he rumbled genially. "Well, it takes a hearty man to fight the war all over again every day in the commission chamber. Three men before me went home with peptic ulcers, but trouble never takes my appetite."

Rick still wondered what he wanted. He said no more of any business until the wine was finished and they had lighted rich blond Cuban cigars. Then he leaned forward to say soberly:

"Young man, I hear you saved my niece's sight this morning."

"She was looking for that flash," Rick said. "She seemed not to know the danger in seetee."

"Do you?"

Rick stiffened, watching him silently.

"She says you want to build a seetee power plant."

"I'd like to see one built," Rick agreed cautiously.

"You spoke to Karen about some sort of bedplate to carry seetee machinery on terrene foundations." Hood's voice was casual, but his hard eyes peered alertly through the pale cigar smoke. "How would a seetee bedplate work?"

"The right answer to that question would be cheap if it cost you ten billion dollars worth of research," Rick told him. "But it's going to involve force applied without contact—"

"Huh?" Hood blinked. "Is that possible?"

"Try holding a magnet over a nail."

"Won't they soon be in contact?"

"They still need engineering." Rick smiled gravely.

31

"But there's the principle. The problems can be solved. Here's one notion I'd like to see tried." He reached for a pencil and a paper napkin. "An arrangement of permanent magnets, half of them terrene and half seetee, interlocked like this—"

"Save it." Hood held up a broad hand to stop him. "I can't read blueprints. But Paul Anders is my expert on seetee, and he was impressed by the way your father used it to move that asteroid. He wants me to put you to work for Interplanet, getting up a confidential brief on seetee. We'll pay you fifty thousand for one year's work—a big figure for a man just out of school, but Karen insisted on it."

"And how am I to earn it?"

"Just make us a full report on seetee. Get together everything known about it. Origin, distribution, total tonnage, estimated abundance of the various elements. And analyze every known scheme for putting it to use."

"For power?"

"Power, too." Hood's shrewd eyes narrowed. "But Karen says you also spoke of seetee bombs."

"She doesn't owe me anything." Anger quickened Rick's voice. "And I won't be bribed to design seetee bombs for anybody."

"This is strictly business," Hood answered smoothly. "Paul and Karen agree that we need you. If you think seetee can be used for peace instead of war, write that into your brief. Go ahead and draw up your blueprints for a bedplate. If Paul Anders says the thing will work, Interplanet has billions enough to build it. Fair enough?"

"I suppose so." Rick nodded uncertainly. "It does seem like a wonderful chance, but still I'd like time to think it over. You see, my father and Rob McGee are expecting me back to work with them."

"All right, think it over." Hood nodded affably. "But if you really want to build a seetee bedplate, you'll tell Max Vickers to write up the contract." He looked at his watch, and rose abruptly. "Sorry, but now I've got to meet

Commissioner Rykov—he's trying to bluff me into upping his uranium quota."

Rick thought it over. He recalled that his father and Rob McGee had no billions, nor even a research license, to try building any sort of bedplate on the bare little rock Ann O'Banion had named Freedonia. Perhaps he was influenced by Karen Hood's bright hair, when she found him at the reception that night and sent him to bring her a cup of tea. It made no real difference who built the first bedplate, he decided, so long as it was built. He signed the contract next morning, to work a year for Interplanet.

Afterwards, he called Ann O'Banion. He knew she wouldn't understand, and he felt almost grateful for the millions of empty kilometers between them.

"Ann, I won't be coming home this year," he muttered awkwardly. "I've gone to work for—for Interplanet." He stammered a little over that, because he knew how she felt about the corporation. "On a special confidential project." He felt glad that he could say no more about it, because he didn't want to tell her what it was, just yet. "I hope my father isn't hurt," he said. "Tell him I'll be writing. Tell him I'm making good money—and I do mean to come home next year."

He waited uncomfortably then for the thread of light to bring her answer back.

"I'll tell your father, Rick." Her voice sounded stifled and strange. "But I'm afraid he will be hurt." For a moment all he could hear was the roar of stray starlight, and then she said faintly, "Good-by, Rick."

He went to work that day. Vickers gave him the keys to a huge, cold, blue-glass-and-bright-nickel office in the Interplanet building. He spent most of the next year shut up there, sifting facts about the drift from dusty mountains of publications in several languages, exploring a thousand unsound schemes for manipulating seetee with electric or magnetic or paragravitic fields, drawing up new plans of his own that Anders always demolished.

"Most of your gadgets look pretty good on paper," the tall Earthman admitted once. "But pretty good won't do, not when you're playing with seetee." He stood frowning at the blueprints that Rick had toiled over for weeks. "I can see that your slab of seetee iron ought to float on that paragravity field—but the known paragravitic effects are all temporary. What happens when a coil burns out?"

"I've provided for three separate circuits," Rick answered. "Any one should hold it safely."

"Till some unlucky mechanic drops a terrene screwdriver on something seetee." Anders grinned cheerfully. "Then your whole installation would go off in a blast hot enough to scorch the planets."

"Men won't be working on the seetee section with terrene screwdrivers," Rick protested. "Everything seetee will have to be remote-controlled or entirely automatic."

"And there's where you have to hoist yourself by your own bootstraps," the Earthman said. "Automatic seetee machines might build more automatic seetee machines, once you had them going. But how do you expect to get the first one?"

"The first tools will be just two natural fragments of seetee iron," Rick told him patiently. "We can assemble terrene machinery around them, to manipulate them with magnetic or paragravitic fields. We can use one fragment for an anvil and one for a hammer—to start shaping more elaborate seetee tools."

"Nothing to it." Anders grinned sardonically. "Not if you can find men with nerve enough to start juggling that stuff barehanded!"

"I know men with nerve enough to try," Rick said quietly. He was thinking of his father and Rob McGee, though he didn't call their names. "Men with skill enough to do it, too—if we can just design the right equipment."

"Anyhow, you haven't showed me the right equipment yet." Anders frowned at the blueprint again, and shook his head. "I can't buy that for Interplanet. If you really want to build a bedplate, better try again."

Rick tried again, with a design in which rows of permanent magnets were arranged to take the load in case the lift of the main coils failed.

"Bootstraps." Once more the Earthman shook his head. "P'raps we could build seetee machinery to manufacture seetee magnets—if we had seetee magnets to build it on. But we don't. 'Fraid you'll have to think of something better."

Rick always failed to think of anything better, yet he couldn't help coming to like the tall engineer. Anders was handsome—Rick had seen the admiration shining in Karen's eyes, and felt a twinge of unwilling jealousy. The Earthman's luxuriant hair was wavy and dark, and his piercing eyes had the gray of steel. Straight and spare, he somehow wore his trim black uniform with a disarming air of casual indolence that concealed a mind quick as reacting seetee.

Although he kept up his courteous, urbane reserve, Rick learned a good bit about him as they worked together. Obviously, he came of a family generations old in the tight, privileged aristocracy of Interplanet—one lifetime, Rick knew, was too short to create such poised assurance. He had traveled on all the major planets. No situation ever found him at a loss. He clearly belonged to the world of Karen Hood.

And Rick didn't—though sometimes, as that year went by, he tried to believe that he could learn to belong. For she was now the assistant branch manager. He saw her often, in the elevators of the Interplanet building, at the few parties to which he was invited, on the street with Anders. She smiled at him—just because he had kept her from staring at that seetee flash, he thought at first, or possibly because he might be useful to the company. But when at last he waited one morning in the corridor outside her office and asked her to eat lunch with him, she accepted graciously. He took her to the Mandate House. The next night they went dancing.

With her, he forgot that he was neither asterite nor Earthman, but lost between two worlds. For a few hours, she was nothing more than a red-haired girl, a little self-willed but still wonderful. After he told her good-night, however, she was clothed again with all the ancient power and the stately opulence of Interplanet. The gulf came back between them in his mind, suddenly more real than ever, so painful that he didn't want to think of it or her. All that really mattered, anyhow, was the bed-plate and the wide new world that men could build upon it. For two weeks he tried to think of nothing but the unfinished plans on his drawing board, but Karen's initials kept turning up among the doodles on his scratch pad. Finally he called her again, and found he had waited too long.

"Thank you, Mr. Drake." Her voice seemed too sweet. "So kind of you to think of me again, but I can't go anywhere with you tonight. Paul and I are going to the Martian ball. And I'm afraid my calendar is full."

Chapter IV
The Admirable Bomb

MARCH HAD COME AGAIN, and the year of Rick's contract was nearly gone, when his desk phone rang one afternoon and he heard Karen's voice. His heart missed a beat, but her tone was crisply distant.

"Mr. Drake? I'm calling for my uncle. You're to be at his office at nine in the morning."

She hung up without saying why, but Rick thought this might be his last chance to see the busy High Commissioner. He worked most of the night to finish his latest set of drawings, but Hood didn't look at them.

"Save 'em for Anders."

He had started to unroll the plans, but the High Commissioner stopped him with an impatient gesture and kept him standing in front of the huge chromium desk that was topped with polished Venusian jadewood to match the lofty walls.

"Can't read 'em, anyhow," Hood said. "But Anders says you haven't hit the mark, not with any sort of safe bedplate. Says you never will."

"I'm still trying."

"You've only ten days left on our payroll," Hood reminded him. "But there's still one more thing I want you to try."

"I'll do anything," Rick promised eagerly. "Nearly anything."

The big man watched him shrewdly for a moment and then asked softly, "What do you hear from your father?"

Rick had to catch his breath before he could speak.

"Not much," he managed to say. "He's living in a pres-

37

sure tent on that rock he saved from collision last year. He seems too busy to write very often."

"Doing what?"

"Just making good his claim." Rick had to gulp. "The rock has to be inhabited and marked, you know, to keep the title clear. He has installed an orbital reflector. The last time he wrote, he was drilling a shaft for a terraforming unit."

Hood's keen eyes narrowed. "You're sure he hasn't been building a seetee bedplate?"

"He has no research license." Rick tried to meet that searching stare. "What makes you think he's working on a bedplate?"

"We aren't sitting on a powder magazine with our eyes shut." Hood shook his balding head complacently. "Your father's asteroid isn't accessible to us—that explosion he set off filled a wide space beyond Obania with a cloud of seetee dust that the Seetee Patrol is still unable to penetrate. But we have our information. Your father and his partner have been coming and going through that cloud —I don't know how—hauling in supplies and equipment they wouldn't need for setting up a rotary marker, or even for terraforming the rock. I've been suspecting that they were up to some new use of seetee. I'm sure of it now, because your father has just come out again. He is suffering from seetee shock."

"No!" Rick stared at Hood. "I'd have heard about it."

"This rock rat McGee brought him back to Obania two days ago," Hood said. "The asterite doctor there gave him first aid, and advised him to see a radiation specialist. McGee is bringing him on here now, to see Dr. Worringer."

"Then he is hurt." Rick nodded reluctantly. "Though I don't know why he didn't call me." He swallowed nervously. "When are they due here?"

"Tomorrow morning," Hood said. "They called Worringer, and he's going to examine your father at ten. I want you to meet them and find out just what they're up to."

Rick flushed. "Do you expect me to spy on my own father? Now when he's hurt or maybe dying!"

"I doubt that he's dying," the big man answered calmly. "But I'm not asking you to spy on anybody. If your father has any seetee know-how worth knowing, I want Vickers to sign him up for Interplanet. Purely as a business proposition—I'm speaking for the company now, and I won't ask what Mandate laws he may have broken. If his injury was due to any lack of suitable equipment or skilled technical assistance, Interplanet can supply such things. I'm simply asking you to put the offer to him, as our agent, because I've found that the asterites of his generation often feel hard toward our company people."

Rick looked hard at him. "Your company owns deposits of uranium and thorium—that once were claimed by the people of these rocks—worth hundreds of billions. Are you really willing to finance a project that might destroy their value?"

"Myself, I am." Hood nodded deliberately. "We do have a few old men on the board back in Solar City who might vote to bottle up seetee power, but out here I'm in charge. If anybody is going to get seetee power—or seetee bombs—I want them for Interplanet. I'll have Vickers back any project that Paul Anders will okay."

"Seetee power can't be cornered like uranium and thorium," Rick warned him soberly. "Not even if my father can build a plant for you. It's too big to be monopolized by anybody. Even Interplanet."

"Tell me why."

"Scientific secrets don't keep well. And you can see that seetee power will have to be generated a long way from anywhere, and broadcast over a Brand transmitter —you can't bring seetee fuel into any terrene atmosphere. That means everybody will be able to tap your power field, free of charge."

"Anders was explaining that." Hood nodded blandly. "But I'll go along with anything he approves. Perhaps we can still come out on top." His eyes glinted blue. "After all, Interplanet didn't conquer space and get possession of our uranium and thorium reserves just because we company people are all made out of gingerbread."

"No." Rick smiled faintly. "You're not that."

"So see your father." The stout High Commissioner rose abruptly, to end the interview. "Find out what he's got. If it's anything Anders says we need, Vickers will pay his price."

Rick didn't wait to answer that, but he knew his father had no price. Nothing mattered much to old Jim Drake, except the challenge of the drift. Perhaps Rick's mother had been more important to him once, but the drift itself had killed her long ago, when a stray flake of seetee fell on Obania. The drift had always been his great antagonist, blind and pitiless, elusive as a shadow. He had spent most of his life trying to tame it. Money meant nothing to him, but Rick thought he might welcome the equipment and brains Interplanet could bring to his aid —if this new injury had left him nerve and strength to carry on the struggle.

The *Good-by Jane* came in at seven next morning, Mandate Time. Five decks high, her rusty hull looked angular and graceless as a twentieth-century railroad box car turned on end and stripped of wheels, but she settled to the gravel of the convex field with the easy precision of Rob McGee's handling. Rick waited impatiently while the port inspectors went aboard, and hurried toward the battered ground gear as soon as they were gone.

"Hello, Rick." Captain Rob McGee greeted him softly from the air-lock, peering down with mild, squinted eyes. McGee's shoulders were broad as Rick's, in an ancient space coat of mildewed green. His head was large and square, with a thick mat of yellow hair and very little neck. His body was short and his legs inconsequential, yet altogether he looked as ready and sturdy and ugly as his ship.

"Come on aboard." He put out a space-burned hand to haul Rick up the narrow ramp. "Jim's up in the cabin."

Plainly but soundly built of square steel plates, the

Good-by Jane had five compartments stacked like boxes on the clumsy skids and springs of her ground gear. Rick climbed up the ladder-well from the air lock, through the holds and the reactor room, to the cabin beneath the pilot-house. He found his father slumped in a chair too small for him, with both hands bandaged. A gaunt, worn, humble man, in a shabby gray coat and rough miners' boots.

Rick had been gone five years from Obania, and he was stricken now to see how time had withered his father's cragged face, thinned and streaked his reddish hair, burdened down his lean, gigantic frame. That distressed Rick more, somehow, than the bandages or the shadow of pain below the hollowed eyes. Not even Worringer could cure the disease of time.

"Dad—I didn't know!" Rick stood staring at the swaddled hands. "My own fault, too." A pang of guilt struck through him. "If I had come on back home to help you—"

"That's all right, Rick," his father broke in gently. "We're only blundering, Rob and I. Maybe you've done better."

"Anyhow, you should have called me."

"No use upsetting you before we got here." His father glanced calmly down at the bandages. "And you can't help this sort of thing, when you're playing with seetee. We were floating a block of seetee iron on a paragravitic field. Must have knocked off a grain of dust so small I never saw it."

"Oh—" Something closed Rick's throat. Awkwardly, he put his arm around the old man's sagging shoulders.

"Now don't get upset," Jim Drake protested. "I've been burned before. Worringer can fix me up so I can try again, and that's all that matters." He stepped back to look at Rick. "Good to see you, boy. Sit down and have some tea and tell us what you're doing."

Rick sat down on a bench, and little Rob McGee poured the bitter tea the asterites always brewed—perhaps to cover the flat taste of synthetic water gone stale

41

in rusting tanks. Rick sipped the tea, but he didn't want to talk about his work with Interplanet, not quite yet. Instead, he asked about Ann O'Banion.

"Ann's all right." Jim Drake's faded eyes lit up again. "She's still running our office on Obania. Getting together the supplies and tools we need for the lab. I don't quite know how, when we're so short of money." A troubled expression overshadowed his wan smile. "She used to talk a lot about you, Rick. She used to miss you. She was always asking when you were coming home."

"But now she doesn't?"

"She was going out the night we left, to a party at the Guard base. She had a date with a young Martian lieutenant named Kurt von Sudenhorst."

"A good thing, maybe." Rick nodded soberly. "There's another girl I know here—" But he didn't want to talk about Karen Hood. "I guess Ann felt hurt, when I went to work for Interplanet. Maybe you did, too."

He saw the truth of that in his father's deep-lined face and haggard eyes. A deep embarrassment reddened him. He caught his breath, and tried to explain why he had taken the company job.

"I'm sorry, Dad," he finished desperately. "But Interplanet offered me a chance to build a bedplate, if I could design one to please their engineers. And I didn't know you had one ready to test on Freedonia—"

"We haven't," Jim Drake broke in softly. "But don't apologize. I've spent twenty years trying to interest anybody in a bedplate. Anybody—I'd even try building one for the Jovians, if I knew how and they'd put up the money, just because I know they couldn't keep it for themselves. So don't think I blame you, boy."

"Thanks, Dad." Rick gulped, and wiped at his eyes. "That makes it easier—what I have to say."

"Yes?"

His father waited, but still he didn't want to say it.

"I don't feel right about it." He shifted his weight uncomfortably, and plunged ahead. "But, anyhow, High

42

Commissioner Hood thinks you're working on a bedplate. He told me to find out. If you do have any sort of workable design, he wants Vickers to buy it for Interplanet."

"We don't." Sadly, the old man shook his head. "Sorry, but we don't."

"But didn't you say you were floating a slab of seetee iron on a magnetic field?"

"We've done that." Jim Drake shrugged heavily. "But that's no bedplate. The fact is, I've given up building any sort of stable bedplate."

"Then what are you making?" Rick saw the watchful look in Rob McGee's squinted eyes, and felt his own face turn crimson. "Or maybe you shouldn't tell me that," he blurted abruptly. "After all, I'm still on the Interplanet payroll."

"That's all right, Rick," his father said again. "I'll tell you what we're doing. I don't mind you telling Hood— if you think he might back us. We're trying to build a pilot model for a seetee reactor."

"But what will it stand on, if you can't build a bedplate?"

"We're trying to dodge the problem of contact," Jim Drake explained patiently. "The same way we did when we moved that seetee asteroid off its orbit by tossing a terrene pebble into it."

Rick bent intently toward him. "Can you do it?"

"Not yet." He shook his head. "But we have floated this block of seetee iron on a variable field, and we looped pick-up coils around it. My idea was to jet a metered stream of some terrene gas against the seetee block, to give us a controlled reaction."

"But it doesn't work?"

"Not the way it should. I don't quite know why. The reaction is never uniform, no matter how we adjust the jet, or what terrene gas we use. The geigers always show a dangerous radiation leakage through the exchanger field. Dust particles blow off, like the one that hit me.

And the seetee block always gets to oscillating, so that we have to stop the jet in a hurry."

Rick frowned thoughtfully. "Your seetee block isn't pure iron," he said at last. "I think that's what the trouble is. The seetee impurities would always react in explosive bursts too intense for any exchanger field to pick up, I think."

"You're probably right," his father said. "But how can we get a block of pure seetee iron?"

"I don't know." Rick shook his head. "Not without a seetee bedplate to build an automatic furnace on."

"I can't build a bedplate," Jim Drake said. "But I'll tell you all about our reactor if you like. You can draw a set of plans for Interplanet. Take your time and make it look good. Sell it to Vickers and Hood, or give it to them. Get them interested in seetee power, before somebody sells them a seetee bomb."

"I'll try." Rick nodded doubtfully. "But their seetee expert is an engineer named Anders, a hard man to sell."

All that day, before they went to Dr. Worringer's office and afterwards, Jim Drake talked of nothing but the crude illicit equipment he had tested on Freedonia and the finer pilot plant that Interplanet money could build. Rick listened to him eagerly, asking a question now and then, sketching rough plans and jotting down specifications.

The old engineer spent an hour with the radiation specialist. He came out with new bandages, and a smile on his gaunt brown face.

"Couple of fingers gone," he murmured cheerfully. "But Worringer says I'll soon be fit to work again."

Rob McGee had spent the day loading his little ship with supplies for Freedonia. They started back that night, thought Rick wanted them to stay.

"Rob will be right back," his father promised. "To pick up more supplies, and find out whether Interplanet is going to finance our reactor."

"Why don't you just wait here with me?" Rick insisted. "At least until your hands get well?"

"Freedonia has to be inhabited, to keep our title good," the old man said. "I'm able to inhabit it, now. Besides, Pallasport is getting a little too big. Too much like Solar City. Rob and I, we like the open rocks like Freedonia, where a man can live without people in his hair. We like the feel of space."

To Rick, Pallasport seemed tiny and open enough. With the naked peaks and airless chasms of the dead planetoid frowning darkly all around the lonely living summit of the town, and stars burning through the thin cap of synthetic air even when the small, far sun hung cold overhead, the feel of space disturbed him. This awesome void was splendid to him, with the hot bright frost of stars burning on the frozen webs and veils and vanishing filaments of the nebulae, but it was too vast for him, too empty, too alien. People didn't get in his hair, not often, anyhow. He was not all asterite. He shook McGee's knobby hand, and squeezed his father's gaunt, bent shoulder, and watched the *Good-by Jane* take them back toward that remote and lonely lump of iron where they could feel at home.

At his desk again, he spent a week turning his hurried notes and sketches into finished drawings for the reactor his father wanted to build. Not very hopefully, he showed it to Anders. He had discovered no way to obtain pure seetee iron, or any safe reaction with impure native iron. He was expecting the Earthman to condemn the project offhand, and he stood silent with surprise when Anders sat soberly down with slide rule and pencil to check every detail of the plans.

"Int'resting." The tall Earthman straightened thoughtfully at last, nodding at a safe in the corner of the room. "Lock'em up. I think we can use'em, with a few modifications. I'll talk to Hood tomorrow, about offering you a new contract."

"I'm not sure I want a new contract," Rick stood staring at him, puzzled. "And I don't see why you're so interested. You must know that this reactor would be far

45

more dangerous than those bedplates you said were too dangerous."

"Which is why I like it." A sardonic smile glinted on the Earthman's hard brown face. "Much too dangerous for any sort of power plant. But a few modifications—to make it more compact and simpler to set off—will turn it into an admirable bomb."

Chapter V
The Light That Went Out

KAREN HOOD's office in the Interplanet Building shared a wide, glass-walled reception room with the district manager's. Rick Drake met her there, unexpectedly, the morning of his next-to-last day with Interplanet. He was stalking restlessly away from a talk with Vickers, so disturbed that he failed to see her coming in. They almost collided.

The manager had called him in to offer him a new contract: sixty thousand dollars for one more year of work on "confidential research and developmental projects to be designated by the engineering department of said corporation." When he read the legal double talk, he refused to sign.

Those projects, he suspected, would turn out to be seetee bombs, though he decided not to say so. Max Vickers was a paunchy Earthman with tight lips and calculating eyes and a mottled, sagging, unhealthy face. He had none of Hood's honest heartiness to balance his aggressive drive, and Rick didn't trust him.

"I'm not interested in confidential projects," Rick told him. "I want to build a seetee power plant. Unless I know I'll be working toward that, I mean to leave the company."

"To do what?"

That abrupt query, and the cold challenge of the manager's eyes, took Rick's breath. Perhaps he could go back to carry on the illicit work his father and Rob McGee had begun on Freedonia, but he couldn't hope for much to come of that. He felt sure they had no adequate equipment, and his own savings would buy too little more. The rival planets, with all their schemes and apprehensions, wouldn't willingly allow the humbled asterites to grasp the power of seetee. Worst of all, he had no workable design for a safe bedplate.

"Well?" Vickers rapped, as he hesitated. "What are you going to do?"

"I haven't decided."

"Decide tonight. See me tomorrow." Vickers leaned across the desk, his splotched face impassive and his pale small eyes warningly alert. "But if you want to do anything with seetee," he added a little too softly, "you'd better decide to do it for us."

"I'll think it over," Rick muttered uncomfortably.

And he stumbled out of the office and across the reception room, blind to everything except that pressing problem. The hard choice, as he saw it, was either to work on those "confidential developmental projects" for Interplanet, or else to give up altogether; and he could accept neither alternative.

"Hello!" Karen spoke a foot in front of him, "In a hurry, Mr. Drake?"

He blinked dazedly at her red hair, and thrust himself desperately aside.

"Sorry!" he gasped. "I was thinking—I didn't see you."

"P'raps you're thinking too much."

Her blue eyes were laughing at his confusion, and her voice sounded friendly. She was suddenly a lovely girl again, and no longer the remote, proud princess of Interplanet. If he left the company, it struck him painfully, he might not see her again. He spoke impulsively:

"Please, may I see you tonight?"

"I'm afraid not." Her smile faded. "Paul's taking me to a dinner at the Guard Officers' Club."

"I—I see." He gulped and tried not to let her see how much he cared. "Please forgive my clumsiness."

And he swung stiffly to go on.

"Rick!" She caught his arm. "Do you have to be so damned superior? I've wanted for a long time to have a good talk with you. Would you let me take you to lunch?"

"If—of course!" He tried to catch his breath. "Or I'll take you."

"I'm going to pay the bill," she said. "Because I don't think you'll like what I intend to say. Shall we meet at the Mandate House?"

He started to agree, but a defiant impulse checked him. That exclusive, expensive haunt of the masters of Mandate was part of her imperial world, and he would not surrender to it.

"I'm not an Earthman, if you remember," he said. "We rock rats don't feel quite at home at the Mandate House. I usually eat at the Seetee Cafe."

Blue anger flickered in her eyes, but she subdued it. "Then I'll meet you there," she said softly. "At noon."

Pallas didn't turn on Mandate time. At noon, it was midnight over the town. Rick had failed to find any answer to his problem, and he strode restlessly down the curving street of glaring fluorescent signs and gaudy glass-and-metal fronts with the black sky reflected on his face.

"Hi, Rick!"

Karen got out of a taxi at the curb, smiling as if her flash of wrath had been forgotten. The way her hair struck back a sign's red glow made a sharp little pain in his throat. He stood for a moment looking at her. Even in her plain green office dress, she was far too beautiful, he thought, to belong on this raw frontier.

The sign of the Seetee Cafe was the huge iron wheel of a Drake marker, spinning on a tower above the flimsy sheet-metal building. Rick's broad shoulders lifted as the flashing signal of the filtered mirrors on that great wheel recalled his father's work, and sagged again when he thought of the inventor now, old and injured and faced at last with failure.

"An odd place." Karen hesitated for an instant, as if she thought it too odd, but then she took his arm. "Let's eat, Rick."

He followed her to a booth at the back of the long, noisy room. Pale letters shone on the chipped glass table: WANT A WALLOP? TRY OUR SEETEE COCK-TAIL! He looked at Karen, with a wry brown grin. The walloping agent, he knew, was a double jigger of synthetic alcohol. He knew she wouldn't want it—any more than she wanted the strong drink of real seetee power the sick planets needed.

The waiter arrived with a dog-eared menu, and he saw Karen looking at the amiable Venusian's grease-spotted apron as they ordered the Blue Plate. Though she said nothing, he thought she seemed uncomfortable in this shabby place, with its rank smells of beer and onions and burned cooking oil, and the coarse loudness of the grimy stevedores at the counter.

"Forgive me, Karen," he blurted, with a sudden rush of feeling. "You don't belong in this cheap joint, and I shouldn't have made you come." He gulped, half incoherent. "I mean it's all no use, because we live in different worlds. I'm just a rock rat, and you were born with an Interplanet coupon in your mouth."

"Stop it!" Karen's nostrils widened and the white skin over her high cheekbones turned pink. "Are you determined to be unfair? Really, we're not far apart. Your mother came from a wealthy Interplanet family, and you know that I'm working for a living."

"I know." His grin was faintly sardonic. "You're the new assistant branch manager—just because you happen to be the High Commissioner's niece."

"I'm counting ten." She paused for an instant, and lowered her throaty voice. "You'll have to admit that I'm a very efficient assistant manager—I could manage the whole branch as well as Vickers does. And I'm not out here just because I happened to be born on some little rock like Obania. I'm here because I like it."

Her flashing eyes seemed almost black. Rick thought her warm emotion very becoming to her, but he decided not to mention it.

"I could have stayed at home in Solar City," she went

on. "I had money of my own—and plenty of chances to marry more, thank you. But I don't care for penthouse parties. I didn't want to be the toy of some playboy billionaire. If you think this frontier town is too rough for women, you don't know what you're talking about. Really, women have a higher place out here than they do at home—and I'm not such a delicate violet. I'm working hard to make my own way. I like it here. I like the people—even their blunt talk." She nodded toward the stevedores at the counter. "And please don't sneer about Uncle Austin!"

"I didn't know you felt that way," Rick said contritely. "Was that what you thought I wouldn't like to hear?"

"Oh, no." She smiled gravely, her anger gone. "I've been wanting to tell you that, but I really didn't mean to quarrel with you. The other thing is more serious, but it can wait until we've eaten."

The Blue Plates came. They were eight dollars each, with the muddy coffee a dollar extra. Such high prices, Rick couldn't help thinking, were mostly hidden taxes paid to Interplanet and the other rulers of the Mandate, whose heavy-handed policies kept the people of the rocks dependent on costly food imports. But he said nothing of that. He didn't want to quarrel; and the sober way she pushed her plate aside and leaned across the little table, after they had eaten, gave him a pang of apprehension.

"Well?" He tried to smile. "What's the bad news?"

"Paul says you're thinking of quitting the company."

"I am." His big bronzed hand fumbled clumsily with a water glass, and spilled a little of it. "Why not?"

Her fine shoulders tossed impatiently.

"Don't be silly, Rick. Interplanet isn't blind. We know your father and his partner have been doing unlicensed seetee research. I'm afraid you're thinking of going back to help them. But can't you see how foolish that would be?"

Rick stirred his cold coffee and looked up unhappily. Karen's blue eyes seemed very serious, but the distracting flow of liquid fire in her bright hair made it hard to remember that her proud old world was so hopelessly far from his own.

"Rick, you just *can't* leave Interplanet. And you ought to make your father give up those reckless experiments, before he kills himself—or gets into trouble with the law. I met him, when he came in the office to sign an order. And his partner—what's his name? The ugly, funny little man who seemed to know the time without looking at a watch?"

"Rob McGee," Rick said. "A real rock rat. Born with a sort of extra sense of time and space."

"Anyhow, I like them both," Karen said earnestly. "They're actual pioneers. But I'm afraid they don't know the danger in seetee—I mean the political and legal danger. I hate to see them blundering into trouble. Can't you stop them, Rick?"

"And sign them up for Interplanet?" He grinned painfully at her anxious face. "To design seetee bombs for your friend Anders? So that he can blow up this crazy old world, before anybody has a chance to build a new one on a stable seetee bedplate? Is that what you want?"

He heard the faint little gasp of her in-drawn breath. Her face went white and her full lips tightened. Sudden tears glinted in her eyes. He sat waiting for some kind of explosion, but it seemed a long time to him before she answered and then her voice was hushed and almost pleading.

"Don't say that, Rick. Nobody wants a seetee war. Least of all Interplanet, because I think we have the most to lose. It's true Paul is studying the military use of seetee—but only because we know the Jovians and the Martians and even the Venusians are all pushing their own seetee weapons projects desperately."

"Chiefly, I imagine, because they know how desperately Anders is trying to push yours."

"All right, Rick." She nodded regretfully. "I was afraid you wouldn't see my point of view. I'm sorry I can't see yours—but Paul says seetee power is just another crackpot scheme, and I trust Paul. So let's not quarrel any more about it. Please!"

He had caught his breath to speak. He wanted to make her see his goal. The mighty reactor on some far-off rock like Freedonia, its seetee parts standing on some kind of safe bedplate. The broadcast energy flowing out to all the planets, like a river of new life. The deserts of Earth turned green with water pumped across continents, growing food for hungry billions. The splendid new cities rising everywhere, even on planetoids now airless and dead. The unbounded abundance, the last emancipation, the priceless freedom of power. A whole magnificent new world—but she could never welcome it, because it meant the end of her own.

"I guess you're right," he said sadly. "I guess it's no use talking."

They walked silently back to the Interplanet Building, and rather stiffly said good-by. He spent the afternoon completing a final report that Anders had requested, summing up all that was publicly known about the intensities and frequencies of the gamma radiation produced by the reaction of the various seetee elements. The facts depressed him as he set them down, because they revealed too clearly the ultimate deadliness of any sort of seetee bomb. He locked up his office at seventeen hundred, and walked outside the town to think his problem through.

The surrounding wilderness of barren, shattered stone seemed to tilt as he walked toward it, because what he felt as *down* was the pull of the paragravity unit in its pit beneath the mountain—the natural gravitation of Pallas itself was far too slight to hold an atmosphere. As the direction of that pull changed, the whole starlit desert seemed to tip. At last he was climbing up the cragged dark face of a world turned vertical.

A lonely, seeking giant, he went on until the town on the terraformed peak was only a glittering knob of metal and glass, far down the up-ended landscape behind. The air grew thin, as he left the field that held it. He stopped to get his breath. Clinging with both hands to the cold, toppling cliff, he turned his head to gaze out into the black mysterious chasm of open space. If he fell, it seemed that he would drop past Pallas, to plunge on forever and forever into that unknowable abyss of suns like diamond dust and galaxies sucked away like snowflakes on a mad, black wind of expanding emptiness.

He shivered, and his fingers tightened on the frosty stone. Yet he enjoyed his sense of that overwhelming infinity—it was what he had climbed to seek. For this was the other half of him. He had learned in childhood to love the dark challenge and the splendid promise of this wild new frontier, and the feel of it now awoke the call of space in him, as old as his life and as strong as anything he knew.

He clung there a long time, breathing consciously and deeply to keep alive in the thin, cold air. All his doubts were washed away, in that clean bright spatial sea. This was his world—and all the mean little schemers of the Mandate were insignificant beside it. Even the untouchable loveliness of Karen Hood seemed less painful, when he looked down at her from here.

Abruptly, he knew what to do. He was through with all the selfish plots of Interplanet. He was going home, to his own people. He would help his father and Rob McGee as far as he could with their desperate undertaking on Freedonia. That would probably fail and fail again, but he could keep on working toward his own goal. If he could ever make a safe bedplate, some bright new future world might stand upon it. If he couldn't—at least the world of Karen Hood would not be shattered with seetee bombs that he had helped design.

He had got his breath and flexed his stiffening fingers and started to climb down, when blue fire exploded in the southward sky. He looked away from it instantly, and dropped into the shadow of the ledge beneath him, but even its reflection on the rocks beyond was bright enough to blot out the stars. It hurt his eyes. It was brighter than the sun, so terribly bright that he had to cover his face and cower back against the shielding cliff.

Was it Freedonia? That cruel fear shook him, when he thought of his father's project there. Had his father and Rob McGee resumed their hazardous experiments, and detonated that suspended block of contraterrene iron?

No, that couldn't be. The blaze reflected from the crags beyond him was far too hot. It kept him pinned down against the ledge too long. The reacting object must have been something larger than that test block. Something as large as the seetee planetoid that his father and McGee had blasted away from Freedonia.

But what could it have struck? McGee had calculated its new orbit to keep it safely away from the space lanes and all the terrene rocks. And McGee didn't make mistakes—not about the things he knew. Besides, the Seetee Patrol had been watching it, ever since the blast, to make certain that its new orbit was really safe. Nothing in its path could have been overlooked. Nothing so big.

Yet that savage blaze kept on burning, and it had to be—something. A nova? An exploding star, long light-years distant but yet already brighter than the sun? He was considering that uncomfortable possibility, and beginning to wonder how long he could stand this searing radiation—how long anything could survive—when it went out.

For an instant he was blind. Then he could see the lighted knob of the town below him, and soon the constellations. But there was no new star fading in the south. No reddening breath of incandescence. Nothing. The abrupt and total extinction of that dreadful light seemed stranger to him than its sudden coming.

He shivered again. The eternal spatial night had reached out to touch him with a bright and frightening finger. Yet what he felt was something else than fear. He felt shaken, but also curiously excited. In the ominous darkness where that light had burned and died, he could feel a veiled and lingering danger—but also an unknown promise beckoning.

His fingers slipped, where he clung to the ledge. Suddenly giddy, he clutched wildly at the frosty stone. He had forgotten to breathe—and the carbon dioxide, at this low pressure, escaped from the lungs too swiftly to stimulate unconscious breathing. He fought weakly for oxygen, until he was able at last to climb back down toward the toppling town.

Chapter VI
"Kiss Your Girl Good-by!"

RICK WENT BACK to his hotel and called Ann O'Banion. It took a long time to reach her—so long that he was taut and breathless with unease before he heard her answer.

"Ann, are you all right?" he whispered huskily. "My father and McGee—do you know if they were hurt? I just saw a terrible flash out that way. I can't imagine what it was."

And he waited, listening to the whispering light.

"That dreadful blast!" Her faint voice came back to him finally, sucked dry of life and meaning by that empty distance. "No, Rick, I can't even guess what it was. But we're safe here. Whatever it was, it happened somewhere on beyond Freedonia. I've just been talking with your father. He's out there alone now, but he says he wasn't hurt."

"When you call him again, tell him I'll be with him soon." Rick thought of all the spies who might be listening in, and tried not to say too much. "You see, I'm through here tomorrow. I want to come back home as soon as I can get passage."

Again he had to wait, while the starlight murmured.

"Rick, that's wonderful! We do need you—" Her faint, far-off voice seemed delighted at first, but then it hushed and became as cautious as his own. "You can get passage soon," she said. "Captain McGee will be landing at Pallasport tomorrow night, for another load of supplies. You can come back with him."

Rick had trouble going to sleep that night. He lay a

long time thinking of his father and McGee and the meager equipment they would have on Freedonia, wondering what steps he could help them take toward building a safe bedplate. Karen Hood's blue eyes kept frowning warningly upon all the hazardous schemes he thought of, however, and he couldn't forget the riddle of that deadly light and its abrupt extinction.

The telephone aroused him, early next morning.

" 'Scuse me, Drake." It was Anders. "Can you come right down to the office?"

That was all the Earthman said, but his slurred voice had an imperative undertone. Rick hurried without his breakfast to the Interplanet Building, and found Anders waiting for him. Still in the trim black dress uniform he must have worn somewhere with Karen, the lean Guardsman hadn't been to bed.

"G'day, Drake." Anders had been working at the drafting desk. He swept a thick sheaf of notes and calculations into his brief case and looked up at Rick with tired, worried eyes. "S'pose you heard about that flash last night?"

"I saw it, and wondered—"

Rick's voice faltered and trailed off, before the challenge on the Earthman's stern brown face.

"D'you know what it was?"

"Seetee, I guess," Rick said.

"How d'you know?"

"I don't know anything." Rick heard the snap of anger in his own voice, and envied the other man's cool self-possession. "All I saw was that flash in the sky. It looked too hot for any sort of atomic fission or fusion reaction. It went out too fast for a nova. So far as I know that leaves only seetee."

"No 'fense, Drake." The suave, dark smile of Anders made him feel a childish fool. "Fact is, it was seetee. That's why I phoned you. As a seetee engineer, p'raps you can solve a riddle for us."

"I'm afraid I haven't done very much to establish myself as a seetee engineer." Rick shrugged. "But that looked like quite a collision! The Seetee Patrol must have been asleep, to let it happen. Do you know what bodies were involved?"

"One of them was the seetee asteroid whose orbit your father tampered with last year." The Earthman's fatigue-reddened eyes searched Rick bleakly, and then fell to a scrap of paper he had left on the drafting table. "Number HSM CT-445-N-812 in the *Ephemeris and Register*. Estimated diameter 90 meters. Composition, from albedo and magnetic readings, b'lieved to be chiefly seetee iron."

Rick nodded. "But what did it hit?"

"That's the riddle—or part of it." Anders blinked at him watchfully. "The Seetee Patrol observed that blast your father set off, and reported the new orbit safe. And luckily that rock was under observation, from the Guard observatory on Pallas I, when this thing happened. Young chap had the three-meter camera pointed at something in Dorado, and he was watching through the guide scope. Flash ruined the plate in the camera. Nearly blinded him, in fact. But he had just exposed another plate that showed the seetee asteroid—and nothing else near that it could have hit.

"What d'you think of that?"

Rick's knuckles had begun an absent drumming on the corner of the drafting table. He saw the Earthman's annoyed expression, and dropped his hand awkwardly.

"I don't know what to think," he said. "But the queerest thing to me about that flash was the sudden way it went out, with no visible afterglow. I wonder if your astronomer got any more photographs?"

For an uncomfortable half-minute, Anders merely looked at him.

"Several more," the Earthman said at last. "What they show is the rest of our riddle. Y'see, that little rock looks different now."

"I'd think so," Rick said. "Most of it must have been turned to radiation."

"Our man thought so." Anders nodded slowly, the

muscles bunching hard in his lean brown jaw. "Fact, he got a reading on that radiation. Figures show the mass of the asteroid should have been all used up—four or five times over. Funny thing, it wasn't. Photos show two fragments flying away from the point of impact. Main one looks larger than the whole asteroid did."

"Huh?" Rick stared at him. "Those fragments—are they still incandescent?"

"By no means, Drake," the Earthman said gently. "Our astronomer took a bolometer reading at twenty hundred—less than fifteen minutes after that flash went out. Temperature of the main fragment was then about thirty degrees absolute—two hundred and forty degrees below zero."

"That doesn't seem possible." Rick shook his head dazedly. "Anything in ten thousand kilometers of that flash should have been vaporized."

"Should have been." Anders nodded cheerfully. "But something did happen, out there. Problem is to find out what it was. I'm asking for active duty with the Seetee Patrol. If Hood will give me a ship, I'm going out to investigate—whatever happened. I'll have Vickers arrange for you to come with me."

Before the Earthman's brittle-voiced assurance, Rick flushed with a needless resentment.

"Vickers can't arrange it." He tried to keep the ridiculous quiver out of his voice. "You see, my contract runs out today. I've decided not to sign another."

The gray eyes of Anders narrowed with a watchful I-thought-so expression. "I've been wondering about you, Drake." The casual tone of his slurred, rapid voice didn't change. "If you quit Interplanet, what are you going to do?"

"That's my own affair."

"Don't upset yourself." With a half-amused smile, Anders offered a long cigarette. "Unless you've reason to!" His voice dropped, with an affable candor. "As you may have suspected, my real assignment here as Hood's special aide has been to size up the military possibilities of seetee."

"I thought so," Rick admitted. "And you know how I feel about that."

"Your heart is pure." Anders grinned sardonically. "But pure hearts make indifferent weapons. With all our enemies scrambling for seetee bombs, we've got to get 'em first." His hard brown face turned grave. "If money'll change your way of thinking, I'll talk to Vickers."

Rick merely shook his head, because he didn't trust his voice.

"S'long, then, if that's the way you want it." The Earthman waved his competent hand, with a meaningless graceful gesture. "Hate to see a good engineer go wrong, but I've got things to do."

He caught up his brief case and hurried out.

Rick watched him go, and stood frowning at that riddle. How could any rock light up space like a sun, and then emerge from its own extinguished conflagration, almost intact but chilled close to the absolute zero?

Rick could see no sane answer—unless his father and Rob McGee were somehow responsible, with their illegal secret project on Freedonia. That was surely impossible, but a cold anxiety took his breath. He called the space port to ask if McGee had arrived.

"Not yet, sir," the control office answered. "Captain McGee is due here late tonight from Obania, but he hasn't yet called for his landing orders."

Waiting for McGee, Rick tried to work on his last report for Anders, on the relative deadliness of the reacting seetee elements, but that exploding asteroid was still a puzzle that he could neither solve nor put out of his mind. He was sitting motionless at the drafting table, scowling over it, when Karen spoke behind him.

"Rick, may I come in?"

Her eyes were hollowed and shadowed, as if she had slept no more than Anders, and her voice seemed dull with trouble. He went to meet her and offered a chair, but she shook her head.

"Rick, Paul just phoned." She came to the drafting table beside him, and stood absently worrying a handkerchief with her fingers. "He says you're really leaving Interplanet."

Her breathing was uneven with disturbed emotion, and her fine skin flushed. He caught a faint scent of expensive perfume. She was lovely and distressed, and perhaps he had made the wrong decision. But then he saw the cold splendor of the diamond on her right hand, with the tiny space ship embedded in it like a fly trapped in amber.

"I am quitting." A sudden tension rang in his voice. "But we agreed not to quarrel any more about it."

"I didn't mean to say another word, before that seetee rock went crazy." Her white fingers twisted the white lace tighter. "Paul doesn't know what happened to it. But he's worried, Rick. We're all worried. We've got to find out the truth, before the same thing starts happening to more important planets! And Paul says you're the best seetee engineer he knows. He says we really need you, Rick. Earth does—and Interplanet. That's why I came."

Her urgent nearness hurt him, and he drew back stiffly.

"It's no use, Karen." He blinked at her uncomfortably, and envied the finished ease of Anders. "I've been trying to be an Earthman—mostly because of you. But it didn't work out. I'm going back to the little rocks where I was born. I'm sorry—I really tried."

Her red mouth was quivering, and her voice scarcely a whisper. "Rick, I can't understand you. You've made a fine start with Interplanet. Uncle Austin likes you. Vickers is willing to double your pay. Paul says you have a brilliant future—if you'll only wake up!"

"I have waked up." He gulped to smooth his voice. "I came out here last year with ideals about my calling as a spatial engineer. I wanted to turn these little rocks into gardens for men. I was stupid enough to believe your great company might help me try to do it. Now I know better."

Karen stared at him. Her long triangular face had

turned pale and something cold was glinting in her troubled eyes and he knew she didn't understand.

"Ideals aren't what you need to work for Interplanet." His voice dropped to a bitter rasp. "Now I know the rules. Get all you can as soon as you can. Sweat and tax and graft the last dirty dollar out of the damned rock rats, and take it back to Solar City, to buy a mistress and a paunch and a granite mausoleum." He saw her face go white, as if he had struck it. "Well, that's not for me. I'm sick of Interplanet—and all the complicated dirty work of the Mandate. I'm going back where I belong."

Then he saw that she was crying, blinking at her angry tears and biting her quivering lower lip. He relaxed his clenched hands and said more gently:

"I'm sorry, Karen. I shouldn't have told you that—though it's still the truth."

"But it isn't!" She tossed a strand of flame-colored hair out of her white face and twisted the handkerchief again. "You're unjust, Rick." Her hurt voice stabbed him with a dull regret. "And Interplanet needs you so. It needs us all, now when our enemies are plotting and arming so desperately against us. A few of our company people may have been selfish grafters. But more men have been, and will be, true enough to die for Interplanet. I expected you to be loyal."

And she stood looking at him with wet, blue-black eyes, angry but yet hopeful. He shrugged unhappily, because he knew she would never understand.

"You have to defend Interplanet," he said hopelessly, "because you're part of it. But I'm not." Awkwardly, he caught her hand. "I'm sorry, Karen. I really tried to be an Earthman, but it isn't any use."

She freed her cold hand and turned away from him. He thought she was going to run out of the room. He took a long, impulsive stride after her.

"Wait, Karen. I mean—may I see you again before I go? Say, for lunch?"

She paused at the door, pushing absently at that bright wisp of hair.

"We'd only quarrel. Anyhow, I'm having lunch with Paul." But she came back toward him. Her eyes were dry again, and dark with anxiety. "Rick, would you consider staying just a few weeks longer, to help him investigate this last explosion?"

"Sorry, Karen." He shook his head. "Captain McGee is due here today, and I'm going with him."

"I'm frightened, Rick." Her distress shook him. "Whatever happened is a danger to Earth and Interplanet. That little rock seems to have broken all the known laws of science. Because, Paul says, it obeyed some unknown law. And that unknown law can give a terrible power to whoever learns it."

Her eyes were dark and imploring.

"Can't you see the danger? We're already fighting for our lives, Uncle Austin says, against the vicious, underhanded attacks of the other Mandate powers—even of the asterite Free Space Party. Won't you go out with Paul, if he can get a ship?"

He wanted to go. The enigma of that exploding but unwarmed rock still fascinated him, and Karen was hard to refuse. She saw him hesitate, and the hope on her white face caught his breath.

"No, Kay." He gulped, and flinched from her wounded expression. "I'm going to be a rock rat, now. Even if I knew that unknown law, I don't think I'd sell out to Interplanet."

"Traitor!" She sobbed the word and ran.

Rick slumped wearily over the drafting desk and tried to be a philosopher. After all, he told himself, you can't have everything. But his philosophy began to crumble. Karen's hurt face kept looking up reproachfully from the blotter on the desk, until he felt sorry he had spoken so harshly. He had reached abjectly for the telephone, to call her and apologize, when it rang beneath his fingers.

"Mr. Richard Drake?" he heard the operator. "Photophone calling you from Captain Rob McGee, aboard the space ship *Good-by Jane*. Will you receive the call, sir? Nine dollars for three minutes?"

Eagerly, he said he would.

"Then please stand by, sir. It will take a few minutes for the call to come through, because your party is forty million kilometers off in the south."

"Forty million—"

He caught himself—but that would put McGee far beyond Obania and Freedonia, near where that seetee rock had exploded. An uneasy suspicion took hold of him, that McGee and his father had been somehow responsible for that mysterious blast. Whatever the truth, McGee ought to know better than to place a call from that point, so far off his course to Pallasport, with the agents of all the planets listening in.

Huskily, he said he would stand by.

"Hello, Rick." McGee's gentle drawl came at last along the endless thread of light, bringing him an image of the thickset little spaceman, brown and squinted, with a short black pipe clamped in the middle of his square, stubborn face.

"So you've decided to quit Interplanet, and join our little outfit? Welcome, to Drake, McGee and Drake! We really need you, Rick. Your father and I have been together since before the war. We've made a good team, too. But we're getting older than we used to be, and now we're going to have some big new projects coming up that are sure to call for a keen young man.

"But three minutes isn't long, Rick, and here's why I called you." The remote, soft voice seemed to hurry, and Rick thought it trembled with a tired excitement. "Something's happened! I left Obania with nothing but bad news for you. Your father had got discouraged about building any sort of—of metallurgy lab, if you know what I mean—and he wanted me to tell you to stay on with Interplanet. But something happened, on the way, and things look better now."

Rick sat up straighter.

"I can't tell you much about it now," the hurried drawl continued. "But I'll be landing at Pallasport tonight at twenty-one hundred. You'd better get your space bag packed and kiss your girl good-by, because it's quite a job that you and I have to do."

Rick caught his breath. The rustle of interfering light reminded him that McGee was forty million kilometers away. The ancient little *Good-by Jane* would need something like a week to cover such a distance. McGee couldn't possibly be landing tonight—but Rick gripped the receiver and listened desperately.

"You'll come to understand why I can't tell you everything," McGee rushed on. "You wouldn't believe me if I tried. But you already know what a really safe bedplate would mean for the metallurgy lab, and there's a working model waiting for us out here in what people take to be the debris of that last seetee explosion. What we have to do is win a race with all the other men who want it— including Captain A."

Rick shook his head, in useless protest. With the spies of every Mandate power surely listening in, that open reference to a bedplate would be enough to start a frantic race to seize it. McGee should have been a little more discreet.

"That's really quite an undertaking," the space-thinned voice ran on. "But don't give up too soon. Remember that the last shall be first, and the first the last. I may even stare and say I didn't call you, but pay no attention to that. Because the bedplate's waiting for us. We're apt to meet some pretty curious difficulties, but I've good reason to believe we can finally beat them all." The three minutes were gone, and McGee finished hastily, "Better not reply."

The receiver clicked and the operator asked:

"Do you wish to call back, sir?"

"Eh?" Rick muttered vaguely. "No, I won't call back."

He replaced the instrument and sat with his elbows propped on the drafting table, staring blankly at the wall. He didn't understand anything about that call—except

66

that it looked like an open invitation for trouble with everybody who knew the value of a safe bedplate. But even though he knew McGee couldn't possibly be landing tonight—and though he had no girl to kiss good-by —he meant to be waiting with his space bag packed.

Chapter VII
The Narrow Footway

LATE THAT SAME DAY, Captain Paul Anders reported to Austin Hood. Announcing him, the male secretary's curt, impersonal voice made a hollow echo in the long, glittering official room. He stood lean and spare in his Guardsman's black, waiting stiffly at attention. He had no good news for the High Commissioner, and he was prepared for a trying interview.

"At ease, old man." Austin Hood returned his crisp salute with a genial, unmilitary gesture. Beyond the polished gleam of the huge jadewood desk, Hood was red and bulky, loud with a bluff assurance. "Karen says you want to run down this trick rock? Take a chair, old man, and let's talk about it."

Hood was smiling, with a politician's ready heartiness. but his ice-blue eyes remained shrewdly watchful and the smile failed to erase the fine web of worried lines in the dark fat around them. Anders sat down uncomfortably on a hard metal chair. He saw his application for active duty with the Seetee Patrol lying on the shining hardwood, but Hood's loud, public voice gave him no time to say anything about it.

"Well, old man, you've had almost twenty-four hours since this seetee rock started playing tricks on the laws of nature." Hood's eyes watched him, less genial than the booming voice. "What have you found out?"

"Too little, Mr. Hood." Anders frowned with his own deep bewilderment. "No more violent seetee reaction has ever been observed. Nothing except a major collision could have set it off. Yet the orbit of that rock had been reported clear, and there simply isn't any known terrene body that could have been involved.

"Two fragments were blown away from the point of impact. The smaller had a fantastically high velocity. It has already disappeared. The larger is moving away from us at nearly fifty kilometers a second—and it was somehow blown out of that inferno of heat with its own temperature still close to the absolute zero."

He moved uneasily on the hard chair.

"Those are the facts—and they don't add up. That main fragment still looks somewhat larger in the telescope than the seetee rock did before the collision—but measurements of the radiated energy show that several times the entire mass of the rock must have been consumed. Any blast terrific enough to scatter the debris at such velocities should have broken it into smaller pieces—and certainly warmed them up somewhat." He shook his head blankly. "I can't imagine what happened."

Hood leaned forward a little, his cold eyes narrowed. "D'you know any more about that smaller fragment?"

"Nothing that makes sense." Anders shrugged. "I had two reports on it from our people at the observatory. The first said it was moving very rapidly in our general direction. The second said it had already passed in a few million kilometers of Pallas—moving at something over a thousand kilometers a second—and disappeared. It's gone —we couldn't hope to overtake it. Our ships aren't that fast."

"But I've got a picture of it." The High Commissioner sat silent for a moment, scowling past Anders at the jadewood paneling and drumming in a disturbed way on the shining desk. "Maybe you can tell me whether the picture makes sense. But before you look, I want to ask you a question."

Anders nodded, but the big man hesitated again, with his red poker-face frozen into a harsh immobility and a strange unease in his eyes.

"Yes?" Anders said.

"Could there be—" Hood paused to swallow, and something hushed his voice. "Do you think there could be—seetee people?"

"Huh?" Anders blinked. "Why?"

"Would it be possible?"

"Theoretically, yes," Anders answered soberly. "Every terrene element has its contraterrene twin, that obeys the same laws and forms the same compounds. A seetee planet, with precisely the right conditions of chemistry and climate, might possibly evolve seetee life. But there's no such planet now. The theory is that the seetee drift must be the debris of some larger seetee body that shattered the original fifth planet into these terrene rocks, but nothing could have survived that smash. You haven't—" A mounting excitement shook his voice. "You can't have any evidence of contraterrene life!"

"You tell me what it is."

Hood bent to unlock a drawer of the desk, and straightened heavily with a tiny reel of three-millimeter film and a compact stereo-viewer. Carefully, his fat, blunt fingers threaded the film behind the lenses.

"Picture through the courtesy of your friend, Captain Franz von Falkenberg." Hood grinned briefly. "He had been out on patrol, around Freedonia—probably had secret orders from the Martian Commissioner to watch those rock rats, Drake and McGee. He was cruising back toward Obania when his watch officers saw the flash behind, and discovered that high-velocity fragment coming after them. He turned the *Perseus* to intercept it, and got close enough to hit it with a test shot. This shows you how it looked."

Anders rose eagerly to reach for the viewer.

"Careful!" Hood warned him. "That scrap of film cost the company two hundred thousand Mandate dollars."

"A lot of money." Anders paused inquiringly.

"But a wise buy, as you'll see."

"Von Falkenberg didn't sell out to Interplanet?"

"By no means." Hood was grinning again, obviously pleased with himself. "He's still playing the old Mandate game. Should have rushed that film to Guard headquarters, for all of us to see, but naturally he wanted to keep the advantage for Mars."

"Naturally," Anders nodded.

"So he landed on Obania, with his crew ordered not to talk, and sent the film by commercial beam to a lawyer here in town, who has been retained by the Martian government. The lawyer was to turn it over to them. But our people had got a private tip from a stooge we have on the *Perseus*, and our Mr. Vickers sent a man to meet the lawyer's price." Hood chuckled. "So we've got the film, and von Falkenberg is still waiting on Obania, expecting secret orders from the Martian commissioner."

Anders raised the viewer and pressed the stud to start its quiet mechanism. He saw a view of space with the stars magnified to tiny, color-ringed halation disks hung in frosty darkness. Out of that darkness a meteor came tumbling. He blinked at its shape.

"A needle!" he whispered. "A golden needle—broken off."

The viewer hummed with a muted vibration, and the spinning object came nearer in the lenses. Glancing in the sunlight, it looked small and near against the stars. The sharp tip of a thin golden cone, broken jaggedly.

"Huh!" His breath caught, as the swinging camera brought a human figure into view: a spaceman in bulky dirigible armor, hanging motionless behind the long thin tube and the intricate sights of a testing gun. The man's nearness pushed that small golden needle back into stereoscopic perspective—and made it huge. A good hundred meters long, Anders estimated; five meters thick across the jagged base.

"You see all that in slow motion, of course," Hood was saying. "Because the *Perseus* might as well have been standing still. Von Falkenberg was just lucky enough— for us—to have his men ready with a long-range gun and a telephoto lens on a high-speed camera, when it went by."

71

The camera swept on past the man and the gun, following that enormous broken needle that came whirling end over end out of the starry emptiness.

"Look at it!" Hood's bluff voice was suddenly hushed, with something close to dread. "Look for anything to suggest that it might be seetee."

"There wouldn't be anything." Anders stopped the film and shook his head. "Every property of terrene matter is faithfully repeated in seetee. A seetee man might look exactly like one of us, theoretically—though he wouldn't last long in terrene air. There's no test except contact."

He stared at the High Commissioner.

"Did that shot show—"

"Watch it!" Hood rasped. "Tell me what you see."

Anders touched the stud again, and saw that the needle was hollow. Sunlight swept inside as it turned, to catch a spiral ramp that wound upward inside the golden shell, with a polished railing high above it.

Something about the ramp and the railing gave him an oppressive sense of wrongness, and after a moment of uncomfortable puzzlement he saw that the inclined footway was queerly narrow, and the bright railing strangely high. Almost apprehensively, he stopped the film again.

"That ramp and rail—they weren't made for men," he whispered sharply. "Is that why you think the thing's seetee?"

"Keep looking," Hood said. "Watch the test."

He started the viewer, and that broken spire came hurtling on toward him, enormous in the telephoto lenses, moving many times faster than the testing shot that had been fired to intercept it. It was almost dangerously near when the tiny terrene bullet struck—and veiled it with a sudden blinding whiteness.

"No question—" Anders had ducked away from the flash, in spite of himself, and he had to gasp for his breath. "It's seetee!"

He watched for a moment longer, while that white blaze reddened and went out. A wide, jagged hole peered darkly at him from the yellow metal, torn by that savage reaction with a few milligrams of terrene iron. The needle flashed by and whirled on away from the camera, until the short film ended.

"Well?" Hood rapped impatiently. "What do you make of it?"

" 'Stounding!" Anders put the viewer down dazedly and stood staring at the mirror-like hardwood, trying to organize his thoughts. "But that object was certainly see-tee."

"Built by seetee—things?"

"Maybe." Anders looked up abruptly. "Or else by men —on the sort of bedplate young Rick Drake has been dreaming about!"

"Think so?"

"Don't know what to think." Anders rubbed uncertainly at his hard brown jaw. "Even granting there were seetee creatures on that alien planet, I don't see how any of their works could have survived so long. But then I don't know why men would build that sort of tower, with that queer ramp inside."

"One proposition or the other must be true," Hood said bleakly. "And either one could wreck Interplanet. We've got to move—fast!"

"I'm ready." Anders looked again at his application for duty with the Seetee Patrol. "That queer tower is gone forever, but I want to investigate the other—the larger fragment, that went the other way. It's velocity isn't quite so fantastic. A fast cruiser, starting now, could overtake it in five or six days. And I think the first men there ought to learn something int'resting." His voice tightened urgently. "If you can get me put back on active duty, in time to get there ahead of von Falkenberg—"

Hood lifted a broad, imperative hand.

"Before we talk about your duty," he broke in, "I want your opinion on another bit of data. A voice transcription from one of our private listening posts. A photo-phone call that was made today by that rock rat, Rob McGee, from out near where that explosion happened. It was accepted and received by young Drake, though he didn't reply. I don't know what it means, and I want your advice."

He leaned to touch his desk transcriber.

"Hello, Rick." The soft drawl of Rob McGee rustled thinly through a crackling roar of starlight. "So you've decided to quit Interplanet, and join our little outfit?"

Anders stood listening in a kind of bleak astonishment, while McGee's recorded voice ran on. Rick Drake was to get his space bag packed, because there was a model bedplate waiting, if he could win a race with Captain A. The last should be first, and the first the last. And Rick had better not reply.

"Well, Captain A." Hood's cold eyes had a brief sardonic glint. "What do you make of that?"

"I think it means we have to deal with men." Anders nodded grimly. "Those damned rock rats! I can't believe they've invented any sort of useful bedplate—but couldn't it be that they found something on that seetee rock, when they were steering it away from Freedonia? Things made by the beings of the wandering seetee world that broke up old Adonis. That golden tower. Probably other seetee artifacts. Possibly even a real bedplate!"

A thin smile crossed his hard brown face.

"Now I know you'll have to get me a ship, to follow that object."

"Has it occurred to you that such a mission might be highly hazardous?" Hood's broad red face turned bleak. "That rock rat knew his call would be intercepted. His broadcast invitation to come out and get a model bedplate looks to me like bait for some kind of trap—and a seetee trap could be uncomfortable."

"I'll keep that possibility in mind." Anders nodded, his lean face hardening. "But still I want to go. And if I'm going to be racing Rick Drake and von Falkenberg and everybody else who might want a really safe seetee bedplate for his own planet—then I want to get started soon."

"Karen told me you'd say that." The High Commissioner rose, and came around the desk to shake his hand.

"And I like your spirit, Anders. The company needs such men. Your fine loyalty won't go unrewarded."

"Then I do get a ship?"

"The new cruiser *Orion*." Hood beamed genially, waddling back toward his chair. "A sister craft to von Falkenberg's, just completed at the yards on Pallas II. Our inside organization will see to the selection of a crew you can trust."

"Trust?" Anders grinned. "You mean, to sell out the Mandate?"

Hood flushed.

"Loyalty to our corporation and our native planet is no fit matter for levity," he said stiffly. "Not even when it does involve technical treason to the Mandate. You know the Guard."

Anders nodded soberly, for he did know the High Space Guard. Under the Treaty of Space, it was formed, like the Commission itself, on a ratio of two men from Earth to one each from Venus, Mars, and the Jovian Soviet. All were required to swear allegiance to the Mandate, but most remained as loyal as he was to their own native worlds.

"Your official orders will be issued at once," Hood continued sternly. "You will be assigned to the Seetee Patrol, to investigate that unpredicted collision and take any required action to protect the shipping routes and inhabited rocks. Of course von Falkenberg will want that assignment, but we can keep him stalled on Obania a few days longer."

"Waiting for orders." Anders nodded appreciatively. "While we're running down that object—whatever it is —and bringing home the seetee bedplate."

"But keep in mind that it looks like a trap." The High Commissioner bent to lock the viewer and its film back in the desk. He straightened, puffing slightly, with a penciled memorandum in his thick, pink fingers. "I want you to do a little confidential detective work on Obania and Freedonia, before you go chasing after it."

Anders frowned doubtfully. "Any long delay might cost us the race."

"Don't forget that the last are to be first." Hood grinned bleakly. "We'll keep the competition tied down, while you find out what those damned rock rats are really up to. Two people I want you to question, on Obania."

He peered down at his memorandum.

"An asterite girl named Ann O'Banion, employed by Drake and McGee. Her father, a decayed rock rat politician—probably involved with the Free Space Party. If you can pin anything on them—either seetee research or inciting discontent—ship them both back to the prison on Pallas IV."

"Yes, sir."

"And then I want you to find out what it is that Drake and McGee have set up on Freedonia that they call a metallurgy lab. Von Falkenberg wasn't able to get inside the clouds of seetee dust they've managed to spread around it, but that girl ought to know how they come and go."

"I'll find out."

"One more suspect on my list." Hood scowled at it. "Young Rick Drake."

"But I know Rick," Anders protested. "He has really been doing his best to design a workable bedplate for us. I don't think he could be involved in any sort of plot."

"But Karen says he's turning against us." Hood's fat face stiffened. "And he did receive that call. Probably getting his space bag packed, right now, to go after that model bedplate. We've got to keep him on the ground, and watch him like a snake."

Chapter VIII
A Sense of Space-Time

KAREN CALLED, at fourteen hundred.

"Mr. Drake?"

Rick flinched in spite of himself, and tried to match her cool remoteness.

"Yes, Miss Hood?"

"I believe you are still on our payroll," she said stiffly.

"Until eighteen hundred today," he agreed.

"Then we have one more job for you. Mr. Vickers wants you to change the tuning diamonds in the terraforming units on Pallas IV. A prison tender will call for you at the space port in half an hour. The job order is ready for you at my office." She hung up.

Pallas IV was one of the six small rocks that had been towed into stable positions, sixty degrees apart in the same orbit, as trailing moonlets of the minor planet, to serve as outposts and bases for the High Space Guard. The Mandate prison was on Pallas IV.

Changing the tuning diamonds there was a routine job that had nothing to do with the seetee research for which he had been hired, but Rick found a set of tools and went up in the elevator to Karen's office. He found her dictating into a machine. She looked up at him with a pale, empty smile, and silently handed him an unsealed envelope.

He took the order back down to a wicket in the supply room, and signed a receipt for three small diamonds, value nine thousand dollars each. They were clear natural octahedral crystals. He dropped them into a small black pouch the armed clerk gave him, and hurried out to the space port.

The prison tender was waiting for him, a slender white torpedo. An alert young Earthman in the uniform of a Guard lieutenant welcomed him politely aboard. Twenty minutes later, they landed on the prison asteroid.

Pallas IV was a thousand-meter block of dark nickel-iron, clad in a frosty breath of synthetic air. Orange lights marked the landing field, but the guns and the barracks, and even the prison, were all buried deep in its hard natural armor.

They left the ship. A guard elevator dropped them to the terraformer room at the center of gravity. There, inside the polar elements, their bodies had no weight, and hand lines were strung to guide and hold them about the machinery. Rick asked the lieutenant:

"Which unit is giving the trouble?"

"None of them." The young Earthman gave him a friendly smile. "You're to change all the crystals. The warden's orders. A safety measure."

That seemed odd. Tuning diamonds were sometimes burned up by accidental overloads, but they didn't wear out. New ones would be no safer than the old. Rick changed all three, however, carefully resetting and testing each unit as he went. He finished and gathered up his tools and nodded at the officer.

"All through?" the guardsman asked cheerfully. "Say, care to see the prison while you're here? I must report to the warden now, and it will save us time if you'll come along."

"If you like," Rick agreed, though he wasn't anxious to see the prison. He showed the little pouch of used diamonds, all as good as new. "But I'm responsible for these, remember."

"They'll be safe," the lieutenant assured him. "We're only walking through the political cell block."

A double set of clanging steel doors let them into a wide gallery, cut deep into the living iron. Faced with open bars, the cells were three levels high. Gray steel ladders and catwalks made an ugly web across the upper tiers. Armored floodlamps filled the whole gallery with a chill blue glare, and the air stank with a bitter musk of human confinement. A glimpse of dead-white faces peering stupidly through the bars made Rick hurry his long stride uncomfortably.

"Slow!" his guide called softly. "Don't get yourself shot."

He checked himself, suddenly conscious of the automatic guns frowning out of slotted turrets. His face must have showed his shocked unease, because the lieutenant told him in a brisk undertone:

"This isn't so bad. These men aren't abused. This is our model cell block, really. Political prisoners, you know. They aren't forced to work, though some of them are allowed to earn tobacco money. The food is good enough, and we give them all the liberties possible. They leave the cells for meals. They have books and writing materials. They get two hours of group exercise daily." His lowered voice had a ring of professional pride. "Modern penology, you know. We don't punish criminals here; we straighten twisted minds."

"I—I see." Rick managed a sickly grin.

"Drake!"

That rasping scream halted Rick, and turned him to see a hollowed ghastly face staring down at him through the bars of a second-level cell. Broken, bloodless hands rattled the locked door furiously, almost drowning that cracked and dreadful voice.

"Drake—have you seen my Mary?"

"Come along." The lieutenant touched Rick's arm. "You'll need special permission, if you want to talk to him."

"I don't know the man." Rick turned away uneasily, trying to shake off the agony of that dry scream. "I never saw him."

"Wait, Drake, damn you!" that blade-keen cry slashed after him. "My Mary—is she dead?"

Rick strode on, hot and breathless. The voice turned

hoarsely foul, cursing them, and then it was thinned again with a frantic mental agony.

"Don't you know me, Jim?" it whined. "Won't they let you speak?"

He stumbled blindly on, but suddenly he understood. Jim Drake was roan-haired and shrunken now, stooped with sixty years, but the prisoner must have known him when he looked more like his son.

"No, I'm sure you couldn't know him," the quiet young officer agreed. "Because he has been here for nearly fifteen years. Life, on a treason conviction. He belonged to the Free Space Party."

That empty husk of a voice cursed again behind them, despairingly.

"Gone simple," the lieutenant said. "He believed this Jim Drake is busy building seetee weapons, with some sort of impossible gadget he calls a bedplate, to arm the Free Space Party and overthrown the Mandate."

Rick blinked at him in dismay, but his pink young face looked innocent. "Seems there really is an old rock rat engineer named Jim Drake," he added casually. "But I guess there's no real danger of him making trouble with seetee bombs, or the Guard would have him in here with his friends."

Following silently, Rick tried not to shiver. He had begun to feel slightly ill from the stale prison fetor and the harsh blue glare and the crushing weight of living iron above. Those wild screams kept ringing in his mind. He couldn't help wondering why this last job for Interplanet had brought him through the political cell block, and he didn't like the only possible answer.

He held himself from hurrying, and forced himself to listen to casual statistics about the prison bake shop and the laundry and the ventilating system. At last they were outside the steel doors again, in air clean enough to breathe.

"Sorry for that disturbance," the lieutenant said. "Most unfortunate, but please forget it. Wait here just a moment while I speak to the warden. We'll have you back at Pallasport in plenty of time for supper."

Rick got back to the Interplanet Building just before seventeen hundred. He unburdened himself of the used diamonds, signed the job report, and carried it up to Karen's office. She looked up inquiringly as he entered, her face pale and thin.

"Here you are." He tossed the job report on her desk, almost defiantly. "And thanks for the prison tour. I saw what becomes of rock rats who don't play ball with Interplanet. I suppose you expect me to sign up, now?"

"Will you, Rick?" She watched him with a tired intentness. "I think Paul has changed his mind about wanting you to go with him out to investigate that last explosion, but we still need a seetee expert here. Uncle Austin says we must persuade you to stay."

He shivered a little, from the lingering chill of the prison. "I don't like your methods."

"Interplanet will pay for services rendered." A quiet determination lifted her faint voice. "You can write your own research budget, and Uncle Austin says he'll see that your expense accounts aren't audited. He told me to promise you that you can put a round million in the bank, if you can give us seetee bombs ahead of anybody else."

"I'm a spatial engineer, Miss Hood." Rick blurted the words in a tight, angered voice. "I came out here to terraform worlds for men to live on—not to graft a fortune."

Karen sat looking up at him with an absent, worried expression, as if she weren't really listening.

"Some things you can't lock up forever, Miss Hood." He knew his outburst was unwise, yet the sudden surge of bitter emotion wouldn't let him stop. "You can keep men buried alive out there on Pallas IV, but there are things that will always make trouble for you—in spite of your scientific modern penology! Things like ideals."

He saw her hollowed eyes flash. She was listening now.

"If your Uncle Austin were living today instead of twenty years ago, he would take the brakes off science and progress. He would let men terraform these rocks—with seetee power. He would give the asterites political equality and a seat on the Commission. That would change the Mandate from a powder magazine to the beginning of a real union for interplanetary peace."

"That sounds like the program of the Free Space Party." Flushed and angry, she stood up. "You had better remember what you saw out there on Pallas IV." She caught her breath, and shook her head at him sadly. "I suppose I'm glad to know what you really think, but please be careful what you say. You're in danger of trouble, Rick. Real trouble."

"Thanks," he said stiffly. "I try to take care of myself."

He went unhappily back down to his office. An unfamiliar guard met him at the door and watched suspiciously while he got his coat and a few personal belongings from the desk. He ate at the Seetee Cafe, and went restlessly back to his room to get his space bag packed.

He had no girl to kiss good-by, but fifteen minutes before twenty-one hundred that night he came striding hopefully into the space port waiting room, with the bag on his shoulder. Watching the clock tick off Mandate time, he waited for the impossible to happen.

It happened. At five minutes of the hour, a speaker blasted out the announcement: "Landing from Obania, the *Good-by Jane*, Captain McGee. Now coming in to berth 81."

Rick burst eagerly outside and followed the port inspectors to berth 81. Waiting outside the barrier he squinted up against the nighttime sun and found the angular, rusty box of the *Good-by Jane*. She dropped alarmingly out of the dark and came down lightly on her creaking gear, landed with McGee's old skill.

There were four inspectors instead of the customary two, and they stayed a long time aboard, as if they had been warned to look for some contraband. They came quietly off at last, however, and one of them lowered the yellow ropes. Rick thought they appeared puzzled and faintly disappointed.

Captain Rob McGee came down the ramp behind them, on small nimble legs. He wore the same mildew-green space coat that Rick remembered, and his sturdy shoulders sagged as if with trouble. When he saw Rick, however, his square leather face tried stiffly to smile.

"Glad to see you, Captain Rob." Rick dropped the bag to seize his stubby hand. "I got your call this morning. Here I am, with my space bag packed. If you know where to find a model bedplate—"

Rick's voice faded, before the blank bewilderment in the little spaceman's squinted red-brown eyes. "My call, you say?" His gentle drawl was puzzled. "I didn't call you, Rick. Bad news will keep, and I had none worth good money to tell."

Dismay shook Rick.

"What's wrong?" he whispered huskily. "My father—"

"Nothing that bad," McGee said hastily. "That last blast did catch him alone on Freedonia, but Ann talked to him afterwards. He says he wasn't hurt."

"Then what is the bad news?"

The little spaceman hesitated, squirming uncomfortably.

"In the first place," he muttered at last, "I am worried about Jim. He couldn't sleep, all the way back. I guess those burns still hurt him, though he didn't complain. Anyhow, he got to brooding. Got discouraged. By the time we landed on Freedonia, he'd decided that his new reactor would never work, not without some sort of bedplate."

"He must have really known it wouldn't, all along." Rick nodded soberly. "But that shouldn't make him too blue. He has failed before."

"He's older," McGee said. "He's giving up. He sent me back to tell you that you had better stay on with Interplanet. That is, if they'll let you do any sort of work that might lead toward a bedplate."

Rick looked down at the little spaceman, who stood uneasily kicking his boots against the pavement. Rick's shoulders drew erect, and his eyes lifted for a moment to the velvet blackness beyond the red sunlit hull of the *Good-by Jane*. His face broke slowly into a hard brown smile.

"No, I'm through with the company." Decision rang in his voice. "I'm going back with you, Captain Rob—after the model bedplate you said was waiting for us, on that splinter from the seetee explosion."

"I'm glad you feel that way, Rick." McGee gave him a weatherbeaten smile that faded into blank perplexity. "But I didn't call you. And I certainly don't know anything about a model bedplate waiting anywhere."

"You aren't trying to joke?"

"Of course not, Rick." McGee shook his shaggy yellow head, his eyes wide and grave as a hurt child's. "I like mathematical puzzles," he admitted. "But I never just joke, the way people do."

"Didn't you see that explosion?"

"I saw it." He nodded uneasily. "The same seetee rock we turned away from Freedonia last year. I was about halfway here from Obania when it blew up like a nova—though there was nothing the size of your fist in a million kilometers of it. It blazed fifty-seven seconds and then went out like a light turned off and started streaking away from the sun."

He stared at Rick, and shivered in the clumsy green coat.

"I saw it," he repeated uncertainly. "And I haven't felt right since."

"How do you mean?"

"Well—" McGee hesitated, kicking at the pavement again. "You know how I am," he muttered faintly at last. "The sense I have. For distances and orbits. The mass of a rock. The time of day." He seemed to grope for words. "I just—just feel them."

"I remember." Rick nodded. "Rob stands for Robot."

"Please forget that." The squinted eyes dropped as if with shame. "People pinned that nickname on me when I was still a boy, fool enough to show how I could work astrogation problems quicker than most robot-pilots.

Dumb enough to be discovered by a Martian scientific expedition. The professors gave me a lot of idiotic tests and wanted to take me back to New Heidelberg like a specimen in a jar. I got away from them, but they did write a paper about me—they called me a long German word that means something like ray-born mutant space-man.

"But please don't think I'm any sort of robot." His low voice was suddenly bitter. "I know I'm different. Not smarter—I can see I'm not as smart as lots of ordinary people, in most ways. Just different. And that gets pretty lonely." He coughed and looked away. "Go ahead and call me Rob, but please forget what it means."

"I'm sorry," Rick told him softly. "Sorry you feel that way. But your sense of things in space looks to me like something to be proud of." His voice quickened hopefully. "Didn't it tell you anything about that exploding rock."

McGee squinted restlessly at the dark sky.

"Just made me sick." He seemed to flinch in the great shabby coat, as if from some internal discomfort. "Always before, when I looked at rocks that were going to collide, I knew just how big they were, and exactly when they would hit, and even which way all the larger fragments had to go. But that explosion was somehow—*wrong!*"

He blinked at Rick, with actual pain in his squinted eyes.

"There was nothing at all that seetee rock could have hit. The main splinter is several times bigger than the whole rock was. It's moving out very fast away from the sun, without any cause."

"And I understand it's still very cold," Rick put in, frowning. "The reflection of that flash was hot enough to blister the back of my neck, here forty million kilometers away. But somehow it failed to warm that fragment much above the absolute zero."

"I don't know about the temperature." McGee shoved his fists into the pockets of the coat, and Rick thought he

85

shuddered. "When I look at it, I don't even know the time of day."

And his hesitant low voice was shaken with a genuine distress, as if he felt lost and blind without that special sense.

"I don't understand that explosion. Or that call you didn't make." Rick stepped back a little, frowning at McGee's perplexity. "But you told me to pay no attention if you said you hadn't called. And you seemed very sure that we could find a bedplate somewhere in that debris. I don't understand anything about it. But I do think we ought to have a look."

McGee's squinted eyes had lifted suddenly.

"Who's your military friend?" he asked softly. "A man as tall as you are, Rick!"

Rick turned to see Captain Anders striding toward them from the military section of the field, followed by the four port inspectors who had already searched the *Good-by Jane*.

"H'lo, Drake." The tall Earthman was careless and assured. He wore Interplanet's ancient greatness, Rick thought, like a badge of high authority. His handsome face broke into a slight, friendly smile, and he looked expectantly at McGee.

"Captain Rob McGee." Rick felt uncomfortably envious of that unshatterable confidence, and he blurted the introduction awkwardly. "Captain Paul Anders, of the Guard."

"G'day, McGee." Anders wasted no title on a rock rat civilian, but his hard gray eyes studied the silent little spaceman with a disquieting intentness. "Might int'rest you to know that I've heard a transcription of your photophone call today, about a seetee bedplate."

"But I didn't—" McGee gulped and checked his protest.

Rick stiffened uneasily. That indiscreet and enigmatic message was going to be awkward to explain, no matter how it came about that McGee denied knowing anything about it.

"S'prised to find you here, McGee." The Earthman's sleek assurance seemed to cover a wary vigilance. "Our listening post reported that you were calling from out near the point of that blowup, forty million kilometers away. How did you get here so fast?"

Rob McGee had turned into a brown, impassive image. "I made no call today." His sudden calm struck Rick with admiration. Anders wore the tarnished might of Interplanet, but the little asterite seemed to share the patient serenity of the stars he knew. He glanced affectionately up at the clumsy hull of his little ship. "And we haven't been near that seetee rock."

"Prob'ly an error in our report." The sardonic tone of those slurred words called McGee a liar. "But I must be your mysterious Captain A." Anders swung back to Rick, and his voice had a brittle rap. "So you think you've got a seetee bedplate waiting for you on that runaway rock? If you can just beat me there!"

McGee stood silent, but Rick caught his breath and blurted impulsively:

"Why not? I'd give my right arm for a good bedplate, and it's just possible we could beat you there." He grinned slightly at the cool Earthman. "Or even if you get there first, that will make you the last, remember."

Anders returned his grin, and he wondered if anything could ever crack the Earthman's iron assurance.

"Sure of that?"

Rick shook his head, frowning uneasily in spite of himself.

"Follow—if you can." Anders paused easily to light a long cigarette, but Rick could hear the frosty snap of danger in his voice. "But you know civilians aren't allowed within a hundred kilometers of any seetee object, and I intend to be in position to enforce that law with spatial guns. Think that over."

Rick thought it over, smiling a little at the shocked protest on McGee's square face. After his year of submission to the company, it was curiously pleasant to make a gesture of defiance; and the inexplicable behavior of that unknown object was still a lure that drew him.

"I think we'll tag along," he said deliberately. "If there really is a bedplate on that object, it can't be all seetee. So I don't think the hundred-kilometer restriction would apply."

" 'Fraid you'll have to think again." Anders nodded casually at the four inspectors waiting silently behind him, and turned to McGee with an air of friendly regret. "Matter of a flawed tuning diamond, in your main drive unit. Seems the port safety office has ordered it impounded."

"Nothing wrong with my tuning diamond." Anger shook McGee's low voice, and his square face turned dark. "A nearly perfect natural crystal. Safe enough, if you don't abuse it. It has pushed the *Jane* for twenty years."

"The inspectors report it dangerously flawed." Anders shrugged indifferently. "Say any sudden overload would burn it out. Anyhow, it's condemned. 'Fraid you won't be leaving Pallasport."

Chapter IX
The Sleeping Spacemen

ABOARD THE GUARD TENDER, on his way out to Pallas II and the new ship waiting for him there, Paul Anders found the riddle of that enormous golden seetee needle growing more imperative than ever in his mind.

A practical spatial engineer, as he regarded himself, he had always accepted the presence of the terrene rocks and the seetee drift without much thought of their origins. The theories of Adonis and the seetee Invader had always been remote and somewhat improbable abstractions. This unaccountable explosion and all its disturbing aftermath, however, had brought that cosmic disaster disturbingly close to him.

He closed his eyes and leaned back in the reclining seat, trying uneasily to picture that ancient cataclysm. Adonis, then the sun's fifth planet, had occupied the Bode orbit between Mars and Jupiter that was now empty except for the rocks. A slightly larger world than Mars, the German theorists believed. He wondered if it had carried terrene life—or perhaps the monuments and bones of life fulfilled and dead before men evolved on Earth. The Invader, from the evidence of the rocks and the drift, must have been slightly smaller than Mars. Some earlier explosion must have torn it from the gravitational grasp of its own contraterrene mother sun, but not even the Martian-German professors had tried to estimate the ages it had drifted through the interstellar emptiness.

It had borne seetee life. The von Falkenberg film appeared to be sufficient evidence of that. Anders was still haunted with the enigma of that too-narrow ramp winding up inside that hollow yellow spire, beneath that queerly too-high railing. Yet his dazed imagination failed to create any convincing image of the seetee beings that must have trod that curious footway.

A contraterrene man, it occurred to him, would never be aware of his plight. Not unless he happened to come in contact with the queer and deadly sort of matter whose atoms were invisibly unlike his own. Anders wondered uncomfortably if the builders of that broken spire had been advanced enough to survive on their sunless, wandering world, until the crash. If so, that must have finished them. Even if they had escaped the collision itself, aboard space ships, they must have found themselves lost among untouchable worlds, with no possible landing place except the dead bits of their own shattered planet.

"Nonsense!"

A man of practical action, Anders had no time or inclination for such fantastic notions. Leave them to the German academicians. The tender landed and he hurried off, impatient to see his new command.

The *Orion* was ready for him. A tall new paragravity cruiser, with two long spatial rifles counterpoised amidships in flat blister turrets. Twelve thousand tons of hard metal and deadly ingenuity, a match for anything in space. At least, he thought, with a momentary lapse of his high confidence, a match for anything terrene.

He was less well pleased with her crew.

Commander Mikhail Ivanovich Protopopov was a huge, shambling, bearlike Callistonian, of Ukranian ancestry. His broad, puttylike face seemed to Anders both sly and stupid. He had a peculiar, blubbery, moronic-sounding laugh. His voice was a hoarse, grating whisper—the result, he said, of some years in the care of the Soviet secret police, before he escaped to join the Guard.

Lieutenant Luigi Muratori was a dark little Martian-Italian, with shifty black eyes in a dried-up face. He walked with a silent limp, and talked bitterly of the Neo-Aryanists who had kicked him half to death in the Hitler

Day riots before they shipped him off to the space labor gangs from which he had enlisted.

Warrant Officer Suzuki Omura was a toothy, spectacled, efficient little Venusian Japanese, who pledged the support of his whole ambitious but unfortunate race.

"So nice, Captain Anders!" He sucked in his breath politely. "So very pleasant that honorable Interplanet Corporation and my poor brave people join together now. We are very poor and humble, captain. Our only wish is to lead the stupid masses of Chinese and Indonesian Venusians into the greater prosperity our wise leaders contemplate. Now that we are associated with your rich company, we cannot fail. Everything is going to be very, very pleasant."

But Anders wasn't entirely sure of that.

The crewmen were as polyglot as their officers, since each unit of the Guard was formed of men from all the planets in the legal ratio.

Hood's insiders—the ranking Earthmen of the Guard —had found twenty-odd men all willing to sell their loyalty for Interplanet dollars, but Anders expected them to be worth little more than they had cost.

He was determined to trust nobody further than necessary. When they were alone in the sealfoam-padded cell of the forward bridge, up in the tapered cone of the cruiser's nose, he told Protopopov:

"Officially, commander, we are merely to survey the new swarms of seetee drift that have been formed by these recent collisions. You may tell the men you trust that we are also to test a secret new device for the spectrographic analysis of seetee bodies at long range."

The Jovian exile nodded, with a glint of cunning in his piggy little eyes. He had already been given to understand, by Hood's insiders, that their real mission was to track down a gang of Martian agents busy fomenting a new uprising of the asterite Free Space Party. In his hoarse and voiceless whisper, he agreed sagely:

"Misdirection is a wise precaution, sir."

"Our first landing," Anders added, "will be on Obania."

"Obania?" Protopopov's waxy, stupid-seeming face looked puzzled for an instant, and then it brightened with an invention of his own. "Then the Martian officers there must be deceived," he rasped. "Shall we inform them that we are engaged in running down an illicit refiner, engaged in bootlegging untaxed uranium?"

"Ex'lent, commander!" Anders grinned.

They were halfway to Obania when the telephone in his cabin awakened him. He reached it from his berth and muttered something sleepily. Omura, the watch officer, hissed apologetically:

"So very sorry to disturb you, captain. But there's a call for you, sir, from some civilian craft ahead. I do not understand it, sir, because this civilian captain says you know him. He says you saw him back at Pallasport, the same night we took off. He will not state his business. He rather insists, on the contrary, that you will speak with him directly. Please forgive my unfortunate stupidity, sir, but I do not entirely understand."

"Neither do I." Anders yawned and sat up on the side of his berth. "But put the fellow on."

The civilian craft was still far ahead. He waited impatiently, listening to the ceaseless hiss of the background light, for almost a minute. By that time he was wide awake, and a puzzled anger stiffened him when he heard the civilian's gentle drawl.

"Captain Anders, this is Rob McGee, on the *Good-by Jane*. Never mind how we got here, without a tuning diamond. But now we're coming back to meet you. We have twenty-eight men aboard. Survivors of a wrecked Guard cruiser. Some of them are hurt, and they're all unconcsious. Under ametine, that new wonder-drug. It does save oxygen, but you know it can also cause serious complications. These men are about to come out of the coma and they need quick medical attention. We're decelerating, for a rendezvous with you."

"Impossible." Anders was annoyed and curt. "We're on an important mission. We can't stop for any rendezvous.

But who are these men? What was their cruiser? How was it wrecked?"

"Ask them when you get them revived," McGee's soft voice came rustling back at last. "You wouldn't believe me if I told you. But they need immediate care, and we're still two days out of Pallasport. When you find out who they are, you'll be glad you stopped."

"I've had enough of your double talk," Anders rapped impatiently. "And I've no time for any tricks. If you rock rats are trying to run circles around Interplanet by the illicit use of seetee power, I warn you that you're running into trouble."

He waited, and the thin line of light brought back the deeper voice of Rick Drake.

"No, we aren't playing tricks," Rick insisted. "And we didn't need seetee power to get here ahead of you—even though we were twice delayed for need of tuning diamonds. But you really must take these men. They must have treatment for ametine shock, as they start reviving. Heat, heart stimulants, oxygen, plasma, massage. Some of them may need iron lungs. You wouldn't want to let them die—not if you knew who they are, and what they know."

"All right," Anders muttered reluctantly. "We'll slow down to meet you."

Twelve hours later, they reached the rendezvous point, a few million kilometers from Obania. Anders studied the other craft, and swore beneath his breath. It was unmistakably the same angular, rusty, meteor-pocked little *Good-by Jane* that he had left behind at Pallasport, apparently disabled.

The two ships drifted side by side. Spacemen from the crusier sealed a fabric tube between the air locks, inflated it, and transferred the unconscious men. Anders stood watching the grimy, unshaven, corpselike figures on the stretchers, strange and white in the saving sleep of ametine, until they began to trouble him. Some of them looked oddly half familiar, like men he had sometime known.

"Geez, Mike!" he heard a spaceman mutter fearfully. "Look at that half-stiff. A dead ringer for you."

"Hell, Smitty!" the other answered. "That one's *you!*"

Anders snatched a hand line to haul himself through the connecting tube, and climbed the ladder to McGee's cramped pilot-house. He found the little rock rat there with Rick Drake, both of them haggard-eyed and beard-stubbled. They listened to his questions, and Rick retorted hotly:

"Since when is it a crime to rescue shipwrecked spacemen?"

"Just a matter of time, Captain Anders," little McGee drawled more softly. "Some of those men already show sign of coming to. If they get the right care through the crisis, they'll soon be able to tell you who they are."

"Don't they have papers? Or their Guard dog tags?"

"Not a thing," McGee said promptly. "We found them unconscious and stripped clean."

"Robbed?" The Earthman's voice turned cold. "By whom?"

"Not by us," McGee protested softly.

"All this looks damned queer to me!" Anders swung abruptly to Rick. "What wrecked that ship?"

"We didn't."

"I'll find out," Anders promised him bleakly. "Now let's see what runs this tub."

Rick climbed silently down with him into the little reactor room, and waited patiently by the ladder while he inspected the antique uranium pile and the paragravity drive. He found no seetee reactor, but the tuning diamond in the drive unit brought a muted whistle to his lips.

"A perfect eight-gram crystal!" He looked hard at Rick's worn face. "The size of those I just signed for, on the *Orion*. Five times bigger than you need, to push this rusty little tub. Where did you get it?"

"You'll find out," Rick spoke quietly, meeting his eyes. "But you'd never believe me, even if I tried to tell you now."

Anders scowled uncertainly, but he was in a hurry. Though the size of that tuning diamond seemed suspicious, he saw no other evidence that it had been looted from any Guard craft. And after all, he reminded himself, the helpless crewmen had been kept alive.

"I've no more time to play games now," he told Rick, bleakly. "I've a number of things to do—besides finding out what these survivors have to say. I'm going to let you go, for now. But I still intend to settle with you, for everything you've done."

"Good enough." Rick Drake's weary grin disturbed him with its easy cheerfulness. "See you soon."

The *Good-by Jane* went on, her presence unexplained, and the *Orion* reached Obania four hours later with her cargo of unconscious spacemen. Anders answered the challenging flicker of a Guard photophone, and received permission to land on the two-kilometer planet. His gray eyes widened slightly when he saw the black pillar of the *Perseus* standing on the field at the tiny Guard base.

"S'prise," he murmured to Protopopov. "I had begun to imagine that our sleeping passengers might turn out to be Captain Franz von Falkenberg and his men. Seems I was wrong—but I've got an idea!" He grinned. "My old Martian friend is going to take these sick men off our hands, while we continue our mission."

Anders phoned the Martian officer. Not unexpectedly, von Falkenberg refused to take the sleeping men aboard. He was courteous but firm. The *Perseus* was not a hospital ship, and he was awaiting special orders of his own. Anders could crowd his patients into the small base hospital, or else take them back to Pallasport himself.

But Anders called the High Commissioner. His brief message must have set Hood's insiders into action, because von Falkenberg was soon on the phone again, hoarse with stifled anger, with the news that he had been recalled to Pallasport. His superiors in the Seetee Patrol were muddy-minded Jovians and dollar-struck Earthmen, but he would take the *verdamnt* survivors.

The sleepers still slept, although their blood pressures

and pulse rates and body temperatures were rising gradually toward normal as the ametine wore off. They were breathing more regularly. Now and then one of them moved or groaned, fighting that temporary death that had probably saved his life.

They were still unknown. None of them had yet awakened to speak his name. Their bodies had been stripped of everything except a few filthy articles of Guard issue clothing. Although twenty-eight men was almost the full complement of a cruiser of the *Perseus*, class, the Guard headquarters at Pallasport insisted that no ship of that or any other class was not accounted for.

And they worried Anders. The faintly familiar look of their lax, beard-masked faces still made him uncomfortable when he tried to place them, and he felt a haunting conviction that they were part of some unpleasant trick invented by the Drakes and McGee, of which he had been the victim.

It gave him a sardonic satisfaction to be unloading them on von Falkenberg. They would keep the Martian occupied for several days, while he began his own investigations, and Hood's insiders would let him know whatever they revealed when they recovered.

He left Protopopov to arrange their transfer to the other cruiser, and walked briskly off the *Orion* in search of information. Above the tiny, convex field, the sky was purple-black. Hot sunlight glared painfully beneath it on the gravel walks, the six-sided tower under the quartered Mandate flag, the tall, twin ships, and everything inside the close horizon.

Enjoying his relief from that oppressive burden, Anders drew his lean shoulders straight. Luxuriously, he inhaled the open air. With a quick and energetic stride, he crossed the military field, toward the commercial docks.

Obania made him feel a conqueror. Once a fragment of dead stone, now it was a man-made island of life. The spatial engineers had triumphed over the cold black eternal enmity of space to claim such bold new outposts for mankind. And he was an engineer.

When he came into the commercial port, however, the pride of the conqueror crumpled. For here, away from the new paint and the brisk efficiency of the Guard base, the deserted merchantile docks and warehouses were sagging with neglect. A row of abandoned ore barges, streaked with red rust, jarred his sense of victory.

He paused a moment, frowning. Here the bright triumph of man over space had led ignominiously to stagnation and decay. Somehow, he felt, the people of this rock had been cheated out of everything the engineers had earned for them.

What had gone wrong?

Impatiently, he shook that vexing question off. For he wasn't half rock rat, like young Drake. He wasn't even a social philosopher. He was just a working engineer, and now he had a job to do. A delicate, difficult job, that had to be done competently, for his planet and his company.

Two shabby old men were laboriously pitching silver dollars at two small holes in the broken pavement. They hastily recovered their coins as he drew near, and stood eying his black uniform with a silent hostility.

"Do you know a family named O'Banion?" he inquired. "A girl and her father?"

The old men looked blankly at each other.

"Friends of the Drakes," he said. "Friends of Captain Rob McGee."

The old men turned back to him doubtfully.

"Guess you mean Bruce O'Banion and his girl," one of them muttered reluctantly. "They live in the big old house on the hill, around beyond the town. But there's her car, agin' the rail. She'd be down toward the *Galactic Queen*."

His bowed head moved vaguely toward the parked car, and Anders went on to inspect it. A queer little makeshift machine, it looked as if it had been assembled from a junkyard, but it was shining with new enamel in the vivid color called seetee blue. Somehow, it made him wonder about Ann O'Banion.

A native of this lonely little ghost rock, what would

she be? The Earthman couldn't imagine the results of such a cramping imprisonment, because his own horizon had extended from the dusty hot uplands of Venus to the eternal icy twilight of Callisto. He felt a dim pity for her.

He found the *Galactic Queen* beyond the rusting barges. Royal in name only, and galactic not at all, she was even smaller and more ancient than McGee's little craft. Bright pits scattered across her rusty hull showed where a few deadly atoms of seetee dust had lately exploded like microscopic atomic bombs.

On the dilapidated platform beside her open valves stood a pile of crates and bags and drums, all stenciled in green flourescent paint, DRAKE & McGEE, FREEDONIA. Beside them stood a huge, blond-bearded man, shouting at a boyish looking girl in blue slacks.

"T'ousand dollar!" The bearded giant, evidently the skipper of the ship, shrugged vehemently. "Million dollar! Keep it. I don't like seetee."

"But you *promised*, Captain Erickson." The girl sounded desperate. "And I just must get these supplies out to Freedonia. Poor old Mr. Drake's out there alone. He has got to have food and air and water. You just *must—*"

Doggedly, Erickson shook his head. "I don't *like* seetee."

"I can get you through," the girl insisted urgently. Her dark head moved, and Anders saw the silver glint of a pilot's badge on her cap. "Now since we've fixed those burned-out deflectors, you won't meet a grain of dust. And you did promise Captain Rob you'd keep Mr. Drake supplied—"

"What's McGee up to, himself?" Erickson broke in dourly. That was what Anders wanted to know, but the angry man gave her no time to answer. "Let him play hide-and-seek in them seetee clouds. I ain't quite ready to die."

"Wait, captain." The girl seemed frantic. "I'm afraid Captain McGee's in some trouble—"

But the skipper didn't wait. He turned and ponderously mounted the narrow gangway to his battered vessel. The girl ran after him, and the rusty valves clanged shut in her face emphatically.

Turning slowly away, she came face to face with Anders. Tears of anger and distress were bright in her gray eyes. A wisp of dark hair trailed below her red space cap. Her face and her round bare arms were freckled and brown, from the actinic sunlight. Tall in the slacks and a snug yellow sweater, she no longer looked boyish at all.

Perhaps she wasn't exactly beautiful. Certainly she was quite unlike the sleek creations of the beauty salons of Solar City. But she looked abundantly healthy and thoroughly angry and not at all as if she wanted pity for being a native of Obania.

"Pardon, Miss Ann O'Banion?"

Anders felt an unexpected awkwardness as he introduced himself. He didn't quite know why, because he had mastered the social codes of four planets. But suddenly he knew he would very much regret it if he had to take this tall, space-tanned girl to the prison on Pallas IV.

Chapter X
No Runaway Rock

SITTING WITH ROB MCGEE, in the pilothouse of the grounded *Good-by Jane*, Rick Drake made a list of repairs and supplies to fit the tiny craft for a long, uncertain voyage. The first item on his list was a new tuning diamond for the drive. The diamond proved unexpectedly difficult to buy.

He was starting out on his shopping expedition, just before midnight, when he saw Captain Anders leaving. Karen Hood brought him down to the valves of the Guard tender, in her new electric runabout. She was devastating in green sports pajamas, and Rick looked away and walked on grimly when he saw the handsome Earthman kissing her good-by.

He took his list to the Interplanet shops at the edge of the field, and wrote a check that used up half his savings. The tender was gone when he came out on the street again, and Karen was driving off the field. Rick stopped and waved an awkward hand, but she whipped by him with only a stiff little nod. It was hard to put her hurt, accusing face out of his mind, even with all he had to do.

His dirigible armor was hanging in a public locker room beside the field. He climbed into the clumsy-seeming lead-shielded steel-and-plastic suit and steered it like the tiny space ship it was into the open air lock of the *Good-by Jane*. He hung it up and shut off the drive and wriggled out again through the belly slit. He found Rob McGee leaning on the ladder, looking very sick.

"Seems we still aren't going anywhere." McGee's soft voice held bitterness. "Somebody just called from the Interplanet shop, about our order. None of it can be delivered, until sometime tomorrow. And they're very sorry about the tuning diamond. Interplanet has none in stock."

"That's not true." Rick's blue eyes blazed. "I checked some tuning diamonds out of the company stockroom, just yesterday, and I know they have millions of dollars worth. It's all a scheme to hold us here, while Anders looks for that mysterious bedplate. I'll see what I can do about it."

He strode across the field to the impressive new red-glass building of the Jovian trading monopoly. The sleepy night man in the office seemed to speak no English. He listened blankly to the hesitant sounds Rick dredged out of a little manual of Russian phrases, and finally shrugged and pointed at an open, empty safe.

The fat blond man at the Martian building said the diamond situation had suddenly become very difficult, but he knew of a fine tuning crystal in private hands that might be bought for forty thousand dollars. He ducked an impulsive left hook, and Rick went on to try the Venusian corporation.

The withered little night clerk had no tuning diamonds on hand for anything larger than a dirigible space suit, but he remembered an occasion in the Lotus Flower Bar a few months before when Rick's fists had helped conclude a rather savage discussion of racial superiorities with a gang of blond Neo-Aryans from the Martian Embassy. He confided that his whole stock had just been purchased by an Interplanet buyer.

"Fresh lot three-four days," he said cheerfully. "Very fine synthetic stones, crystallized by the Brand process. Hold one special for you, please?"

"Thanks, but that would be too late."

Rick climbed heavily back over the curve of the terra-formed hill with his anger ebbing into bleak despondency. This seemed to him a remarkably ignoble abuse of Interplanet's ancient power. But he could think of nothing more to do about it.

He found an Interplanet delivery truck backed up to

the valves of the *Good-by Jane.* A paragravity loading tube was sucking up the crates and bags and drums of supplies Rick had ordered, to stack them aboard. Wrestling with the twisting tube, as if it had been an enormous metal-armored snake, was Karen Hood.

It was early morning now, Mandate time, and the setting sun struck red lights in her hair. A broad streak of grease made a black wound across her shoulder, where a rivet in the writhing tube had torn the green pajamas, and her flushed and breathless loveliness struck Rick like a meteor.

"You're wonderful Kay!" He climbed eagerly into the truck. "I had begun to think—"

She had stopped the loading tube and swung to face him, standing back against the huge rusty springs and beams of the ship's ground gear. He forgot what he had begun to think, and moved impulsively to take her long body in his arms.

"Your order!" She gestured wrathfully at the stacked cargo. "Take it and go."

Anger became her. It flushed the fair skin over her high cheekbones and turned her eyes a frosty blue. Rick paused to stare at her, with a choking ache in his throat. She fumbled inside her torn green blouse, and tossed him a small black bag.

"Your damned tuning diamond!"

"Karen!" He caught the bag automatically. "Thank you—"

"Don't!" Her brittle voice checked him. "That's your own diamond—if you think it's safe to use. Your money for the new one will be refunded. You'll get everything else for which the company accepted an order. And don't blame Paul for the delayed delivery. He wouldn't sink to such tricks. I'm sure he wouldn't."

He caught her trembling arm. "Please, Karen—"

"You have your diamond." He saw the angry glitter of her tears. "The rest of your order will be delivered as soon as possible. I'll see to it that the port authorities permit you to take off when you are ready. But that's all I owe you. Now let go!"

She twisted savagely against his grasping arm, but Rick was strong enough to hold her. He dropped his other arm to pen her against the rust-red steel.

"Listen, Karen." He had to gasp for his breath, and his voice was harshly uneven. "I can't sign up again with Interplanet. I'm going out after that bedplate—if it exists. But now—since you've done this—I want to say I love you."

"You're too late," she whispered. "Too stubborn and too late."

"Can't you even try to give me some sort of chance?" he begged huskily. "Even though perhaps I do seem like a traitor to you, can't you try to understand? This knocks me over, Karen. I mean, it shows you're really different from the rest. Can't you—please!"

She made no other struggle against his confining arms. Relaxed against the great steel beams, she looked pale, withdrawn from him. The bright flame of her hair was suddenly incongruous. Very white beneath the grease and the ripped blouse, her shoulders dropped with a tired little shrug.

"It's no use, Rick." Her voice was spiritless. "I may as well tell you—tonight I promised to marry Paul. Whenever he gets back from that queer object in the sky."

The faintly spoken words were a blow. They took Rick's breath and left him dazed and cold and ill. He lowered his arms and let her slip off the truck. She walked stiffly away across the field. He stood watching her blankly until she disappeared inside the Interplanet shops. Then, the diamond in his hand, he climbed heavily aboard to look for Rob McGee.

He found the little asterite waiting in the hold, at the other end of the cargo tube. They finished unloading the truck, and then McGee drove it back to the Interplanet shops while Rick began replacing the tuning diamond. By noon, they were ready to seal the valves and call the tower for permission to take off.

"Destination?" the port office called back.

"Freedonia." McGee grinned at Rick.

"Wait for your clearance." There was a delay, while Rick began to fear that Karen's angry aid had failed them, but at last the abrupt order came, "*Good-by Jane*, you are now cleared for Freedonia. You may proceed at once."

"By way of that object!" Rick breathed triumphantly. "To look for a model bedplate."

"If you think it's any use." McGee stood over the controls in the low gray-padded pilothouse, lifting the ship on the soundless thrust of its drive field, and his tired voice came muffled through the black periscope hood over his head. "With that damned Earthman twelve hours ahead of us."

"That's the way we want it," Rick told him cheerfully. "Because the last will get there first, as you didn't say!"

For a time he felt elated. He had taken orders from other men too long, and it excited him to be driving through the still and deadly night of space with a goal of his own ahead. He found that unknown object in the dark field of the periscope, as soon as McGee had the automatic pilot set, and stood watching it until its faint gray point came to stand for all the ultimate mystery of space and time and being.

"Don't look at it," McGee begged gently. "I can't, myself. Because it's somehow wrong. It makes me sick and lost. I had to use the instruments, to find its position and velocity. I don't know why I can't—feel them." He shook his head uneasily. "When I look straight at it, I don't even know the time of day."

Rick laughed. He had no special sense of lose, and he was not afraid to look. Yet a gray loneliness crept over him, even after he left the periscope and found a bunk in the upper hold. Karen's flaming hair and her blazing anger still haunted him. He couldn't forget her angry generosity, or quite give her up to Anders.

He slept a little at last, and tried to fight that bleak

depression. He made McGee tell him more about all his father's heartbreaking failures to build a stable bedplate. He learned to operate the ship. He helped in the galley, and once even offered to brew a pot of the weak bitter tea that the little asterite sipped unceasingly—but making tea, McGee insisted, was an art beyond teaching.

They were three days out—it was nearly midnight, March 28, by the ship's chronometer—when Rick heard the buzzing signal of the photophone.

"The *Good-by Jane,* of Obania," Rob McGee answered. "On our way from Pallasport to Freedonia. We're running out here a little off the shortest route, to avoid this new drift. But who are you?"

Rick had been sitting in the cabin below, frowning over a sudden notion that seetee objects might be manipulated, without contact, by radiation pressures. He had thought of mounting enormous concave mirrors about the reactor, to hold and operate it with the reflected thrust of its own radiation, but he could already see that the resulting force would be uselessly feeble, and the whole arrangement suicidally dangerous. He put aside his calculations, to listen to McGee's bewildered voice:

"Men? What men? . . . No, I haven't seen twenty-eight unconscious spacemen. . . . No, we certainly didn't speak you two days ago near Obania. . . . We don't know anything about a wreck. I tell you we haven't met anybody . . . All right, I'll let you talk to Rick."

Rick climbed into the pilothouse, with a question on his face. McGee shrugged blankly, and handed him the receiver.

"Rick Drake speaking."

"Paul Anders." The Earthman's curt voice snapped back with no perceptible interval of time. That meant that he was no more than a few thousand kilometers ahead, in spite of his earlier start and his faster ship.

"Where did you get those men?"

"Huh?" Rick was utterly bewildered. "What men?"

"Don't get funny, Drake. After all, we're now in easy firing range. One square hit would scatter your little tub from here to Mars." The Earthman's slurred voice dropped, suddenly hoarse and cold. *"Where did you get those men?"*

For a moment Rick couldn't answer. He stood listening dazedly to the background sounds in the receiver, the hissing, crackling, crashing rays of far-off suns. At last he stammered awkwardly:

"I don't quite—I don't know what you're talking about."

"Then I'll remind you of a thing or two." The Earthman's voice was harshly imperative, yet still tempered with his old assurance. "You spoke us, two days ago, near Obania. How you got there ahead of us is something I intend to find out—I still b'lieve you burn seetee in that old tub!"

"Not yet," Rick said. "And we didn't speak you."

"So you've forgotten all about it?" Anders rasped sarcastically. "You've forgotten that we met you and took off twenty-eight unconscious men because you couldn't care for them? And you still claim you don't remember where you picked them up?"

"No!" Rick protested sharply. "We've landed nowhere since we left Pallasport, and met nobody."

"Would it refresh your recollection if I warn you that now you're apt to meet those men again?"

"Why should it?"

"Your problem, Drake," the Earthman murmured, too carelessly. "But if I had been robbed of everything on me —maybe even of a seetee bedplate—while I was under ametine, I think I'd try to run the robbers down. And seems to me those men are apt to think you robbed them."

"I don't know what you're talking about."

For a long half-minute, there was only the rustle of the starlight. When Anders spoke again, his voice was curiously hesitant. Rick knew he was afraid.

"Rick—*who* are those men?"

"I don't know," Rick insisted patiently. "I really don't know what you mean."

"Say what you please, Drake." Anders paused an instant, as if struggling for his lost self-confidence. "I'm not going to arrest you now—I've no time to waste, because those men you don't remember will soon be too close behind us. But I warn you I'm operating on special orders that give me a good deal of authority, which I intend to use. Think what you're doing, Drake—and try to remember what you've done. It would be painful to some of your old friends to learn you had wound up on Pallas IV."

Rob McGee took the dead receiver out of Rick's hand and replaced it on the rack. His seamed brown face asked a mute question. Rick shook his head.

"Either Anders has gone crazy—which isn't very likely —or else there's been a reasonable facsimile of the *Jane* cruising around with our doubles aboard." Rick's lean face broke into a brief, uneasy grin. "Must have been that double of yours that called me from out where that explosion happened."

"Please, Rick," McGee protested gently, "this is nothing to joke about. We've got too much at stake. Think what a real bedplate would mean to your father—to everybody. It wouldn't be very funny if Anders locked us up on Pallas IV, for things we'd never done."

"No," Rick agreed very soberly, "that wouldn't be a joke."

Silence hung in the cramped gray room, disturbed only by the occasional soft click and hum of the robot-pilot. The hush of space was getting on Rick's nerves. He had envied the little asterite's calm, but now Rob McGee himself seemed uneasy, fumbling nervously for his pipe. Rick reminded him that he had left it on the table down in the cabin, but he didn't go after it.

"Rick, I don't like this thing. Not any of it." His squinted eyes seemed dark with some dim foreboding. "I've lived all my life in high space, and I don't think I'm easy to panic. But this—" His voice dropped to a husky whisper. "All this is—*impossible*."

"But still it's happening." Rick tried hard to seem

107

cheerful. "The riddle of it has to have an answer—probably some very simple and obvious fact—if we can only solve it."

McGee looked ill.

"I can't quite tell you how it makes me feel." His leather face twisted painfully as he paused to grope for words. "But—that call I never made. These men we never saw. That—*thing!*" He shrugged, in a baffled way. "The way it blazed up and went out and ran away. It hurts my head."

Rick nodded slowly, trying to understand. McGee's special sense was like some delicate measuring instrument, he thought, and some jarring wrongness about that object threw it out of order.

"It's upsetting," he agreed. "But let's carry on." He grinned hopefully. "After all, Anders seems as much upset as we are."

And they went on. A day later—it was just after midnight of March 29th, by their log and chronometer—they were less than half a million kilometers from the thing that hurt McGee's head, decelerating. Standing with his head in the periscope hood, straining his eyes to make some shape from the faint gray point of its image, Rick didn't hear the photophone. McGee tapped his shoulder and gave him the receiver.

"H'lo, Drake." He heard the voice of Anders, clipped and cool as ever. "S'pose you'd still claim you don't know anything about this peculiar object? Well, no matter what you may say you've forgotten about it, I'm presuming it's seetee. The legal safety zone will be in effect around it. If you approach within a hundred kilometers, I'll open fire on you without further warning. Is that clear?"

"I suppose so."

"Then don't forget it," Anders rapped, but then he turned abruptly friendly, like a veteran actor changing roles. "I don't mean to be unreasonable, Drake. I like you, personally. I can even understand your asterite sympathies. I admit that I still have no more than suspicion and circumstantial evidence against you. If you're willing to surrender now—and give me an honest explanation of all these queer things you've done—I'll promise you a full pardon. What y' say?"

"No," Rick blurted desperately. "I mean, I've done nothing at all that needs explaining."

"As you please." Anders dropped the sympathetic role. "But watch your step."

The receiver clicked and Rick hung it up.

McGee whispered uneasily, "What did he want?"

"Information," Rick said. "Somehow, he thinks we know something we don't. I believe he's afraid of us. I think he's acting tough, trying to bluff us into talking."

"Maybe." McGee looked uncomfortable. "But a good many rock rats have been arrested—and some of them sentenced to life on Pallas IV—on no more than suspicion and circumstantial evidence."

Rick said nothing. For a time the only sound in the small gray room was the murmur and click of the robot-pilot. The stillness of space became a smothering oppression. Rick caught himself tapping at the keyboard of the calculator, just to make a noise. At last McGee climbed down the ladder to make himself some tea, and Rick turned back to the periscope.

That gray fleck of that unknown object was nearer now, and not quite so faint among the stars ahead. He refocused the lenses and blinked his straining eyes, until at last he began to see its shape. What he saw was no runaway fragment of any shattered rock, either terrene or seetee.

Chapter XI
The Barrier of Dust

STANDING WRATHFULLY STRAIGHT among the crates and drums that Captain Erickson had dumped off his drift-battered ship, Ann O'Banion stared up at Anders. As she saw his trim black uniform and the bars of his rank, the anger in her gray eyes changed to a cautious watchfulness.

"B'lieve you're with the engineering firm of Drake and McGee," he told her easily. "I'm looking for Captain McGee. D' you happen to know where I'd find him?"

"So you're the Interplanet man?" Her cool tone indicated that Interplanet men were quite unnecessary. "No, I can't help you find Cap'n McGee," she said. "Because he isn't here."

"Don't you know where he is?"

She merely watched him for a moment, warily.

"He's gone to Pallasport," she said at last, and Anders thought she seemed uneasy. "He meant to come right back, but he called from there two days ago to say he had been delayed. He didn't say by what. But now, captain, my father's waiting for me."

She walked quickly away from him, toward her parked car.

"Wait, Miss O'Banion." She looked back inquiringly, and failed to hide the tears of trouble in her eyes. "I—I overheard your talk with Captain Erickson," he said awkwardly. "You were trying to charter his ship?"

Hesitantly, she came back to him. He grinned at the wet streaks on her tanned, firm face, and suddenly she

110

smiled in return. Her teeth were fine and even. Her wet gray eyes seemed clear and warm and honest.

"I think you know Rick Drake," she said. "Maybe he told you his father has a little metallury laboratory out on Freedonia? Well, Mr. Drake is out there now, alone. Cap'n McGee has been ferrying supplies for him and the shop. When McGee was delayed, I hired Captain Erickson to take this load. But we ran into a grain or two of seetee dust, and he turned back. I don't know what to do about it."

"P'raps I could help," Anders murmured hopefully. "Y' see, I've just been assigned to the Seetee Patrol. We're making a new survey of the dangerous drift around Freedonia and beyond. Since we're going out that way, s'pose we just take your shipment on to Mr. Drake?"

"Would you?" For an instant Ann O'Banion was beautiful with gladness, until a sudden hard mistrust chilled her face again. "But why must you go to Freedonia?"

"Orders," he said. "But the patrol's s'posed to help civilians in distress—and besides, I rather like the freckles on your nose. Want me to take your cargo?"

She drew back a little and then decided not to be offended.

"Mr. Drake will soon be desperate, and I don't know when Cap'n McGee's coming back." She nodded suddenly. "I'll go with you."

"You?" He gave her a somewhat startled grin. "We were talking about your cargo."

"I must go, because—" Some troubled urgency hushed and checked her voice. She looked at him uncertainly for a moment before she went on, "Because Mr. Drake is hurt, you see, by—a laboratory accident. I want to stay with him, if he'll let me, till Cap'n Rob comes back."

"In that case—" Anders paused to peer at her with a new astonishment, because the women he had known weren't quite the sort to go out to nurse an injured man on such a lonely and hazardous rock as Freedonia. "Pleasure," he murmured. "I'll enjoy your company."

111

"Thank you, captain." She smiled doubtfully. "When are we leaving?"

"Sometime tonight. I'll have your cargo loaded."

"I didn't want to trust you, captain, but maybe I was wrong." Candidly, her gray eyes searched his face. "Maybe I was prejudiced, just because you're an Earthman. Maybe you're not—" She flushed and looked confused, until he smiled. Then she said impulsively, "Captain, won't you come home with me for supper?"

"Pleasure," Anders said instantly.

He returned to the *Orion* and left orders with Muratori to load her shipment for Freedonia. She waited for him in her car, and drove him south over the toppling near horizon. For all its homemade look, the little machine ran smoothly, and her tanned hands were skillful at the wheel. Watching the grace of her bare arms, and all the pleasing hints of courage and honesty and humor on her firm brown face, he wondered more than ever what she really was.

"Obania comes from O'Banion?" he inquired.

Her red cap nodded toward a rusting derrick above an empty, abandoned pit. Hanging from it was a fading sign that read:

URANIUM PRINCE NO. 1
O'Banion Mining Co.

"My father was the pioneer here, back before the war," she said. "He brought Mr. Drake to terraform the rock and help install a little paragravity ore separator. The mine was never rich, but it made a little money and he kept the separator plant running for the public until the Mandate seized all the reactable deposits. That ruined us."

She spoke without bitterness, as if simply stating an obvious fact. "Rick Drake and I both grew up here. Rick was never quite content. He wanted me to come to Earth and finish my education, after he went back there for his engineering degree. Dad offered to scrape up the money, but I didn't go. I like it here. The last two years, I've been working for Drake and McGee. Cap'n Rob has taught me to pilot his ship, and I've run machines for Mr. Drake, but mostly I just keep the office open here."

She looked suddenly aside at his interested face.

"I don't know why I'm telling you all this."

"Because I really want to know," he said.

The road dipped under black iron bluffs, and they drove through the town. It was a single street of flimsy buildings, half of them abandoned now. On the rusty false front before one long sheet iron shed, he read another faded sign:

DRAKE & McGEE, SPATIAL ENGINEERS

"Quite a difference."

He was thinking of Karen Hood's spacious office, back at Pallasport, and her own sophisticated loveliness, so unlike the tanned and sturdy simplicity of this unspoiled frontier girl. Something made him smile.

"Am I amusing, captain?"

"Sorry," he murmured. "Just wondering what you are."

"And now you know?"

"I think I'd like to know."

She drove faster. The tiny car dropped over the tiny planet's curve, so abruptly that he wanted to clutch at the edge of the seat. She brought it to a skidding stop, in front of the O'Banion mansion. Massive and angular, the old house was perched boldly on a dark iron crag. Its chromium gingerbread, in style forty years ago, was stained and tarnished now.

Ann was out of the tiny car before he could extricate himself. He followed her up the wide steps between the rust-streaked but stately columns. She seemed out of breath, but she gave him a quick little smile before they went in.

She introduced her father. Bruce O'Banion was a big, shaggy man, who still lived in the better times gone by. His lips had a bitter sag. His sullen eyes were bloodshot and veins on his nose and temples were red and bold as if from too much drinking.

These two rock rats were the first suspects on his list. Anders was hoping for some chance reference to Drake's illicit seetee research or McGee's mysterious voyages or perhaps even to the plots of the outlawed Free Space Party, but Ann fixed the stooped old asterite with a warning glance.

"Captain Anders, dad." Her faintly malicious smile made the Earthman wonder if her unspoiled simplicity had been merely a lapse of his own perceptions. "The Interplanet man who wants seetee bombs. Probably looking for them here, but anyhow he's eating supper with us."

As charmingly demure as Karen Hood had ever been, she led them into the long front room, which was old-fashioned and threadbare and very clean. Anders made a confused effort to revise his ideas of sophistication. Perhaps it was something that could be acquired as readily on this frontier rock as in the penthouses of Solar City.

"Yes, I've done a bit of seetee research with young Rick Drake," he said hopefully, when the girl had left him alone with her father. "Rick has told me about the interesting work Drake and McGee are doing. S'pose you've seen this new lab of theirs, out on Freedonia?"

Old Bruce O'Banion made a derisive snort and began to talk about the prosperous times before the war. Never a hint of contraterrene artifacts or the baffling activities of Drake and McGee or the riddle of that exploding rock. Anders rose with relief when Ann called them to supper.

She had cooked the food herself, and it was good. The young green peas and mashed potatoes didn't taste dehydrated, or the steak vacuum-frozen. Anders accepted a second portion of dried-peach cobbler, and observed that Ann looked charming in a blue apron.

The *Orion* was standing where the bright-pocked *Galactic Queen* had been, when they drove back to the space port. Ann's cargo was already aboard. She parked her car, and they took off for Freedonia. He let her come with him to the bridge. She looked at the instruments as if she understood them, and watched with a lively interest as Omura set up their course on the robot-pilot. He offered to find her a cabin.

"Thanks, but I'll stay up," she told him. "It's only five hours, at this acceleration, and I'm not sleepy. Besides, you'll need me for a pilot when you come to the clouds of seetee dust that frightened Captain Erickson."

Omura retired politely to the after control room, and Anders enjoyed the flight. He left the little Venusian and the robot-pilot to hold the course, and encouraged Ann to talk. It was mostly of her childhood on Obania. She and Rick Drake had attended a one-room school that her mother taught. Her father had a library, and Mr. Drake had been her math instructor. She admitted that the little rock had begun to seem lonely as she grew up, with the mines worked out and the plant shut down and everybody leaving.

"But things could be wonderful again, if—if anybody can ever build a seetee power plant."

Her gray eyes shone hopefully, as if that dubious project had already been achieved in her mind, and her eagerness brought Anders a pang of sharp regret because he couldn't share her faith in that old utopian rainbow. He felt relaxed and happy with her, and he had been talking more than usual about his own early years, when his time was divided between his mother's expensive apartment in Solar City and the long trips to space with his engineer father. He found it unexpectedly difficult to remember that she was a suspect enemy of Earth and Interplanet.

Presently, he had a midnight supper set for them down in the wardroom. He ordered a bottle of wine, but Ann wouldn't let him open it.

"I feel gay enough, just from talking to you." She smiled, and her tanned face had a glow of excitement. "Besides, the approach to Freedonia is really dangerous. Remember Captain Erickson. You'll have to let me pilot you in."

115

They returned to the bridge.

The *Orion* had none of the broad ports of a liner's observation deck, which enemy fire or a seetee particle could shatter so easily. Anders went to the hooded periscope, whose narrow tubes penetrated the steel armor and the lead radiation shielding and the gray sealfoam lining of the tapered hull. He spun the vernier wheels and found Freedonia.

Just a tiny mote at first, lost in the frosty night of space, but identified by the stabbing green-and-blue flashes of the automatic signal reflected from its orbital marker. He increased the magnification until it became an enormous, jagged cube of iron, rolling like a giant's die on frosty black velvet. He was looking for Jim Drake's laboratory when he saw the sudden gleam of danger.

A bright new star swam out from behind that square mass of iron. It burned red and orange and red again—the colors that meant seetee. He stiffened when he saw the sequence of the colors, and his lips moved silently, counting the seconds between them. He flung off the black hood, and swung accusingly to Ann.

"So that's how you guard Freedonia?" he rapped at her. "That signal says there's a cloud of seetee drift all around the blinker, dangerous in every direction for ten thousand kilometers."

"There is," she said.

Her voice was calm and her face looked innocent, but their precarious sense of comradeship was already lost. Anders stood frowning at her sternly.

"This cloud's new." His voice had a brittle ring. "It hasn't been officially surveyed—that's part of my assignment now." His gray eyes narrowed. "Who placed that blinker?"

"Drake and McGee," she said. "They were afraid of a wreck before you got around to placing your official blinker."

"How come Freedonia's right at the center of the cloud?"

116

"Nothing so very strange about it." She smiled uncomfortably, as if puzzled and hurt by his accusing stare. "You know this dust was shattered off the seetee planetoid, when we blasted it away from collision with Freedonia."

"Maybe so. He grinned sardonically. "But still the stuff makes an effective screen against intruders—no wonder Captain Erickson decided to turn back! It also gives you a very convenient reservoir of material for your seetee experiments!"

She tried to answer, but she couldn't. All the color drained out of her face. She stood blinking up at him with terror dilating her eyes. He had an uncomfortable picture of her standing so, behind the bars of a cell in the nickel-iron heart of Pallas IV. It made him feel faintly ill.

"Ann—" He gulped uncertainly. "Please, Miss O'Banion—"

She didn't move or speak. Without quite meaning to, he reached out to pat her stiff shoulder. She struck savagely at his hand, and turned quickly from him. Still she made no sound, but he could see that she was sobbing.

Apologetically, he offered his handkerchief. She took it with an angry clutch of her strong brown fingers, and dried her eyes. She looked back at him at last, with a sad, apologetic little smile.

"I'm a fool," she whispered faintly. "I thought you were really just surveying the drift. If you're looking for some sort of evidence to pin on poor old Mr. Drake—please take me back to Obania."

" 'Fraid not." He liked her smile, and he felt a stab of regret that she had to be an enemy. "No time to turn around. We're going on to Freedonia."

"You can't get through without a pilot."

"We can try," he said cheerfully. "After all, we're equipped with paragravitic deflectors."

"They'll stop the fine stuff," she agreed. "But there are swarms of bigger lumps—big enough to burn out your coils and blow your ship to dust."

"We'll get through," he insisted. "We're better equipped than McGee's old tub."

"But no better equipped than McGee," she said softly. "He has a—feeling. He didn't need instruments to pick the open rifts in the cloud. He showed me a safe way, but you'll never find it."

"P'raps not," he murmured. "But we can try."

Facing him in that silent conical room, whose foam-lined walls muffled every sound except the occasional muted murmur of the robot-pilot, she stood visibly uncertain and afraid. Her pale tongue moved across her full, paintless lips. She didn't speak.

"So don't you worry." He grinned sardonically. "If anything happens to us, the Guard can always send another ship."

"You can't—" she began breathlessly.

But then she must have seen that she was beaten, because she stopped abruptly. Her blue-sweatered shoulders made an eloquent little shrug of defeat. Her fine teeth bit into her quivering lip, and the pain in her eyes made Anders look away.

"You win, captain." Her voice was small and flat. "Of course I could let you kill yourself, but I guess that would only make things worse. Give me the controls, and I'll take you down through those rifts to Freedonia."

"Take over." He nodded pleasantly. "And thank you, Miss O'Banion."

"Don't thank me!" she told him savagely. "I wish I'd never seen you.

But she took his place at the periscope, and brought the cruiser down a twisting curve, through the clouds of invisible dust and the deadly swarms of contraterrene meteors, to Freedonia.

Chapter XII
The Untouchable Ingot

THE *Orion* settled into a shallow depression at the south pole of the iron planetoid.

"We've installed a small paragravity unit," Ann O'Banion's taut voice came through the periscope hood. "Just strong enough to anchor our equipment and to hold the nearer seetee particles in safe orbits around us. There's no atmosphere, so don't go outside without your armor."

"Naturally." Anders grinned. "If you're operating seetee machinery, you have to do it either in seetee air or none at all. But thanks just the same for your solicitude."

Her only answer was an indignant sniff, and he turned back to the auxiliary periscope. He saw that she had set the cruiser down beside a low wharf. Beyond the platform stood a long sheet metal building, so skillfully camouflaged with blended grays that he was startled to discover it.

"The metallurgy lab?"

Still she didn't answer, and he looked out again. Across the shallow hollow, hidden beneath the low iron cliffs, he found a little cluster of dome-shaped, inflated tents, also splotched with concealing paint. The rude little camp had a deserted look, but he asked sharply:

"How many men have you here?"

"Now there's just old Mr. Drake," she insisted quietly. "Of course we had a crew of mechanics to set up the buildings and the terrene machines, but that's all finished. Here he is!"

A thick-limbed suit of silver-painted dirigible armor had soared into view beyond the long building. Hanging in the shadow of the rock, it was scarcely visible until the photophone transmitter that crowned the helmet began flashing red. Anders turned to the communications board, and brought in the rusty voice of old Jim Drake.

"Cruiser ahoy!" he was rasping huskily. "What do you want?"

"H'lo, Drake," Anders answered quickly. "We have a freight shipment for you. Transportation free of charge, courtesy of the Seetee Patrol. And better not set off any seetee bombs before you see who our charming pilot is. I'll have our main lock opened, for you to come aboard."

The flying armor dropped toward the platform. Anders dialed the watch officer, in the after control room, and ordered the lock made ready for a visitor.

"Have him sent up in the elevator," he added. "I'll receive him here on the bridge, while we're unloading his cargo."

And he came at last up the short companion from the deck below to the bridge, a stooped and apprehensive giant, clumsy-seeming in the thick knit garments he had worn inside the armor. Two fingers were gone from his left hand, Anders saw, and the others still bandaged. He looked at Ann, with hollowed blue eyes that were oddly like Rick's.

"I'm—I'm sorry, Mr. Drake," she whispered bitterly. "We—I guess we just played a game. And Captain Anders won."

"That's all right, Ann." The old man's faded eyes turned warm with kindness. He limped to the girl and put his arm around her as if she had been a troubled child. "There's not much harm you could do."

"True enough," Anders agreed cheerfully. "We were coming out here anyhow. Nothing she could do about it. 'Course she did pilot us in. But even if we'd been lost in the drift, you'd still have to deal with men like von Falkenberg."

"My son was telling me about you, captain." The old man looked at him keenly. "A real engineer, Rick says.

120

. . . Does this visit mean that he interested you in our work here?"

"We're int'rested." Anders found his voice clipped and brittle, as if what he had to say were somehow painful. "I've information that you've been doing illegal research on a seetee bedplate. First thing, I want a look at all your shops and equipment."

"You won't find a bedplate."

"P'raps not." Anders stiffened himself against the old man's air of injured honesty. "But we have reliable information that a working model for a safe bedplate has been built—"

"And now you've come to steal it!" Ann's face was pale beneath her tan, and her stifled voice had a savage snap. "So that you can use seetee power to hold the rocks in slavery to your great company for another hundred years." She swung trembling to the old man. "Don't give him anything, Mr. Drake!"

"Aren't you pretty bitter at the company?" Anders tried to grin at the defiant girl. "After all, it was our engineers who developed the fission reactors and the paragravity drives and the terraforming units that opened up these rocks for you to live on."

Her gray eyes remained cool with scorn.

"If you're such wonderful engineers," she inquired softly, "why don't you set up your own laboratory and invent your own bedplate?"

"We've been trying." He nodded soberly. "So've all the other Mandate powers. And we've all run into the same paradox. The unlike elements of any stable bedplate obviously must touch—and obviously can't. Any fool can see that no safe bedplate can be built. Yet now we have these seetee artifacts turning up—"

"What?" Ann broke in, her puzzlement almost too grave to be assumed. "What are artifacts?"

"Products of workmanship." Anders frowned at her uneasily, thinking of that narrow footway. "If the workmen were men, they must have used bedplates. Even if

121

those seetee things were made by seetee creatures, we still have this open reference to an existing bedplate." He swung abruptly upon Drake. "What d' you know about it?"

"Nothing." The lean man blinked as if bewildered. "We've built no bedplate here."

"P'raps you found one," Anders rapped. "Among those ruined towers of a lost seetee civilization you and McGee discovered on that seetee rock—while you were steering it away from collision with Freedonia." He thrust an accusing finger at Drake. "Didn't you?"

"We found no ruins." The old man shook his bent, graying head, with an air of blank astonishment. "I'm sorry, captain, but I don't know what you're talking about—"

"I intend to get that bedplate," Anders cut in coldly. "I've no time to play guessing games, but I don't want to seem unreasonable. If you're willing to do business, I can promise you fair treatment from Interplanet."

"You expect us to sell out?" Ann whispered hotly. "To you?"

"Rather sell to the Martian Reich?" he inquired sardonically. "Or p'raps the Jovians? Think they'd be better neighbors?"

The girl's face whitened, and old Drake's great gaunt frame stiffened protestingly.

"Better sell—whatever you have." Anders tried to smile. "Commissioner Hood can keep you out of prison. I have authority to offer you anything in reason for a safe bedplate—or even a good seetee bomb. I can go so far as to promise one of you a place on the Interplanet board."

"So?" Ann whispered sharply. "And what's your promise worth?"

"Better sell out," Anders said softly. "Before our offer is withdrawn."

The girl had caught her breath defiantly, but the old man took her arm and drew her back with an awkward, weary gentleness.

"No use fighting, because we've nothing at all to sell."

He turned back to Anders, with a heavy shrug. "Nothing but the reactor I told Rick about." His haggard eyes brightened with a faint spark of hope. "If you're interested in that—"

"I'm looking for a bedplate."

"You won't find it here." Old Drake's rusty voice was edged with a tired bitterness. "I guess the best way to prove that is to show you through the shop."

"Thanks, Drake." Anders grinned with relief. "To play fair with you, I'll come alone. My crew will have orders not to follow me for—say three hours, if that's time enough?"

"One's enough," the old engineer said wearily, "to show you why we've failed to build any sort of bedplate."

Anders called Commander Protopopov to the bridge, and the huge, hairy exile shambled up the companionway, with a cunning leer at Ann. She shrank from him, flushing.

"Take over, commander," the Earthman rapped. "I'm going off the ship."

Protopopov stood blinking his sly little eyes at the old asterite. He appeared to believe that Drake was a Martian agent, and Freedonia a secret invasion base, for his hollow whisper came anxiously:

"But, captain, will your life be safe?"

"If I'm not back in three hours," Anders told him, "you will send Mr. Omura after me with an armed search party. But keep every man aboard until then. That's an order."

"Aye, sir." He looked at his watch with a moronic-seeming deliberation, as if to fix the time in his mind, and lifted his arm in a clumsy, slow salute as they went down the companion.

Down on the valve deck, Drake climbed back into his outsize space armor. Ann put on the suit she had shipped with her cargo, and Anders found his own. They came out of the lock together, and Ann glanced at her little pile of crates and drums already unloaded on the wharf, neatly covered with a silver-painted tarpaulin against the chill of space. Anders couldn't see her expression, beyond the face plate of her bucket-shaped helmet, but the red flash of her photophone brought him one curt word:

"Thanks!"

Walking in that cumbersome gear was laborious and slow, but the battery-driven paragravity units lifted them into easy flight. Anders followed Drake and the girl into the dark building beyond the platform. The interior surprised him.

The floor was sunk deep below the doorway, and the lofty walls painted white. A long row of heavy machines stood end to end along one side of the bright-lit room. The other side was vacant, the floor dug with shallow, empty pits, as if for the mounts of a second row of machines. Old Drake dropped his flying armor on a white-railed catwalk that ran along that idle production line, and Anders came down beside him, whispering apprehensively:

"Seetee?"

Before Drake could answer, however, he had seen the diamond-framed space ship of the Interplanet trademark on the red-painted shielding of the massive old uranium reactor that fed electric power to those ore-separators and furnaces and turret lathes and milling machines.

"Terrene." His helmet receiver picked up the flicker of Drake's photophone, the deep voice tired and slow. "All terrene. Just a pilot model for the seetee shop we once hoped to build—on those bedplates we failed to invent."

He gestured toward the empty pits.

"That was to be the seetee shop."

The old engineer leaned to touch a switch, that started that production line. Anders felt a faint vibration through his boots. He saw bright ribbons of metal curling silently from the cutting tool of an automatic milling machine, and turned to watch the operation of a heavy drop hammer that fell without a crash. In spite of himself, he shivered.

He knew well enough that the hard vacuum of space carries no sound, yet suddenly the total silence frightened him. He shrank back from the inhuman deftness of an automatic turret lathe that picked rough gray beryllium castings from an endless conveyor and turned them soundlessly into intricate and unfamiliar shapes.

"What—" He paused to gulp at the uneasy tremor in his voice. "What are you manufacturing?"

"Nothing, now," old Drake told him. "But we built most of these tools ourselves, on the first two or three units we brought from Obania, and they're still set to turn out patterns."

"What d' you mean?"

"Terrene patterns, for the seetee devices we can't build. All this was designed and built just as a working model, you understand, for the seetee workshop. Everything runs under remote control, from the ore separators and induction furnaces, all the way down to the assembly jigs."

"But your control board will have to be terrene." Anders tried to see the old man's worn face, inside the helmet. "How'd you mean to bridge the gap?"

"Induction," Drake answered patiently. "That requires no contact of conductors. We've designed push buttons and verniers to act through induction relays. And there's the terrene half of our main transformer."

He pointed at a tall, unfinished bulk of laminated iron and insulating plastic and condulloy conductors, near the row of empty pits. "Induced current in the seetee half was to operate the shop with power from our old uranium plant—until we could get some sort of seetee reactor going."

"Beautiful!" Anders turned to study that long line of gleaming machines, all running silently and unattended, and he felt an admiration stronger than his first illogical alarm. "A lovely shop."

But the old asterite engineer was staring moodily past him at the half-finished transformer and the empty hooks hanging beneath the great beam of a traveling crane, above those vacant pits. Even the clumsy armor couldn't hide his mood of abject defeat.

"We tried." The light on his helmet glowed feebly with his faint whisper. "We failed."

"Failed?" Anders echoed harshly. "When you've built all this in just the year since you claimed this rock—how can you say you've failed?"

"This model shop has cost me nearer twenty years than one," the old man answered heavily. "All the basic units had been finished and tested before we moved here from Obania. All but the bedplates to mount them on. Of course we had to leave the bedplate problem until we had this airless lab—and even here we've been forced to give it up."

"McGee says something else." Anders let his voice ring hard. "Let's see your seetee machines."

The old man turned silently to Ann. The light reflecting on their thick lead-glass face plates concealed all expression, but he could imagine a suspicious hostility.

"Why not show him the hammer?" the girl whispered harshly. "If he thinks we're forging bedplates!"

"Then come along, Captain Anders." The old engineer reached calmly for the switch to stop the ghostly motion of those soundless machines. "The hammer is around at the other pole—just in case of accidents."

He lifted in his armor. Anders and Ann swam after him, over the empty pits and out through another doorway at the back of the long building. For a moment the Earthman could see only darkness, but then the diamond splendor of the stars burst out, and the tall shadow of the cruiser against them. Halfway around the rock, in another shallow iron depression, they found the contraterrene hammer.

Anders had expected something small and crude, but the massive red-painted frame beneath the metal shed was three times his height. All the terrene parts were cleanly designed and accurately machined, but the hammer and the suspended anvil were rough native masses

126

of meteoric iron. Red fluorescent paint glowed on the guard rail around them, and small signs warned: DANGER—SEETEE!

The Earthman shrank quickly back from the railing, staring at those unfinished natural ingots with a sick fascination. Although he had spent years on the theoretical problems of working seetee, he had never been so near the actual stuff of the Invader. He shivered in spite of himself.

"It looks like iron," he whispered stupidly. "Just like terrene iron!"

"So long as you don't touch it," Ann reminded him gently.

"The hammer itself and the anvil are splinters we shattered off that seetee rock." The old engineer moved calmly to that glowing rail, explaining patiently. "McGee located them, in this new drift around Freedonia, and we towed them into place with magnets wired to the batteries of our suits."

Anders stared uncomfortably across Drake's shoulder at the long uneven hammer and the more massive block of the anvil. He knew what would happen if anything terrene touched them, and he felt numbed by the mere notion of towing them with magnets.

"The anvil weighs fifteen tons," old Drake's tired, rusty voice went on. "It is floated between negative paragravity fields, that repell it from six directions. The coils draw power from our uranium reactor in the other building."

He pointed at an armored cable.

"The hammer was to slide in similar repulsion fields." His steel-clad arm indicated the vertical ingot. "There's a reversible paragravity unit at the top of the frame, that was to lift it and drop it."

His blank face plate turned slowly to the Earthman. "That's it, captain. Could you forge a bedplate with it?"

Anders didn't think so, but he merely asked:

"How do you hold the work?"

"We don't," Drake said. "I once hoped to design seetee tongs with terrene handles, but my attempts at that were even less successful than the hammer."

"What's wrong with the hammer?"

"Do you want to see it run?"

Anders was conscious of a quietly ominous difference in the old man's rusty voice, and he drew back quickly toward the girl. A pretended accident would be very easy here, and he knew that any human life was worthless against the prize of tamed seetee.

" 'Fraid?" Ann's low voice was mocking now. "Then I'll hold your hand."

He felt her glove touch his.

"All right," he muttered huskily. "Let's see it run."

Awkward in his armor, the old engineer moved behind a massive parapet of lead and iron that would be useless as tissue paper if anything went wrong. He bent over a simple switchboard, watching a mirror above it. Anders wanted to move back, but the girl stood bold and angry against the glowing rail.

The jagged-edged bar of the hammer lifted very slowly. It hung still, while Anders felt a sudden sick desire to stop the demonstration. It came back down to the angular mass of the anvil at last, with a soundless impact. The girl touched his elbow as it struck, pointing calmly.

He looked—and terror caught his throat. For that great dark splinter of contraterrene iron had begun to wobble as it recoiled from the blow, as if too loosely held in its guides. The anvil tossed like a cork on uneasy water, rocking toward the field coils that held it.

"See how it works?" Ann was asking softly. "Could you forge anything—"

That was all he heard, because he thought that huge seetee block would touch the terrene frame. He snatched the hanger strap of Ann's armor, and flung her backward toward the doorway. His whole body tensed for the blowup he would have no time to feel or see.

128

But it didn't happen.

"Please, captain!" Ann flung herself free of him, with a scornful little toss of her helmeted head. "Now you see we've no bedplate."

"I—I thought—" He tried to get his breath. "That seetee splinter almost touched the frame!"

"If it ever did, the reaction would vaporize Freedonia," she said quietly. "You're safe as anywhere, there against the rail."

"Sorry," he whispered shakenly. "S'pose you're right."

When he turned to look, Drake had stopped the hammer. The uneven bar and the massive block were quivering in the fields of repulsion that held them, still intact, coming slowly back to rest.

"There was no great danger, captain," the old engineer murmured calmly. "We've tested it for as many as five impacts, without blowing up the planetoid. Yet you can see that it's quite useless, because we can't damp out that vibration."

Anders nodded silently, moving farther from the guard rail. Even at rest, those great untouchable ingots were still awesome. Seetee machinists, he was thinking—if such a calling ever came to exist—ought to draw high pay.

"Int'resting." He nodded his head in the helmet, trying to steady his voice and recover himself. "Very int'resting, Mr. Drake. And now let's see what else you've done here."

"Nothing, captain," Drake insisted softly. "Nothing that would interest Interplanet."

"How about your seetee reactor?" Anders straightened in his armor, more confident since that fearful hammer had ceased to move. "The one that hurt your hands?"

"There's nothing much to tell about it." Drake shrugged in his armor, and his old voice seemed dull with hopelessness. "When I saw this hammer would never work, I tried to rebuild it into a reactor. A tiny orifice arranged to meter a fine jet of terrene gas against that anvil. An exchanger field, with pick-up cables. But as you know, it didn't work. The reaction was as dangerously unsteady as that hammer—my son says because of unavoidable impurities in the native seetee iron."

"No doubt," Anders rapped impatiently. "But where are your cables and your jet?"

"I've torn them out since I got back." He gestured calmly at the motionless hammer. "If the power in those coils ever went off, you understand, those seetee splinters would fall against them. I want to get the thing dismantled, before that happens. As soon as McGee gets back, we'll put that seetee back where we got it."

"A good idea." The Earthman nodded uneasily. "But where is McGee?" He peered again to see old Drake's seamed and haggard face. "P'raps you've built no bedplates here—but hasn't he found one?"

"I hope he has!" Ann whispered eagerly. "But you won't learn anything from us."

Chapter XIII
The Alien Voice

ANDERS FROWNED at the defiant girl.

"Better be careful," he warned her softly. "Men like our Martian friend von Falkenberg could find out anything you know."

She merely stiffened in her silvered armor, and he turned to old Jim Drake.

"Set that thing so it's safe to leave." He gestured uncomfortably at the hammer, and tried to recover his crisp, official voice. "Come back aboard the cruiser. No matter what you found on that seetee rock, we still have to reach some understanding."

He waited for Drake to adjust the fields that held those seetee blocks suspended, and followed alertly as the two asterites soared back around the night side of that small iron world, toward the *Orion*. He flew his armor silently, wondering what to do with them and Freedonia.

The scientist in him felt an awed admiration for the bold enterprise of their long effort to tame the untamable fury of seetee. He couldn't quite believe that they had altogether failed, and in spite of himself he almost wished them success.

But he was still an Earthman. He was in the race to win seetee for Interplanet, because he knew that its loss would break the company. And in spite of Drake's seeming failure here, there was too much evidence that these asterites had somehow got far ahead. McGee's call about a model bedplate; the ominous arrival of his rusty little tug where fission power could never have brought it; the ugly riddle of those stripped, unconscious spacemen.

All those things were far too ominous to be ignored, and Ann O'Banion's hostility was too open.

The girl was flying ahead of him, close beside old Drake. Her helmet light was dead, and her armor only a tiny silver atom, as remote from him suddenly as the cold dimensionless points of the stars. Yet he was annoyed to discover how much her mere presence disturbed his logical processes.

He still felt shaken when he thought of her reckless challenge to him, to let old Drake demonstrate the hammer. The little fool, she might have been killed. But then so would he, if those floating seetee blocks had rocked against anything terrene. He began to wonder why he felt such a sharp concern for her.

She had surprised him. Not at all the slatternly brat he had expected, she had the poise and pride of Karen Hood. Though she was only a stiff robot now, flying in the bright armor, he yielded for a moment to warm impressions of her. The young grace of her lithe body, so becoming to the slacks and blue sweater. Her brown, competent hand, so skilful on the wheel of that homemade car. The perfume of her dark hair when she stood beside him on the cruiser's bridge, expertly piloting the cruiser down through the invisible rifts in that cloud of deadly dust.

She was too competent, he thought. Too serious. He couldn't remember that he had heard her really laugh. Even when she had tried to seem friendly, there had always been that barrier of veiled conflict between them. He tried to picture her gray eyes warm with a real friendship—and then he caught himself.

He couldn't fall for a rock rat girl—an open enemy of the company. That was fantastic. No doubt she was attractive. Perhaps she was even honest enough in her mistaken loyalties. But still she was as utterly different from him, in birth and culture and experience, as any girl could easily be.

Opposites attract.

That ancient law came to his mind and he dismissed it

almost angrily. It might hold true of magnetic poles and electrical charges and paragravitic fields, but he thought it couldn't apply to human beings. Not really. Human opposites merely clashed.

No, he told himself sternly, any sympathy for this rock rat girl was the most dangerous sort of folly. He was an Interplanet man, and the way of duty plain. She must have justice, but he owed her nothing more. If it came to that final hard decision, she must go to prison with the rest.

Ahead of him, she waited with Drake on the little platform beside the cruiser until the valves opened for them. They left their armor, and the little elevator lifted them to the bridge companion. There Anders climbed ahead, and Commander Protopopov met him with a leer of moronic cunning.

"You're too bold, captain." The huge Callistonian lowered his voiceless whisper, with a crafty glance down the steps. "I expected them to trap you, but I see you've turned the tables on them." He touched his pistol. "Shall we take them now?"

"Not yet, commander!" Anders caught his arm. "You see, the whole situation has taken a very delicate turn. To avoid dangerous interplanetary complications, these people must be handled with the utmost care. I'm going to have another talk with them, alone."

"Ah, so they have confederates!" The cleverness of that deduction brightened the exile's broad putty face. "And you wish to set a trap for the whole gang? You're very ingenious, captain! If they cause you any trouble, I'll be waiting on the deck below."

Protopopov descended the steps with the rolling gait of a walking bear. and the two asterites came up. The old man was limping wearily, holding his bandaged hand with the other as if it pained him. His thin, red-stubbled face seemed cold and gray, and his haggard eyes dull with resignation.

"Well, captain," Ann said. "What now?"

Her voice was taut and flat, her tanned jaw stubbornly

set. For all her cool defiance, however, the dark, unruly wisp of hair curling from beneath her red space cap made her look more than ever like a troubled child. Anders tried to smile at her, but her gray eyes checked him with their level hostility.

"That's more or less up to you," he said soberly. "You must understand that the Guard can't condone your unlicensed seetee research here—no matter how unsuccessful you say you've been. That hammer might work better if I weren't looking on, and these curious recent activities of Rick Drake and McGee are still unaccounted for."

He tried to soften his voice.

"On the other hand, I don't want to send you back to Pallas IV. I'd be greatly pleased it you'd prove to me that you're not involved in any treasonable schemes against the Mandate. I'm perfectly willing to overlook all the evidence I've seen—if we can only get together."

He turned again to meet the old engineer's patient disapproval.

"P'raps I could leave a couple of company men here," he suggested hopefully. "And let you carry on, under their supervision. If you ever produce anything worth money, you'll be well paid. But you must tell me now what Rick and McGee are up to. Where they got those men, how they drive that tug, what about that bedplate."

Drake shook his head, with a convincing imitation of tired bewilderment. The girl's gray eyes narrowed oddly, but she said nothing.

"Better talk," Anders rapped. "The alternative is prison."

Old Jim Drake stood gripping his bandaged hand as if to stop some throbbing pain. His gaunt frame sagged and swayed, and the life went out of his hollowed eyes.

"Bully!" Ann O'Banion straightened angrily. Her lips were pale, and Anders noticed that the freckles on her attractive nose had become oddly distinct. "But haven't you forgotten something, captain?" Her voice was bit-

134

terly scornful. "You're in no position to issue such ultimatums."

"Eh?" Anders liked the fighting courage in her eyes. Wishing again that chance had not made her so utterly his opposite, he felt a painful stab of loss. "What have I forgotten?"

"The drift." Her white lips smiled at him defiantly. "Your safety fields might stop the finest dust, and your detectors might show up the largest fragments, but there are splinters enough in between, too large to be deflected and too small to be detected and avoided. You can't get out of here alive without one of us for a pilot."

"I could call the base for a meteor sweeper."

"But you won't." Her head lifted triumphantly. "You're in too big a hurry to investigate that runaway rock—if you really think there's a seetee bedplate on it. And you're too much afraid of tipping your hand to somebody else." Her voice was a cool challenge to him. "How about it, captain?"

"That's an ace, Miss O'Banion." He gave her a hard little smile, as if in polite pleasure at her victory, and made her an ironic little bow. "But how are you going to play it?"

She glanced at the worn old man, and stepped quickly forward.

"Just leave us alone." The grave, half-pleading urgency of her low voice seemed childlike again. "That's all we want. I'll pilot you safely back outside, if you'll only give your word to go on and forget us. Won't you, captain?"

She paused, and he looked into her breathless face. The color had come back beneath her tan. Her full lips were parted. Her eyes were bright with eagerness. Now he knew that she was beautiful—and far too fine for prison.

And old Jim Drake—surely his stubborn, patient, daring efforts to work seetee had earned him something better than a cell in the cold iron heart of Pallas IV. Anders was suddenly afraid that he would have to yield to the girl's bold stand.

Yet he couldn't.

Because, somehow, old Drake's weatherbeaten features had become his own father's face, younger and thinner and darker as he remembered it. And his father's precise, quiet voice came back across the years, all the way from their trips to space in his childhood, to remind him that he was an Interplanet man.

"So you really mean to be a spatial engineer? Well, Paul, that means you're going to have to study very hard, to master many fields of science. It means your life will always be in danger, because human bodies—or human minds. either—weren't engineered for high space. Most of all, it means you must never forget the company, and the duty you owe to all our people who have died to make it great."

A few years later, his father had become one of those people—when he was lost with the disastrous Interplanet survey expedition which discovered that the trailing group of Trojan planetoids were nearly all seetee. Now, remembering that, Anders looked squarely back into the girl's eager face.

"Sorry." Her look of crushed disappointment caught him like a stab of pain. He wanted desperately to tell her why he had to be a company man, but he knew she would always hate the company too much to understand. "Sorry," he repeated stiffly. "But we've a card of our own."

Her face turned white and cold again.

"You'll die without a pilot."

"We've this ace you gave us, and a good gambler's chance." He grinned at her puzzled look, and explained cheerfully, "Y'see, every turn you took on the way in here was recorded by our accurate instruments. We'll just follow the same way out."

"But the drift is moving," she protested quickly. "Different clouds moving at different velocities. You'll meet deadly splinters where the way was open before."

"P'raps." He nodded easily. "But we haven't been here long, and I think the odds are still fair enough that we'll get through." Watching the bright confidence fade out of her, he felt a sudden sting of pity and added hopefully, "Unless you want to accept my terms."

She merely shook her head.

"Sorry." His voice turned harsh with his own regret. "But you can see that you've left me no choice. I'll have to arrest—"

The sudden hum of the ship's telephone interrupted him. He picked up the receiver and heard the thin nasal whine of Luigi Muratori, now on watch in the after control room.

"Captain Anders?" The little Italian-Martian officer sounded puzzled and uneasy. "Communications is picking up a signal, sir. An unusual signal. The security machines do not unscramble it. Perhaps it is not intended for us. But the matter is so strange, sir—"

"What's strange about it?"

"It was beamed from the runaway seetee body that I understand we are to survey, sir. A very faint signal. Impossible to tune clearly. It seems to be a voice, sir. Communications says it is in the clear. But nobody seems to know what it is saying."

"Put it on."

The receiver clicked. For a moment there was only the hiss and crash of interference, but then the voice came in—if it was a voice. A ghostly rustling, so thinly drawn in transmission that all its human character was lost—if it had ever been human at all. He stood for an endless half minute straining to catch some known sound, and then he shivered, suddenly, as if the black chasm of outer space had somehow breathed its frigid breath upon him.

"Listen!" He thrust the rustling receiver at Ann O'Banion. "Isn't this for you?"

She listened, with a wondering apprehension on her face. An accomplished actress, he thought bleakly. In a moment the rustling ceased. She returned the receiver silently. He thanked Muratori and hung up.

"Well?" he demanded. "What was it?"

"That queer noise?" She shook her head.

"I know it was meant for you," he insisted curtly. "Your asterite gang. Because it was beamed at Freedonia —and it takes a narrow beam to reach twenty-five million kilometers. What was it saying?"

"I don't know." She shrank a little from his imperative voice. "If it was saying anything—it didn't sound quite human!"

"P'raps it wasn't." He glanced aside at old Drake's calm worn face, and stared at her again, looking for some shocking guilt beyond her air of innocent perplexity. "P'raps it was something seetee?"

Her brown face tightened. For a long time she stood motionless, and then she gasped a little, as if she had forgotten to breathe. At last she whispered faintly, "Then there are seetee—*people?*"

"There was a seetee tower." He nodded slowly, watching her taut, defiant face. "It was blown off that object that you asterites had steered away from this rock. *Something* built it—the same something, I think, that was calling you just now!"

He swung abruptly upon Drake.

"Something very tall?" he said. "Taller and thinner than a man?"

"Don't ask me." The bent old man had straightened, and a new, enormous interest was shining in his eyes, but he gravely shook his head. "I've no seetee friends."

"They were calling you." The Earthman's eyes had narrowed. and he nodded suddenly. "And p'raps intelligence would make a better bridge across that gap between untouchables—better than magnetic and paragravitic fields. P'raps that's how to build a bedplate. You make the terrene parts. They turn out the seetee parts— and help you fit the thing together. Is that what you've been doing?"

"It is not!" Drake's haggard eyes flashed indignantly. "I've never seen any trace of seetee life."

"The evidence says you're lying." Anders looked hard

at the girl. "I'm taking both of you with me, under arrest. By the time we investigate that object and get you back to Pallas IV, you may decide to talk."

The old rock rat flushed and caught his breath, but Ann O'Banion lifted a cool hand to stop him. Her gray eyes met the Earthman's stare, unflinchingly level. Her tight lips smiled slightly, without warmth.

"You're forgetting the drift again, captain." Her voice seemed curiously quiet. "But I'll pilot you through, if you'll take me with you to investigate that seetee body. I'll be glad to go. But you'll have to leave Mr. Drake."

"To answer that call from his seetee friends?"

"Please, captain." Her dark head tossed scornfully. "We have no seetee friends. But don't you know what would happen if anything shut off the power to that seetee hammer? The first explosion would blow the terrene debris of Freedonia out into that seetee drift, and touch off a thousand more. You'd have a whole new cloud of high-velocity dust for your Seetee Patrol to survey, spreading all the way from here to Pallas."

"Are you trying to threaten me?"

"Just suggesting, captain, that you had better leave Mr. Drake to keep our cranky old uranium reactor running, until Cap'n Rob gets back to help him dismantle that hammer."

"P'raps I had." Anders rubbed at the lean angle of his jaw, and gave her a hard little grin of admiration. "But why are you so anxious to get me away from here?"

"I want to go with you, out to that—object, as you call it." She paused, with a hesitant glance at Drake, and then went on impulsively, "Because, you see, I really have had a call from somewhere near it."

"Huh?" Anders searched her smooth, space-tanned face again, and still he found no shadow of guilt or shame. "When was that?"

"The day after that last blowup."

"I'd have heard about it." Anders shook his head unbelievingly. "Through our listening posts."

"The long distance operator who received it on Obania

139

is a friend of mine. She didn't relay the call through your spies. She just recorded it, and brought the tape to me when she came off duty."

"Where's the tape?"

"Right here." She dug into the pocket of her slacks. "I was bringing it out for Mr. Drake to hear, because I didn't understand it—and I knew your spies would pick up anything I tried to say about it on the photophone. It's the real reason I was so anxious to get here."

"Let me have it."

She gave Anders the flat little spool, and he threaded it quickly into the recorder on the communication board. Amplified starlight blasted from the playback speaker, and then he heard the voice of Rob McGee, calling faintly through that storm of light.

". . . because it's personal, operator. No particular business of anybody else. Please just hand her the tape, and then forget all about it. Better if she doesn't try to reply."

For a moment there was only the roaring of the stars.

"Ann . . . I don't know quite what so say." Tossed on the waves of light, McGee's far-off voice was hard to hear, and it seemed oddly hesitant and slow. "But we've found the thing we wanted most for the metallurgy lab. Rigid as one piece of metal. Permanent, so it won't blow up when the power goes off. Tell Jim about it, when you get a chance to see him."

He paused uncertainly, and there was only the crashing of the stars.

"Tell him it's all we want—if we can get home with it. Men from all the planets are scrambling for it. There's going to be trouble. Men fighting. Fighting themselves. Dying in ways you wouldn't believe. But I mustn't talk too much, till you get here."

Anders had swung with narrowed eyes to watch the two asterites. McGee had already talked too much, he thought—about a seetee bedplate.

"Because we need you, Ann," the faint voice continued. "We've got to have you, to help us deal with all these desperate enemies. That's why we're taking such a chance to call you now. Don't try to answer. Too many listening posts would be reporting what you say. Just come on after us when you can.

"You'll find us on this object Captain Anders is following, and you'll know what to do when you get here. I don't like to be so vague, but you'll understand in time. Come when you can. That's all I can say. . . . End of message. Thank you, operator."

The hurricane of light roared again for a moment, and was cut abruptly off. Anders stopped the recorder and swung bleakly back to Ann O'Banion.

"So that's why you want to go with us?" He nodded sardonically. "And you'll know what to do when you get there?"

"Please, captain!" she protested huskily. "I don't understand anything about that message."

"I think I do." He stabbed a wary glance at the silent old rock rat beside her. "Taken with that queer call we just intercepted, I think it's enough to prove that you asterites are dealing with some sort of seetee monsters—"

"But we aren't!" Ann's wide gray eyes looked convincingly distressed and bewildered. "And Cap'n Rob couldn't have made that call—not from that runaway rock. Because he had started out to Pallasport just the day before, and he called me from there next day. He couldn't have been out to that rock, and he didn't say anything about this message." Her tanned hands clenched uneasily. "I don't understand it, captain—unless we're being framed!"

"By whom?" He snorted. "Wasn't that McGee's voice?"

"It sounded like him," she admitted reluctantly. "But with all that interference, you couldn't really tell."

"But anyhow you want to go with me out there?"

For a moment she stood pale and still. Then her smooth throat pulsed to an uneasy swallow. She glanced uncertainly at old Jim Drake's tired, baffled face. He gave her no sign, but she turned slowly back to Anders.

"I must go," she whispered. "Because I don't understand . . ." Her eyes widened anxiously. "You will take me, captain? If I promise to pilot you safely through the drift?"

"I'll take you." He looked hard at her brown, breathless face, and tried to remember that she was an enemy of the company. "Though the presence of unattached women on a ship of war in action isn't officially approved of, y' know." He gave her a wary grin. " 'Cause I'm afraid to let you stay!"

Chapter XIV
The Seetee Ship

RELUCTANTLY, Anders agreed to let Jim Drake stay to keep his antique reactor going and that frightening hammer safe. The old asterite put his arm around Ann O'Banion's shoulders as if she had been a beloved child, and limped silently down the companion. When he was off the ship, Anders nodded curtly at the girl. Calmly, she thrust her head into the periscope hood, to pilot the cruiser out through the blinkers and the wheeling drift.

The Earthman stood watching her deft brown hands on the instruments, wondering what she was and what to do with her. He disliked to have his ship encumbered with a woman on this desperately uncertain mission, but there was no time to take her back to Obania. He had to keep his promise. He debated locking her in the brig, and decided in the end to vacate his own cabin for her.

She relinquished the controls at last and assured him quietly, "You're safe now, captain."

"Thank you, Miss O'Banion."

His careless tone must have seemed ironic to her, because her tired gray eyes looked suddenly alarmed.

"I've kept my promise," she whispered anxiously.

"And I'll keep mine." He turned briskly to the automatic pilot, to set the ship on a course to intercept that unknown object. Over his shoulder, he told her, "I'll have a cabin cleared out for you."

"I hope I won't be too much trouble."

"None at all. I'll just move into Commander Procopopov's quarters, and he'll take Lieutenant Muratori's, and Muratori will take Mr. Omura's— and I s'pose the last man in line will have to swing a hammock some-where."

An hour later, speaking through the scrambling de-vices that were intended to defeat the spies of rival powers, he talked to High Commissioner Hood. He re-ported the interception of that not-quite-human voice and all his other enigmatic findings, and asked for news about the sleeping men he had transferred to the *Perseus*.

"No news, captain," Hood's blunt voice came back at last. "No report from our people aboard since they took off, and they aren't due here until noon tomorrow. But I've an apology to make."

Hood's voice turned suddenly harsh.

"Karen admits she helped those rock rats follow you. Returned the tuning diamond we'd confiscated, and de-livered supplies they'd ordered. My own niece—I don't know what's got into her. Now she's quit her job with the company, just when we needed her. Says she's go-ing back to Earth. Thought she was engaged to you, but she says that's all a mistake."

"P'raps it was." Anders nodded slowly. "P'raps she wasn't the one for me."

"Can't understand her," Hood's annoyed voice came back. "Blowing up about the same sound business meth-ods that made her own fortune. But I'm sending her home on the *Planetania*. And counting on you to undo the damage. Carry on, captain."

"I'm carrying on, sir," Anders answered. "Think I can handle Drake and McGee. But I'm still worried about those spacemen. Want to know who they are. What wrecked their ship. How those rock rats got them. Soon as they're able to talk, please let me know what they have to say."

The huge Callistonian commander was on the bridge, inspecting the robot-pilot, when Anders returned from the communications room. He straightened, with an in-quisitive gleam in his small animal eyes.

"Yes, commander, we've left Freedonia," Anders told him. "Now we're going to run down that object ahead—

144

which was listed in the *Ephemeris* as a seetee rock before it blew up and ran off its orbit."

"So it is not really seetee, sir?" The broad stupid face broke into a sudden grimace of crafty admiration. "And these Martian agents and their asterite allies have doubtless terraformed and fortified it for a secret base against the Mandate? Ah, it's a deep and clever game you're playing, captain!" The face leered knowingly. "Now I see why you've installed that pretty little asterite stool pigeon in your own cabin!"

Anders tried not to flush. He gave Protopopov a cigarette and fumbled with his lighter, trying to conceal a sudden, unreasonable anger. At last, when he could trust his voice again, he said stiffly:

"Miss O'Banion knows this drift. She's aboard only as a pilot."

"I understand, sir." Protopopov made his bubbling chuckle. "Aye, captain, you've quite a way with the women!"

"Commander, this is a dangerous operation." Anders couldn't help his voice turning brittle. "In spite of whatever aid or information we may get from Miss O'Banion, we are likely to encounter hostile action, on or near the object ahead. We must take all precautions."

"You are very wise, captain."

"The ship will be blacked out, at once. Except for emergency calls, we'll keep signal silence. The crew will remain on twenty-four-hour alert. Periscope lookouts will be doubled. The thermalarm, photophone, and paragravity detectors will be maintained at full sensitivity. Gun crews will drill on every watch."

"Aye, sir."

"It is quite possible that we will encounter the Guard warship from which those unconscious spacemen were taken, now in hostile hands. If any vessel is sighted, inform me at once and sound battle stations."

"Aye, sir," came that rasping whisper.

"Also, commander, we must be prepared for another encounter with the *Good-by Jane*." The Earthman paused, frowning. "I . . . I don't know quite what to expect from these rock rats, but they don't seem friendly toward the company, and we must be prepared to blow them out of space."

"Aye, sir!" The Callistonian made his fat, moronic grin. "And I want to say I think your strategy is admirable, captain. You'll be winning medals and a juicy Interplanet bonus for us all!"

Anders left him on the bridge, ate a solitary breakfast in the cruiser's tiny wardroom, and went to sleep on a cot in the chart room—he hadn't really started that threatened chain of evacuations.

All that day and most of the next, while the ship followed the faint gray fleck of the object ahead, he waited for news of those unconscious men. He knew they should be recovering, enough of them at least to identify themselves and their lost ship. Even if von Falkenberg had discovered and silenced the company men among his crew, he would be landing at noon. But noon came and passed. It was seventeen hundred, Mandate time, when Anders was called at last to the communications room to receive a secret call from the High Commissioner.

"Anders speaking, sir." He was alone in the soundproofed room, with the scrambler humming on the line. "Those men, sir?" A tormented anxiety edged his voice. "Have you any news from the *Perseus?*"

He had a long time to wait, and Hood's voice seemed hushed and hoarse with strain when at last it overtook him.

"No good news, captain. A grave disaster for the company, I'm afraid, though the details aren't yet clear. Your ametine-victims woke up and talked to our Martian friend, von Falkenberg. I don't know what they told him, but it made him a mutineer. He has turned his ship around, in barefaced defiance of his orders to land here. He is now following you, captain, with those men still aboard—the ones still alive.

"Because there was fighting on the *Perseus*. Venus and

the Soviet had agents of their own aboard. Seems they joined forces with our insiders when von Falkenberg turned back. Tried to seize the ship. Took the bridge. Held the signal room long enough to send back an incomplete account of the trouble—but even then our people weren't allowed to say who those sleepers were or what the trouble was all about. Guess their allies didn't trust the company.

"Seems the awakened sleepers took sides with von Falkenberg. Not clear what happened, but I gather one of them broke the stand of the loyal men on the bridge with what he said was a seetee weapon. Then the Martian used ametine in the ventilator ducts, to smother those in the signal room.

"Last thing we picked up was our chief agent's voice. Already half unconscious, but he said the loyal men were beaten. Said von Falkenberg had the ship. Said the Martian was following you to get a seetee bedplate. Then he tried to tell us something else, but he was too far gone to make any sense.

" 'They're chasing the *Orion*,' he mumbled at the end. '*Chasing . . . themselves . . .*'

"Don't know what he meant, because that's the last thing he said. He laughed, a crazy-sounding laugh. It was broken off in the middle—perhaps the ametine hit him. For another minute or two we could hear the hum of the carrier ray. Then the mutineers must have stopped the transmitter. The ray went out. We've heard no more from the *Perseus*."

Hood's hoarse voice paused for a moment.

"What's happening, captain?" he whispered huskily. "I don't know. Those ametined men are still unidentified —except as enemies of the company. They are following you now, with that Martian mutineer, but you'll reach that object a day or two ahead of them—unless they've invented some sort of seetee drive.

"You're out there on your own. I don't know whether you'll have to deal with Martian agents or rebellious rock rats or invading seetee monsters—or all of them together

—but our insiders can't do much more for you. You will have to go ahead at your own discretion, captain. And if any sort of seetee bedplate exists, you will get it for Interplanet."

"Yes, sir." Anders gulped uncomfortably. "I'll carry on."

Later that same day—it was nearly midnight, Mandate time, March 28—the thermalarms picked up heat radiation from some faint source far behind the cruiser.

"Probably a ship, sir," Protopopov reported. "No meteor would be catching up with us, now. Assuming it's a ship our size, the readings show it's around eighty thousand kilometers behind—and overhauling us steadily."

Anders frowned sternly to cover his unease.

"We'll keep on our course," he decided. "We'll maintain signal silence and total blackout until they come in range."

When the estimated distance of that following object had shrunk to forty thousand kilometers, he called the crew to battle stations, and broke the blackout with one cautious sweep of an infra-red range finder. The reflected pulse gave a measured distance of only nine thousand kilometers.

"Then it's no Guard cruiser." He grinned at the Callistonian commander, faintly relieved. "A smaller craft. Already in easy range." He turned to the communications board. "We'll soon know who they are."

His photophone call was answered at once, by the gentle drawl of Captain Rob McGee. "The *Good-by Jane*, of Obania. On our way from Pallasport to Freedonia. We're running out here a little off the shortest route, to avoid this new drift. But who are you?"

"The Guard cruiser *Orion*," he said harshly. "With guns trained to blow you out of space. Seems to me you're running pretty far off your course to Freedonia. But what I want to know is where you got those men."

McGee knew nothing at all about twenty-eight unconscious spacemen. Neither did Rick Drake, when Mc-

Gee called him to the telephone. They had landed no-where since they left Pallasport, and met nobody.

"Would it refresh your recollection," Anders snapped, "if I warn you now that you're apt to meet those men again?"

"Why should it?"

"Your problem, Drake." Anders tried to seem at ease. "But if I had been robbed of everything on me—maybe even of a seetee bedplate—while I was under ametine, I think I'd try to run the robbers down. And seems to me those men are apt to think you robbed them."

Rick Drake answered innocently, "I don't know what you're talking about."

Struggling not to show his own baffled apprehension, Anders murmured a warning and hung up.

"Well, captain." Protopopov stood blinking at him hopefully. "Shall we blow them out of space?"

"No, I don't think so." Anders scowled thoughtfully. "Seems the High Commissioner's niece has some sort of weakness for •Rick Drake, and I still can't prove he's broken any law." He shook his head. "No, we'll just keep our rifles trained on those rock rats, till we get a better look at that object ahead."

The asterite craft came a little nearer, and then began falling slowly astern. Although its speed was still high, it had already begun decelerating at a rate well inside the limits of its ancient uranium reactor. Reluctantly, Anders let it drop out of accurate range, but still it followed steadily.

At noon next day, he was dining with Ann O'Banion in the cruiser's narrow wardroom—the disciplinary conventions of the Guard forbade him to sit down with his subordinate officers, but he had invited the asterite girl to join him. Sometimes she had seemed almost light-hearted and entirely charming, as if this strange mission were merely a holiday cruise, and they no longer need be enemies, but now he found her staring at him over her teacup, in troubled silence.

" 'Smatter, gorgeous?"

Her tense brown face met his cheerful question with a shy, uncertain smile, as if she didn't quite know how to take his half-sardonic admiration.

"I don't quite know." She dropped her voice, and looked quickly around as if to be sure they were alone. "Except that I don't much like your fellow officers."

He stiffened. "If any one of them have been improper—"

"I don't mean that," she broke in hastily. "I can take care of myself. I was thinking of you."

"Huh? What do you mean?"

"That little Muratori—" She hesitated, and then went ahead suddenly. "I guess you'll think it's just my nerves, but yesterday I saw him looking after you, up the companion steps, as if he would like to shoot you in the back. And Omura. He's always polite—much too polite—but you can't ever tell what he's thinking. And Commander Protopopov. That ghastly whisper and stupid, gurgling laugh. He gives me the creeps!"

She leaned urgently over her forgotten plate.

"Captain, how can you trust such men?" she whispered anxiously. "When you're looking for the secret of working contraterrene matter? If you ever found it, why wouldn't they murder you for it?"

He grinned at her solemn concern.

"I shouldn't trust any one of them out of sight," he admitted cheerfully. "But then, y' see, none of them can trust any of the others. Divide and rule—that's the way Interplanet runs the Mandate. Set a spy to catch a spy. I don't think we'll be murdered in our sleep—so smile again, beautiful!"

She didn't smile.

"Then I suppose the High Commissioner doesn't trust even you?" Her wide gray eyes studied him naïvely. "I mean, if anything ever brought you over to our side, so that you wanted to help me get that mysterious bedplate for Drake and McGee—your whole crew would be against you?"

Anders caught his breath. He was first surprised and

then angry and finally moved to sardonic laughter. The moon-faced Venusian steward looked inquiringly into the wardroom, and he ordered another pot of tea before he turned back to the girl's pink, embarrassed face.

"Well, bewitching, you're a little optimist," he told her softly, when the steward was gone. "I come from three generations of faithful Interplanet men. How d'you think you're going to charm me into turning traitor now?"

"I'm not bewitching!' she told him hotly.

She pushed away her plate and ran out of the wardroom.

He drank his tea alone, shaking his head in amazement at the rock rat girl, and then climbed thoughtfully back to the bridge. He found Protopopov crouched at the main periscope. At the sound of his footsteps, the commander turned with a shambling, ursine swiftness to face him.

"This object ahead, sir!" The voiceless man was hoarse with excitement. "I had assumed it to be only an ordinary terrene planetoid, which had been wrongly identified as seetee—perhaps as part of the plot to use it for a secret Martian base."

"A logical assumption."

"But you knew it wasn't?" The huge exile lowered his grating whisper, confidentially. His small eyes flickered watchfully at the companion, and came furtively back to the Earthman's face. Meeting that bright, blank stare, Anders wished that Hood's inside organization had been able to provide him a crew of Earthmen. For all his careless assurances to Ann, he knew that men bought for Interplanet dollars could be bought again, for rubles or rupees or marks.

"That object has not behaved like any ordinary rock," he agreed calmly. "There have been evidences of the application of some entirely new engineering principle. I'm going to tell you now, commander, that our real mission is to secure that unknown principle for Interplanet."

The Callistonian brightened.

"So those rock rat engineers used their new discoveries

to arm this fortress against the Mandate?" rasped Protopopov. "But the asterite girl knows the password—which she has gladly revealed to you?" His broad fat face broke into a hideous smile of admiration, and he brought his immense black-haired hands together with a startling crash. "Ah, my clever captain, no woman can oppose you!"

Anders managed a thin smile.

"Please forget Miss O'Banion," he said softly. "That object ought to be enough to keep us busy, and I'm still afraid of hostile action. Even though we've outrun those asterites, they can't be far behind. The mutineers on the *Perseus* are following them, don't forget. There's the Guard ship on which those men were ametined, still to be accounted for. The object itself is no doubt defended —perhaps by inhuman things and seetee weapons."

He gave the hulking Callistonian a stern little grin. "With all that, commander, I'm expecting trouble. Every lookout device must be kept fully manned. I'll take the main periscope myself. I want the men off watch to get what rest they can, before we call them back to battle stations."

"Aye, sir." But Protopopov's crafty little eyes narrowed doubtfully. "We ought to have a story for the crew, sir. Despite all our precautions, there may be Martian agents among them." His dough-white face smiled suddenly, at his own ingenuity. "I have the answer, sir! I'll inform them that this object ahead is the headquarters of a band of rock rat outlaws, who have stolen a new process invented by yourself for the manufacture of terraforming diamonds."

"Very good, commander." Anders nodded grimly. "But when we get there, I want every man ready for action."

The Callistonian saluted like a trained bear, and lumbered down the companion. Impatiently, Anders pushed his head into the periscope hood and found that gray fugitive speck in the dark ahead. It was growing now, and he waited anxiously to see its shape.

The riddle of it held him fascinated. Every asteroid had its own spell of wonder—a tiny world, complete, unchanged by erosion or decay since the dawn of human knowledge, untrodden since its cataclysmic birth. The contraterrene rocks, the shards of that unknown Invader from some far, unthinkable beyond, held the strong allure of bright and sudden danger. But this one dark body was now a mystery beyond all the rest.

Unaccountably, it had exploded like a nova and then frozen instantly almost to the absolute zero. It had changed its shape inexplicably. It fled spaceward now, away from the pull of the sun. It had spoken with an inhuman voice to the asterites on Freedonia, and its dull point glittered in his mind with the incredible promise of a seetee bedplate.

He refocused the periscope with anxious fingers, and waited impatiently for his eyes to adjust to the dark. He saw its shape at last—and trembled a little at the hooded instrument. Because it was no jagged rock.

Still tiny-seeming, it was bright in the sunlight and suddenly very sharp and clear against the dusty dark of space. It reached out to chill him with the mysterious cruel cold it had somehow brought from the flaming heart of that super-atomic inferno. Staring at it, he forgot to breathe.

It was almost egg-shaped. His engineer's mind found the better word, ellipsoid. But soon he could make out puzzling surface features. A wide flange circled it, around the smallest diameter. Thick supporting ribs arched away from that, converging toward the poles. Each pole was a jutting cylinder.

The color of it was equally baffling. All one end, including half the wide equatorial rim, was a dull, dark red, as if with the rust of ages. All the other half was bright as new-polished chromium.

A seetee space ship? That seemed possible, though the only test was contact. The projecting polar cylinders looked like air locks. The color of it, dark on one side and bright on the other, might be only a crude sort of

153

temperature control—the dull surface could be turned sunward to absorb solar heat, or spaceward to radiate surplus heat.

But he couldn't understand the golden spikes. Four slender yellow needles, each about the length of the smallest diameter, were thrust straight out through equally spaced ports near the bright half of that broad flange. What could they be?

Nothing more, perhaps, than some queer sort of radio antennae. Yet, shining against the silver-dusted dark, those golden spires sharpened his awed sense of alien mystery. They challenged his engineering intuition. They promised him the mysterious fruits of an unknown science. They shook him with the recollection of that rustling, alien voice.

Were they seetee weapons?

He was scowling at that disturbing possibility, when the thing's slow rotation brought a fifth yellow needle into view and he realized abruptly that he had seen something like it before. That hollow, broken, contraterrene tower, in von Falkenberg's film!

That yellow tower must have been blown off this machine. But no—all the needles in his sight appeared undamaged. Strangely, he could see no evidence whatever of that recent vast explosion that had flung the ship spaceward from its old path around the sun.

He forgot the riddle of that blowup, in his sudden wonder at the ship's dimensions—for that broken golden tower had been at least a hundred meters tall. Dazedly, he tried to imagine the builders of it—the whining things that had been calling their terrene friends on Freedonia; the tall, thin beings that must have walked that narrow contraterrene footway and clung to that bright, high contraterrene railing.

But they were still beyond imagination.

Chapter XV
The Vanishing Enemy

THAT OMINOUS SHIP swelled ahead of the decelerating cruiser. By midnight, its radiation-echo in the finder showed that it was only three thousand kilometers ahead —in easy range of the *Orion*'s long guns. Anders wondered if the *Orion* had also come within the range of something deadlier, but he had seen no sign of any life about the alien ship, terrene or seetee, hostile or not. The bright half of it shimmered in the glare of the distant sun. It was more immense than anything men had ever made, cold and strange against the gulf of space, utterly baffling.

The *Good-by Jane* had fallen far behind, beyond the reach of the thermalarms and even outside the vast sweep of the infrared search beam. Brooding over its inexplicable antics, over McGee's disturbing boast that the last would be first, over all the evidence that linked those impudent rock rats to this seetee machine, Anders began to regret that he had let them go. They might be circling to get ahead of him now, using some sort of super-drive borrowed from their seetee friends!

He yielded, in the end, to that mounting unease. A little after midnight, with the cruiser's main photophone beam pointed at the spot half a million kilometers behind, where they would be if they were still decelerating with their old uranium plant, he called them. Rob McGee answered promptly. Somewhat relieved, he asked for Rick Drake.

"H'lo, Drake." He tried hard to conceal his apprehensive wonder at that monstrous mechanism. "S'pose you'd still claim you don't know anything about this peculiar object? Well, no matter what you may say you've forgotten about it, I'm presuming it's seetee. The legal safety zone will be in effect around it. If you approach within a hundred kilometers, I'll open fire on you without further warning. Is that clear?"

"I suppose so."

"Then don't forget it." He was trying to be officially stern, but when he heard the known, human sound of Rick Drake's hesitant low voice, he gave way to his own bewildered dread, blurting an impulsive plea for help. "I don't mean to be unreasonable, Drake. I like you, personally. I can even understand your asterite sympathies. I admit that I still have no more than suspicion and circumstantial evidence against you. If you're willing to surrender now—and give me an honest explanation of all these queer things you've done—I'll promise you a full pardon. What y' say?"

"No," the rock rat stammered. "I mean, I've done nothing at all that needs explaining."

"As you please." His stumbling incoherence had a guilty sound to Anders. "But watch your step!"

More confidently now, since he knew the *Good-by Jane* was still behind, Anders held his course. That alien machine grew ahead, incredibly gigantic, but nothing moved about it. Nothing deadly came from those golden needles. Nothing monstrous emerged from the twin polar cylinders, and no eerie voice challenged the cruiser.

But Anders halted cautiously, at a hundred kilometers. He watched the great ship's slow rotation until his eyes were aching, and found no target for his guns. Reluctantly, at last, he surrendered the periscope to little Muratori.

"It looks dead, Mr. Muratori," he muttered huskily. "I don't think it is. I expect to have to fight the things that built it, and their rock rat allies. At any sign of life, recall the men to battle stations."

"Aye, sir." The little Martian limped quickly to the instrument.

"I'll be right back." Anders stretched himself, and rubbed at his weary eyes. "But I've got to have a cup of coffee."

He was walking into the wardroom when the alarm burst over the cruiser. Gongs snarled, whistles shrieked, bulkhead doors clanged shut, running feet hammered the decks. He went back up the companion steps by threes.

"A Guard vessel, sir," Muratori whispered from the hooded periscope. "Or the wreck of one—lying on that machine!"

Anders strode to take the instrument. That monstrous machine looked enormous in the lenses, bright and unbelievable against the black of space, but he could see no man-made vessel.

"Where?"

"Lying flat," the little Martian said. "On the north hemisphere, but near that flange. Half in the shadow of the needle by it—"

"I see it," Anders breathed.

It looked tiny as a broken toy, flattened against the dark half of that alien craft. In contact—yet they had not reacted! He whistled softly through his teeth. That meant the thing was not seetee. The dull hemisphere, at least, must be terrene. But the bright parts—could they be contraterrene, and joined to the rest with those bedplates the rock rats had found?

He adjusted the focus and blinked his eyes and stared again. Slowly, as the vast thing turned, the wreck crept out of the ink-black shadow of that enormous needle. He saw that it had been a Guard cruiser, of the *Perseus* class. The lean black hull was crushed and torn, the ground gear battered to useless scrap. A pale breath of vapor veiled it.

"Still smoking," he called softly to Muratori. "P'raps it just crashed there. Get me a voice beam on it."

And he spoke the wreck.

"H'lo, cruiser aground!" He swallowed, trying to smooth the anxious tremor in his voice. "Can you identify yourself, D'you receive me? Make any signal—"

The wrecked vessel answered then, but not with any friendly signal. One of its flat turrets was crumpled underneath, but the other moved. The long spatial rifle lifted to point like a black finger at the *Orion*. Red flame erupted and expanded into darkness.

"We're under fire!" Anders rasped at Muratori. "Begin evasive action."

The little Martians prang to the controls, and he felt the cruiser heel. He pressed the button again, to put his voice on the photophone beam.

"What's the meaning of this attack? Piracy and treason, I s'pose? A damned rock rat plot to wreck the Mandate? P'raps with the help of seetee monsters? I don't know how you got that Guard craft, but you won't have it long. I demand your immediate surrender, or we shall open fire."

The reply was another gush of vicious flame.

"Evasive action under way, sir!" Muratori shouted. "Shall we return their fire?"

"Not yet," Anders said. "First, I want to know what that thing's made of. Fire a series of testing shots. Against both sides of it, and those yellow spikes. Spectrograph the flashes. Meantime, continue evasive action to take us back five hundred kilometers."

"Aye, sir."

"Better surrender!" He spoke the wreck again. "I can see you're crippled, and we've all the advantage. We've got you motionless, in silhouette. We can hammer you to junk before you touch us. Cease fire at once!"

That long gun blazed again.

He ordered communications to black out the beam.

"Testing shots on the way, sir," Muratori reported.

He bent to the periscope, and dropped a filter between the lenses, watching anxiously. The tiny iron pellets were invisible in space. Those that must have struck the dark half of that huge ellipsoid made no visible flash. But the rest exploded against the bright hemisphere and the long golden needles, blindingly.

Dazzled in spite of the filter, he turned slowly away from the instrument. His knees felt weak. A sudden sweat chilled his face. A dry tightness caught his throat. He lit a cigarette carefully, and burned half of it with three long inhalations.

"Test report, sir." Muratori's voice sounded faint and shaken. "No reaction observed on the dark side, sir. But the bright side and the yellow spikes are seetee. I'll get the spectroanalysis. . . . Bright surface mostly iron and chromium. Stainless steel, sir—but seetee! Yellow surface shows an alloy of heavy metals, platinum, iridium, and gold. All seetee!"

"Thank you, Mr. Muratori." He wiped his wet face. "That means we'll have to be careful. 'Parently the unlike halves of that thing are held apart by some sort of bedplate, but a shot in the wrong place could touch off a general reaction—and cook us to vapor."

"Yes, sir." The little Martian gulped. "I see why you don't return their fire, sir!"

"Now we're going to," Anders said. "Warn fire control that one hit on those seetee surfaces would probably finish us. But silence that gun."

The flash of that defiant gun made a bright bull's-eye against the dark machine, and the *Orion* fired twenty salvos at it. The first shots fell dangerously near that dividing flange, Anders saw, in spite of his warning. But none of them struck anything seetee. The alien ship didn't dissolve into consuming incandescence, and soon his gunners found the range. Exploding flame veiled the wreck, until it ceased to reply.

When the smoke cleared, Anders peered at that hostile cruiser, and stiffened with astonishment. Though its image was vanishingly small in the lenses, at this greater distance, he could see that it now stood upright, somehow, on its broken ground gear.

Its unknown crew had obviously made a desperate effort to get away to the safety of open space. They had failed. Their guns were still silent. Yet their captured craft showed no new damage, so far as his straining eyes could see. In fact, it now appeared rather more space-worthy than he had thought at first.

The photophone on its black tapered snout began flickering furiously.

"Get their message," he told Muratori. "P'raps they're ready to give up."

The little Martian ran to the communications board. He tuned the incoming message, and his thin dark face was pinched with a look of sudden wild alarm.

"Well? Don't they surrender?"

"Listen, sir!" Woodenly, Muratori held out the receiver. "Listen. . . ."

Anders listened. What he heard was the same unintelligible drone he had intercepted on Freedonia. It seemed queerly semihuman, yet it uttered no sound he knew.

"What is it, sir?" Muratori whispered huskily. "What language—"

"No human language," Anders said. "But get me a beam to them." And he spoke to the captive ship, his voice brittle and edgy. "Better speak English if you want to give up."

The red light shivered again, but not with English.

"Continue evasive action," he told Muratori. "To carry us back a thousand more kilometers."

"Aye, sir." The Martian reset the robot-pilot, and looked up at Anders anxiously. "But . . . sir?" His lean throat pulsed. "That inhuman-sounding voice!"

"It isn't human."

The thin man gulped again, and waited silently.

"This—mechanism was built by seetee creatures." He turned to stare at the Martian, thinking aloud, speaking in a hushed uneven tone. "By the people of the Invader, before it struck Adonis. P'raps they'd predicted the crash. P'raps this thing was their ark."

"Does the captain really mean—" Muratori's sudden question trailed off into a troubled silence. He wet his thin lips, and looked back at Anders. His twisted face had a sick expression.

"Anyhow, they've survived on it," Anders rasped. Prob'ly just a few of them—it's a long time since the crash, p'raps a hundred thousand years. But these rock rats have found them, and managed to communicate. And now they've got that ship."

"Seetee creatures?" Muratori blinked. "Could they board a terrene ship?"

"That would call for engineering—but you can see they're engineers." Anders nodded grimly at the periscope. "Prob'ly got their rock rat friends to valve off the terrene air—and remove the terrene spacemen we found on the *Good-by Jane!* Prob'ly walking on some version of their bedplate. Working our terrene gadgets with special terrene tongs. Safe enough—so long as they're careful!"

"I—I see, sir." Muratori moved restlessly, as if to ease his stiff legs. "I hope we're getting out of here."

"Not yet." Hard muscles tightened in the Earthman's jaw. "That captive cruiser's knocked out. Unless they throw something drastic at us from their own ship, we can go back in."

"Back, sir?" The little Martian shuddered. "Why, sir?"

He was a little too fearful for a man of his hard experience, it occurred to Anders, too eager for information that might sometime be turned to rupees or rubles or marks.

"You'll get your orders when I'm ready, Mr. Muratori," Anders told him flatly. "For the time being, just continue evasive maneuvers and keep every instrument manned."

"Aye, sir." Muratori limped away, looking hurt.

The captive cruiser was carried slowly across the face of that enormous object by its slow rotation, but the guns fired no more. That uncanny voice had fallen silent. Nothing attacked the *Orion*. Anders stared through the periscope, and wondered what the asterites had found inside that alien ship, and finally decided to talk to Ann O'Banion.

She must have been listening for his footsteps in the

161

corridor, for she unlocked the cabin door before he reached it, and stood waiting for him with a look of worried expectation. She let him·in, and locked the door behind him.

"Tut, tut!" He gave her a tired little grin. "What will Protopopov think?"

"Please, captain! What's all the shooting about?" Her voice trembled anxiously. "I heard the gongs, and the men running, and felt the guns go off. Was it—"

"No, it wasn't the *Good-by Jane.*"

"I'm glad." She gave him a quick little smile of relief. "I was afraid—"

Her low voice trailed back into anxious silence, as if she were afraid to state her fears, but she stood so near him that he could catch her faint perfume. Her slim tanned body filled out the blue slacks and sweater sufficiently, and her dark hair was pleasantly disheveled. No, he couldn't much blame his fellow officers for whatever they suspected.

"We were firing on a warship." He watched closely for her reaction. "A Guard cruiser. in enemy hands. I think in the hands of seetee monsters. What d' you know about that?"

"Nothing." She flushed and caught her breath. "Why should I?"

" 'Cause I think your rock rat friends have been out here before." His stern eyes narrowed. "How else did they pick up the spacemen from that captured cruiser? Or know about the bedplates in this seetee ship?"

"Ship?" She caught at the word, breathlessly. "Then the object is a ship? And still seetee?"

"Half seetee. I can tell you more about it if I can get aboard."

"Please, Paul!" She moved toward him urgently. "May I—"

"Not this time," he interrupted firmly. "For plenty of reasons. Number one, you admit you're with the opposition."

162

Yet, even as a declared enemy, she looked lovely and beguilingly innocent and somehow far more trustworthy than Luigi Muratori. He saw the glitter of angry tears in her gray eyes.

"Listen, captain!" she whispered hotly. "I don't think you're really bad. You aren't like most of your men. But we aren't so very wicked, either. It's true we did try to build a bedplate without a license from your Mr. Hood. But we aren't traitors. We aren't in partnership with any kind of monsters—and I really don't know anything about that queer voice that called Freedonia."

"P'raps you don't." Anders grinned at her earnest vehemence, and lighted a cigarette to cover a sudden uncertainty. "But your asterite friends have several things to explain."

"We can't explain what we don't understand," she whispered bitterly. "I know something strange is going on. And I suppose you do have to suspect us, because we're just rock rats. But everything will be cleared up when we find out the truth." She gave him a shaken, hopeful little smile. "That's one reason I must go with you aboard—"

"Listen, precious, Commander Protopopov already thinks I have snared you with my irresistible fascination." He grinned at her quick flush. "Might misunderstand."

"Paul, you must let me come—"

"You haven't seen that—mechanism," he told her solemnly. "Dunno what it is. An ark from the Invader, maybe. But it doesn't look quite friendly. Half seetee, remember. No place for you, gorgeous."

"Careful, Mr. Interplanet." She mocked his warning tone, and then her voice dropped urgently. "But you must let me go with you—and I can take care of myself. You didn't know that it took three of us to assemble that hammer on Freedonia?"

Her gray eyes challenged him.

"Ever work any seetee yourself?"

163

He shook his head, looking at her with reluctant admiration. The Interplanet heiresses he had known didn't even dress themselves.

"Never did," he said. "Though I used to try—on paper."

"Seetee *looks* just like terrene matter," she reminded him gravely. "When you're going about that ship, how are you going to tell what you can touch and what you can't?"

"We've fired tests."

"But you can't shoot at everything you're about to touch. You'd be blowing yourself to atoms. Touching off the whole ship, probably."

He peered into her eager eyes. "Can you identify seetee without contact?"

"Only Cap'n Rob can do that," she said. "But I do know how to make safe short-range tests. With special bullets. I have equipment in my armor. One thing Mr. Drake did invent on Freedonia."

"What sort of bullets?"

"Alpha particles. From a speck of radium. They react with seetee, just like larger bullets. Mr. Drake designed a special geiger, set to detect the gamma rays from those small explosions."

"Sound idea." He nodded. "Ought to work."

"It does." She smiled triumphantly. "So you see you'll have to let me come."

"P'raps I do need you, darlin'," he admitted reluctantly. "But I think you'll change your mind, when you've seen that ship. It wasn't built for human beings."

"I'm coming." She looked at him silently for a moment. "No matter what we find—or what happens to us —I'd rather be with you than back here alone with your noble fellow officers."

She was still his enemy, but that made him uncomfortable. Restlessly, he crushed out his cigarette in the ash tray, before he saw her hairpins in it.

"Sorry, gorgeous." He recovered himself, and gave her a quizzical grin. "But you win. If you're really so eager to help me get hold of that bedplate for dear old Interplanet, come right along. Glad to have your charming company."

He heard the quick little catch of her breath. He thought she was going to answer, but her quivering lips tightened suddenly. Tears made a bright sudden glitter in her eyes. After a moment she gulped, and turned silently to unlock the door.

"I'll be calling you," he promised her. "But first we'll have to land on that machine alive. It's a couple of thousand kilometers away. We could have trouble even getting there."

She locked the door behind him.

On the bridge, he took the periscope from Muratori to study that monstrous machine again. Spinning on its own axis like some minor planet, it had carried that toy-sized cruiser far back toward the dark, but nothing else had changed about it. The five enigmatic spires glittered with their untouchable gold. The thin sunlight shattered into white frost on the bright hemisphere, and spilled like drying blood across the age-rusted iron of the terrene half. It looked ancient and strange and dead, yet still alive with unguessable danger. He began to regret his promise to let Ann O'Banion go with him aboard.

For another hour, he kept the *Orion* blacked out and wheeling through erratic patterns of evasive action, but nothing moved except that slowly spinning ship itself. No alien voice spoke again. The dark hulk of the captive cruiser stood where his bombardment had left it, until at last it disappeared beyond the turning bulge of that enormous rusty dome.

"Enough evasive action, Mr. Muratori." He swung briefly from the periscope, with a tight-lipped smile. "I've seen nothing else for us to evade. Now we're going in for a closer look—before those rock rats catch up with us."

"Aye, sir." The little Martian peered at him with a furtive sharpness. "Is the captain expecting trouble?"

"I don't know what to expect," Anders told him. "But

put fresh men on all the instruments. Alert the gun crews and fire control. Stand by for anything."

He took the controls at the periscope, and steered back toward the alien ship. It grew ahead, turning slowly against the starry dark, unknown and huge and deadly. Yet nothing came out to stop the *Orion*. The range was eight hundred kilometers . . . eighty . . . eight. The thing swelled in the lenses, stupendous, until all he could see was the rust-red dome ribbed with those enormous beams that converged upon the jutting polar cylinder. He was turning cautiously toward the wide joining flange, where the bedplates must be, when the telephone jangled.

"That Guard craft, sir!" It was Protopopov, speaking from the after control room, his voiceless whisper hoarse with panic now. "The craft we fought! Slipping around to meet us!"

"Take over, commander." Anders released the controls. "Meet them fighting!"

The *Orion* heeled, as Protopopov brought the guns to bear. The deck shuddered, as he let the first salvo go. Anders read the bearing of the guns. Clinging to the periscope, he searched for the attacker. That contraterrene dome flashed across the lenses, immense as a planet. One yellow spire glittered and vanished. The familiar stars of the crooked Southern Cross—and a shadow that blotted them out!

The shells must have gone wild, for that black shadow swept on to meet the *Orion*. It came so near that Anders could see the faintly reflected sunlight on the tapered dull-black hull and the counterpoised flat black turrets and the long black spatial guns tipped with the ugly black recoil brakes: all the black-camouflaged detail that made it a Guard warship of the *Perseus* class.

The salvo had gone wild, and it was too late for another. Yet, as that swift black shadow came on to the point of collision, he had time to see the massive, black-painted skids and struts and cylinders of the captive's landing gear, all somehow repaired since that first engagement. He even had time to wonder why the unknown masters of the craft had chosen to ram stern-first, with the long guns flat in their turrets and trained ahead . . .

But that was all. Dark-painted steel blotted out the stars. The ship paused and shuddered. The hooded periscope struck his face, flung him back. Staggering, he caught his breath and rubbed at his bleeding cheek . . . and realized slowly that he was still alive.

The telephone rang.

"It's gone, sir!" Protopopov croaked faintly. "That hostile craft. I saw it coming at us, backwards. I thought it was ramming us. I thought I felt it strike. We aren't damaged. But the enemy—"

Anders heard the big Callistonian catch a rasping, shaken breath.

"But the enemy has vanished, sir!"

Chapter XVI
The Iron Mushrooms

HOWEVER IT WENT, the attacking craft was gone.

"P'raps it went on past us after that glancing impact," Anders told Commander Protopopov, on the telephone. "Must have got out of sight behind this mechanism, while all our periscopes were still trained ahead. Anyhow, we don't seem damaged. Keep every man alert. If it doesn't come back, I'm going to try a landing."

The enemy cruiser didn't return. He set the *Orion* down on that vast rusty dome—near where the crippled captive must have lain when it began firing, though now he could find no sign of the shelling. He telephoned Ann O'Banion to meet him on the valve deck, and went down in the tiny elevator to the after control room.

Protopopov turned to face him, with the ponderous swiftness of a frightened bear. The ungainly Callistonian looked far too large for the tiny, gray-walled room, his pale hands too fat and clumsy for the fine precision of the instruments. His blubbery face shone with apprehensive sweat.

"A strange stronghold!" he rasped. "Does the captain expect another attack?"

"I don't know," Anders said. "I'm going scouting. You'll be in charge while I'm gone. Wait for me here unless you are attacked. If you are forced to leave, come back and watch for my signals. Allow nobody off the ship. I'm going alone, except for Miss O'Banion."

"Aye, sir." The huge exile chuckled hoarsely. "So her pretty face is to be your safe conduct into the fortress? A superb stroke, captain! These asterite engineers and their Martian friends have armored their secret base against our guns, and doubtless armed it with seetee bombs. But you attack with one clever kiss, and find them undefended!"

Anders managed a bleak little grin.

"I'm not so sure of that," he said. "Hostile action of one kind or another is still very likely. You will take every precaution against attack. Unless you are attacked, wait here twelve hours. If in that time we have not called or returned, you may consider that we are lost."

"The captain underestimates himself." Protopopov's small bright eyes glittered slyly. "You won't be lost, sir. Not if that girl can help it. I know a conquest of the heart when I see one, sir!"

Anders stiffened with annoyance.

"Don't send out a rescue party," he said curtly. "Don't let anybody leave the ship, under any circumstances. Too much danger of stepping on a piece of seetee and blowing everything into gamma radiation."

"I understand that, sir." The Callistonian nodded uneasily.

"If we don't come back within twelve hours," Anders continued, "it will be your duty to return to Pallasport at full acceleration. Maintain strict photophone silence. Keep the crew aboard when you land. You report to High Commissioner Hood, in person. Tell him all you know about this object. Tell him it's half seetee, held together with some sort of stable bedplate. You'll remember that, commander?"

"Aye, captain." Protopopov saluted like an educated bear, and his immense putty face brightened with conclusions of his own. "Then the High Commissioner will order this base destroyed. That will start a war with Mars. War means quick promotion."

His hollow chuckle bubbled.

"You know how far you can trust me, captain!"

"I know." Anders grinned. "But I intend to come back."

Ann O'Banion was waiting for him on the valve deck,

as clumsy-seeming as Protopopov in the silvered bulk of her dirigible armor. She watched silently as he snapped special equipment to the belt of his own suit: a lead-shielded camera, a plug-in headlamp, a luminous pencil and pad, a hand testing gun. Smiling gravely, she held out her arm to show him her own testing device, no longer than a watch on her armored wrist.

He climbed into his armor, clamped down the helmet, snapped the face plate shut. Ann followed him into the air lock. The inner valve clanged shut. Roaring economy pumps sucked the air from around them—and all sound with it, so that they were left in a sudden chasm of silence. At last the thick outer valve swung open, noiseless as a shadow. They swam out of the ship, into the diamond-sifted spatial night.

Some troubled impulse made Anders look back at the cruiser. It stood soundless on that enormous bulge of rust-red iron, black against the pale Galactic clouds. The last bright glint of bare metal vanished as the valve swung shut, and left it dark and strange as that attacking shadow-ship had been. He was afraid of it.

But that light-absorbent camouflage was meant to make warcraft look ghostlike, he reminded himself impatiently. Even though he didn't quite trust Commander Protopopov, the commander himself probably couldn't trust Muratori and Omura. He shrugged impatiently in his armor, and guided it after Ann's.

Flying silently side by side, they left the cruiser and lifted away from the alien ship to get a whole view of it. The thin sunlight struck down from above, cold on their silvered armor. Anders knew that the temperature inside his suit was automatically right, yet something made him shiver and glide closer to the girl.

She was silent, the steady red glow of her helmet light only a warm red star, a little nearer than the rest. A wave of loneliness made him glad to have her with him. Suddenly he wanted to speak, to hear her voice, but there was no time for nonsense. He swung resolutely to study the seetee ship.

Against the stars and the thin silver fog of suns too remote for the eye to separate, it hung stranger than the farthest nebula. Those bright spires of untouchable gold burned under the pale sun with a heatless glitter. The massive vastness of the equatorial flange and the arching ribs made the tall *Orion* a futile toy.

"Paul?"

Ann's tiny muffled voice startled him at first, and then he was infinitely glad to hear it. He turned his drifting suit to face the red flicker of her photophone light, and asked quickly what was wrong.

"Nothing, I guess." Her voice came in more clearly when he faced her, but it was still husky and uncertain. "I just wanted to talk. This thing makes me feel so terribly young and small and lonely. I'm frightened, Paul—but still glad you let me come. You don't mind talking?"

"Not a bit, beautiful. Felt the same way."

"Queer, to think how old it must be. Cap'n Rob says the Invader hit Adonis nearly a hundred thousand years ago, and this—thing—I don't know what to call it—has got to be at least that old." Her hushed voice paused. "I wonder why the seetee half didn't rust?"

"Dunno." He shook his head. "P'raps the beings that made it were still having trouble with their terrene metallurgy. The seetee part is all special alloys, but p'raps they had to use native terrene iron. P'raps it was never polished bright."

"It's so big!" she breathed. "I never imagined anything —" Her awed voice trailed away, and she hung silent, staring.

"It is enormous." With his engineer's eye, he was estimating its dimensions against the scale of the tiny-seeming *Orion*. "The long axis must be a full six hundred meters. Between those cylinders—locks or hatchways, whatever they are. Short axis half that. Those yellow spires must be a couple hundred meters tall. Ribs twenty meters thick. Beside it, we're no more than gnats."

"It feels so dead!" Her voice was hushed. "So terribly

171

dead. What do you think could have happened to the things that made it?"

Anders looked at her sharply. He couldn't see her face in the helmet, but her breathless wonder sounded real. Suddenly, he wanted very much to believe in her innocence, not altogether because he needed her aid. Yet the evidence damned her.

For all her seeming astonishment, this ship was the same object that Drake and McGee had steered away from collision with Freedonia, a year ago. Their seetee know-how must have been learned here, from this awesome work of actual seetee engineers. Their loyal employee and ally, she must have shared this fantastic secret.

"Aren't they dead?" He hadn't answered, and she spoke again. "They couldn't be—" Her low voice shuddered convincingly. "Surely, Paul, those—things couldn't still be here?"

Certainly the ship looked dead enough. It ought to be dead—how contraterrene life could survive a hundred thousand years here amid the untouchable terrene planets of the sun, he didn't understand. Yet he had heard those alien voices calling, and they had to be explained.

"I dunno," he whispered harshly. "But what do you think, Miss O'Banion?"

She turned quickly toward him, as if stung by his accusing tone.

"Oh, Paul!" Her breathless voice seemed more shocked than angry. "If you're thinking of that weird call to Freedonia—please believe it wasn't meant for us! I don't know anything about it."

The words meant nothing. But the cold sunlight swept into her helmet for an instant as she turned, so that he saw her young brown face, so hurt at him, so grave with trouble, yet so firm with courage.

"Sorry." He shrugged abruptly in the chafing fabric, as if to break the grasp of his own invincible perplexity. "Now let's get moving, gorgeous." He grinned stiffly through the oval lens. "We ought to have six or eight hours to get that bedplate for dear old Interplanet, before your asterite friends can get here."

Ann said nothing audible, but she followed him down toward the wide equatorial flange that hooped the ship. An immense ring, standing twenty meters thick above the massive ribs that bound the unlike domes, it was double, really. As they dropped toward it, the thin black line between the bright half and the dull half of it became an open space of more than half a meter.

Anders glided down toward the rust-colored band, reaching out with his gloved hand to grasp it. He was intent on the dark gap between the unlike bands, peering to see what held them apart, but Ann flashed in front of him.

"Just a minute, reckless!" She mocked his own bantering voice. "P'raps you're an engineer, but you've still a trick or two to learn. You'll find out you can't take anything for granted. Not with seetee."

Poised above the dull metal, she extended the tiny device on her wrist gingerly toward it. She seemed to listen, as if for the warning click of the detector, but Anders heard no sound.

"It's all right," she said.

Anders nodded his half-sardonic thanks, and they alighted on the unpolished flange. It was like an iron roadway, fifteen meters wide, curving around a metal planetoid. Anders shuffled cautiously across it, to that dividing gap.

"Those disks!" Ann was ahead of him, and a sudden taut elation of discovery trembled in her voice. "Aren't they the bedplates?"

Leaning eagerly, balancing the ship's gravitation with the thrust of his drive pack, he saw that the gap between the unlike flanges was spaced with thousands of thick disks. Wide mushrooms of shining seetee steel—but all of them stemmed. somehow, with thick rods of dark terrene iron! The crowning disks were fastened to the seetee flange. The roughly welded terrene stems held the unfinished terrene flange in place.

"They are bedplates!" Anders gasped. "Real bedplates!"

He bent as close as he dared, trying to see the actual junction, where the dark stalk of the nearest unit met the shining crown. He could see no gap between. That startled him, and he drew apprehensively back. The terrene stem was in visible contact with the seetee cap. An impossible weld. Though he knew it had already endured for many thousand years, he couldn't resist a feeling that it ought to erupt into solar fury.

"Well, Mr. Genius!" Ann's voice was softly mocking now, and he thought her gray eyes looked quizzical beyond the heavy plate. "You've found a bedplate for your company. What are you going to do with it?"

"Dunno." He gave her an uneasy grin. "S'pose the only way is to take one of 'em apart, to see what keeps it from coming apart on its own. But that strikes me as a slightly ticklish undertaking."

"Slightly?" She stared at him. "One slip would set the whole works off, with a blaze like we saw last week."

"Might do it, beautiful. What would you suggest?"

"I'm not on the Interplanet payroll," she said sweetly. "It's all your problem, Mr. Handsome."

"And I still intend to solve it." He straightened. "That looks like some sort of lock or valve, up at the end. The answer could be waiting for me, right inside. Coming, Miss O'Banion?"

The dirigible suits lifted them away from that broad band of ancient iron. He saw the warm red star of Ann's helmet light flying close to him. It trembled, and her low voice reached him:

"I'm coming, Paul. And I don't mind, really, if you want to call me beautiful."

He laughed, with a sudden release of nervous tension, and reached out impulsively to catch her armored hand. She clung to him, as they rose above the immense, dark-ribbed dome. In spite of all the evidence, she seemed a very friendly enemy.

"Thanks." He grinned through the leaded glass. "Glad you're along."

The small, pointed shadow of the cruiser sank out of sight, below the near iron horizon. Alone with the stars and the riddle of the ship, they dropped toward that jutting polar cylinder.

"If anything goes wrong," he muttered abruptly, "don't wait for me. There won't be any rescue efforts. Y'see, Protopopov has orders to leave us if we aren't back in twelve hours."

She said nothing. Her armored hand clung to his for an instant, and then she darted ahead to test the thick, dark rim of that projecting cylinder. It was terrene, and they alighted upon it.

"Odd!" he whispered. "There's something more than gravity, holding us here. Dead as it seems, this thing still has a paragravity field of its own, like a terraformed rock. I wonder if the builders of it hadn't got around the field-loss problem, that we've been fighting ever since Maxim-Gore first found that the forces in sun spots aren't all magnetic."

The heatless rays of the far sun still found them, where they stood on the wide lip of the cylinder, but the inside of it was a chasm of faintly starlit mystery. They turned up their helmet lights for illumination, and Anders plugged in his spare head lamp, but even that was too feeble to dispell the frozen, clotted gloom.

Ann stood on the rim, staring down the rosy beam from her helmet. Tiny-seeming, even in the inflated fabric, her figure gave Anders a scale of size. That black opening, he estimated, must be sixty meters across.

As his eyes became accustomed to the darkness within, he began to see the outlines of huge flaps and hinges, down inside the rim. It was oddly difficult for him to puzzle out their purpose—and he realized, with a chilly discomfort, that the very thought-patterns of their designers must have been completely alien. But at least he could see that they were the parts of a kind of gate or valve, arranged to close the top of the cylinder. They were half open, now.

He stepped off the rim, toward that yawning opening. "Wait, Paul!" Ann called huskily. "Shouldn't we be careful? I mean, if there *is* anything left alive—" Then she must have seen that he didn't mean to stop. "Wait for me!"

Chapter XVII
The Frozen Mutineers

SHE JUMPED AFTER HIM. Slowly, balancing the pull of the ship with the flexible power of their suits, they floated down between the half-opened leaves of that tremendous valve. The inside of the cylinder was a black, enormous cavern. At first their feeble probing lights found nothing but dead emptiness. Slowly, their eyes adjusted. A ramp and a railing loomed out of the dark.

"A footway!" His voice fell, almost as if he had glimpsed some thin, untouchable thing upon it. "I've seen another like it, in a film—"

It curved down around the dark wall of the cylinder, descending into bottomless night. At intervals there were wide platforms, with immense doorways gaping behind them. Dark iron boxes were stacked high on the nearest platform.

"I've got it!" he whispered abruptly. "Cargo. Means this was a berth for some kind of tender or auxiliary ship—one with a hundred times the tonnage of the *Orion!*"

He swam toward that burdened platform.

"The loading docks—they came level with the hatches." His voice was quick, excited. "The creatures—the Invaders—went up and down that narrow walk. Wonder what they were like? Or should I use the present tense?"

He glanced uncertainly at Ann. Her wide gray eyes, behind the heavy glass, seemed to reflect his own bewildered awe. He felt suddenly certain she had not been here before, and somehow equally sure that nothing at all had walked that strange footway for many thousand years.

He had used the past tense unthinkingly, because of the feeling of antiquity and death that came up through the bitter dark from everything around him, yet now, when he paused to search for the source of that abrupt conviction, he could see no positive evidence that the Invaders were really dead.

The ship seemed utterly silent, but because it was half terrene it had to be airless and consequently soundless. It was dark, but perhaps the Invaders had required no light. The polished rail above that sloping ramp shone like new metal, though of course there had been no atmosphere to tarnish it. He saw no dust of time on the dark platform, though perhaps ages here would leave no dust. He and Ann had been allowed to enter, but only after the *Orion* had silenced the guns of that captive cruiser.

"The past tense is right," the girl was whispering. "From the feel of everything, I think they were dead and gone a long time ago. Maybe killed when their planet hit Adonis."

"Prob'ly." Anders nodded in his helmet, suddenly confident. "Even if this was meant to be their ark, they couldn't have lived forever in it. P'raps they thought or hoped our planets would turn out to be seetee. P'raps they died, in the tender ship from this berth, finding out the truth. Or most of them, anyhow."

His voice fell uneasily again, when he thought of those alien voices still to be explained. Perhaps there had been some few survivors left, just enough to seize that terrene cruiser and fire on the *Orion*. Perhaps the last of the Invaders had used their ancient skills to repair that battered wreck, and departed upon it.

He nodded doubtfully to himself. That might explain the swift disappearance of the captured warcraft—if they had replaced its fission power plant with some sort of seetee reactor. But where could they be going? All the major planets of the sun were still terrene, and no conceivable rebuilding would fit a *Perseus* class cruiser for an interstellar voyage.

"Dunno where they went." He shrugged impatiently and turned to look at Ann. "But let 'em go, gorgeous." He gave her a thin little grin. "Seems they left all their secrets for the company—"

"Don't, Paul!"

They had floated close to that narrow ramp, and as he turned to face her he had reached out unthinkingly to catch that high, bright railing. Ann checked him, with that sharp cry of warning, and flung herself to brush him back.

"Huh?" he gasped. "What—"

His startled voice dried up, when he saw the bedplates beneath the footway. Thick silver disks, like geometric mushrooms on long crooked stalks. The terrene stalks were welded to the wall, but he saw now that the footway didn't touch it anywhere. The railing didn't, either. And something else was odd about that railing. It seemed to be on the wrong side of the ramp, until he saw that it was there to guard the things that walked it from the deadly terrene wall.

Cold in the heated fabric, he watched her return to test the railing. At a cautious distance, she moved her wrist to sweep it with the beam of invisible alpha particles. The explosions when they reacted with the shining metal were too small for him to see, but her helmet light brought him the sudden whirr of the gamma ray detector, precisely like the whirr of a striking rattler he had seen in a zoo on Earth.

"Thanks, Ann." He gulped, and his voice came back. "Wasn't thinking. But of course they had to have seetee walks, wherever they wanted to go."

They retreated from the railing.

"This was something else." She frowned at him, her own voice strangely unshaken. "Something besides an ark, I mean. Or why would it be half-and-half?"

"Guess you've got something." He nodded uneasily.

179

"If they had been building it just to carry them away from the big blowup, they would have just made it all seetee. Or else, if they wanted terrene armor to turn terrene gas and meteors without reacting, they would have armored the whole ship."

"Why would they build anything half-and-half?"

He floated for a moment, peering down into the yawning dark.

"The same reason Drake and McGee would," he said suddenly. "Power! Of course they couldn't land on our terrene planets, or even touch a terrene rock with their hands—if they had hands! But everything alive needs energy, and there's no source like annihilated matter. B'lieve this whole thing is nothing but a big reactor! Terrene shops in this end. Tools to maintain the terrene parts. Machinery to gather and process the terrene half of the fuel."

Eager now, he caught his breath.

"Let's have a look below!"

They sank cautiously into that shadowy chasm, peering ahead with their feeble lamps. That untouchable narrow ramp wound around them. Dark platforms emerged from the gloom and slipped dimly upward and were lost again above. And they came at last to the floor of that vast cylindrical pit.

He waited, this time, for Ann to make her test. There was no deadly rattle, and they dropped warily upon the floor. It was dark iron, cluttered with untidy piles of terrene rock. Anders stooped clumsily, to study the broken stone with his head lamp.

"Ore! he called. "Mostly meteoric nickel iron!"

He looked up again with a better understanding at the winding footway and the wide platforms and the giant valve half open to the stars—it gave him a brief sense of comfort to recognize the familiar battered W of Cassiopeia.

"This was a berth for a terrene ship." He swung excitedly to Ann. "Equipped with a seetee bridge, or p'raps for remote control. Anyhow, they used it to collect terrene meteors. Spilled this waste. Left it here, because moving it was dangerous. But yonder's where they dumped the ore."

He moved eagerly toward the center of the pit, where a circle of huge iron stanchions supported a massive ring, many meters above, that must have cradled the vanished ore-ship. Beyond the stanchions yawned a deeper pit, wide enough he thought to swallow the *Orion.*

"The ore-chute, of course."

He leaned to look into that darker abyss, and his voice turned triumphant.

"Means we're getting places, darling! The mills and furnaces and terrene machine shops will be down below. We can prob'ly get all the new know-how we need just by seeing how they work. Might even take the whole thing over, for the company. Just tear out these catwalks we can't use, and build some of our own in the seetee sections, on the same bedplates! What a prize for Interplanet—"

Ann screamed.

It was no ladylike yelp, but a deep-lunged shriek that carried terror at high tension. Anders groped for the gun at his belt and crouched to fire a terrene shot into some seetee attacker. But Ann had not been attacked. She stood still, merely pointing.

He moved to her side. "What happened?"

"Sorry." She laughed nervously. "I'm all right. Just getting jumpy. Didn't mean to scare you. But yonder—" She gulped, and something hushed her voice. "Yonder is a man."

Anders swung the pale beam of his head lamp, and found the man. An armored form, sitting on a dark pile of terrene rubble near the foot of that untouchable ramp, and hugging the dark iron stalk of a bedplate. The sight was grotesque. The white, air-swollen fabric looked like some kind of clumsy toy, sitting beneath a bright metal mushroom. Anders had to choke back a shocked, mirthless laugh.

He snapped the gun to his belt again, when he saw the

extinct helmet light and the queerly rigid limbs and the white frost inside the face plate. He turned to peer sharply at Ann.

"Dead," he rasped. "Who was it?"

"A Guardsman, I think." Her voice was almost calm again, and entirely innocent. "Anyhow, that looks like regulation armor."

"Guess you're right," he muttered apologetically. "Would you test it—and that disk?"

The armor was terrene, and the stalk in its stubborn grasp, but the bright disk above made a warning whirr in the detector. Anders started forward cautiously, and stopped when his light caught the black letters stenciled across the silvered shoulders.

Mandate Property
Size Five
SS PERSEUS HSG

"That couldn't be!" His voice shrank to a whisper, and the stiff fabric felt cold on him. "Hood did warn me that von Falkenberg had mutinied and started after us, when those unconscious men recovered. But that wasn't forty-eight hours ago. The *Perseus* couldn't have got here ahead of us—not without some kind of seetee drive!"

Ann crouched back from the frozen Guardsman.

"I don't like von Falkenberg," she said huskily. "I think he got himself assigned to the Seetee Patrol, just so he could spy on our work. His men broke into our office on Obania. He tried twice to follow Cap'n Rob through that drift to our shop on Freedonia. Maybe he had found this thing before."

"We'd have known about it." Anders shook his head, and leaned to read that stenciled legend again. "But von Falkenberg is an able agent. He's the one who took that film I saw. I don't know how he got here ahead of us—but that must have been the *Perseus* we fought."

He nodded in the helmet, not quite convinced.

"P'raps it all makes a sort of sense. I'd still like to

know where your asterite friends picked up those ametined spacemen, but it must have been out here. Seems they woke up and joined that Martian and somehow got here in time to meet us with a shot—"

His voice trailed doubtfully away, because after all nothing really quite made sense.

"So he's off the *Perseus*." Ann looked back at the man and the iron mushroom, her voice dry with dread. "But what was he doing with that bedplate?"

"What we're all doing." That much at least seemed obvious, and he spoke more confidently. "Trying to learn why it doesn't blow up. Prob'ly meant to carry it off and try to take it apart."

"There!" Ann had swung her pale helmet light to the foot of that narrow ramp, and she pointed to a gap where one support was missing. "But what—" Her low voice caught. "What could have killed him?"

"Prob'ly just a dead power pack," Anders said. "Must have used an arc to cut that rod. Too excited to watch his gauges. Or p'raps he just forgot this paragravity field. Anyhow, when he finally got his prize cut loose, he didn't have power left to lift it."

Ann shivered. "But he couldn't put it down!"

"Not without setting off the whole installation." Anders stared at that anonymous, white-frosted face plate with a sudden sympathy. "The ramp's too high to lean it on. When he failed to lift it, all he could do was to sit and hold it balanced on its stem, till his power pack gave out completely and his air unit quit. Waiting, maybe for his friends to come back. Only they didn't come."

Ann turned away.

"A ghastly way to die!" she whispered. "Even for that mutineer."

"Wonder if any others came off the *Perseus*?" He moved uneasily to sweep those dark mounds of spilled terrene ore with his inadequate head lamp. "With mutiny already against them, and all this precious know-how in reach, they'd be desperate—"

"They'd be dead!" Ann broke in, her ragged voice

near hysteria. "They'd all be dead. Because this whole monstrous machine has been dead ever since the Invader killed Adonis, and there's nothing here but death."

She caught his stiff glove, urgently.

"Please, Paul," she whispered, "haven't we seen enough? Can't we go back now? Couldn't we just turn this bedplate over to the Drakes and Cap'n Rob? They know seetee. I think they could take it apart without getting killed. That would be enough. There's nothing else we need."

He stood silent, watching the man it had already killed.

"Let's get out," she begged softly. "While we can. This whole terrible machine is too strange for us. Anything we touch is apt to be deadly as that railing. If we stay we'll only trap ourselves, the way *he* did."

Anders turned slowly away from the silent mutineer. The glow of his head lamp filled her helmet, to light the brown curve of her cheek and the tilt of her freckled nose but not the frightened dark of her imploring eyes.

"P'raps you've got something, gorgeous." He inhaled deliberately, trying to relax. "Not sure myself we need anything those dead things made. Might be a stroke of luck for the human race, if we blew this damned machine to gamma radiation."

With the thin white beam of his head lamp, he followed that winding footway upward until it was lost again in the thickening dark. His eyes hurried back to Ann. He smiled again at the warm human planes of her anxious face, and squeezed her clutching glove.

"Dunno what they were," he muttered. "Taller than we are. Prob'ly different in more important ways. Hard to say what their dead culture would do to ours."

She watched him silently, her gray eyes puzzled.

"Dunno." He shrugged against the cramping weight of his armor. "No social philosopher, gorgeous. Can't even state the question, except in engineering terms. But I do know that when you mix up unlike things or forces, you're pretty sure to get a reaction."

She looked at the dead man uneasily, and anxiously back at his face.

"Sometimes constructive," he said. "Sometimes destructive. Sometimes neither. Unlike poles attract. A light metal and a poison gas react to give you common salt, plus a little incidental heat and violence. A set of equations that old Maxim-Gore fished out of the sun, acting on the old corporation laws, made Interplanet. Men in high space become spatial engineers—or mutineers, when you add the fission power shortage and a jolt of interplanetary politics. One terrene ship plus one seetee rock equals one blinding flash." His voice fell gravely. "So what are we going to get, if we inject the know-how in this ship into our civilization?"

"I'm not quite sure I know what you mean." She leaned in the clumsy armor, trying to see his face. "Unless you're afraid the Martians would make seetee bombs. I think they would. But if we can help the Drakes unlock seetee power for all mankind—"

" 'Fraid not, gorgeous." He straightened briskly. "Don't get yourself excited over anything I said. I'm just an engineer, working for the company. The final philosophical consequences of what I'm paid to do are outside my field."

He glanced at the watch on his sleeve.

"So let's try the ore bins, next. Want to come along?"

"Paul—" She choked back her hurt protest, when she saw that he was moving. "Yes, I'm coming."

She followed him away from the frozen mutineer, between the massive stanchions and on to the lip of that vast chute. The Invaders hadn't died for any want of terrene fuel. Searching that dark lower chasm, his head lamp found a vast gray mountain of ore.

"So on we go, darling," he murmured a trifle too casually. "For dear old Interplanet—"

He had stepped off the rim when he heard a tiny dry sound in her throat, as if she had tried to scream and failed. He felt her snatch the hanger strap of his armor, and the thrust of her own hauled him back on the floor.

"Listen, gorgeous." He grinned at her sardonically. "If you can't bear to watch me doing an honest job for the company, you'll just have to go back and wait with our fat Callistonian friend—"

Still she couldn't speak, but her trembling sleeve was pointing at that black rim. He saw where his boots had started a little pile of spilled ore to pouring in a thin stream down the chute, but that was nothing very strange.

"Don't you see?" she gasped at last. "Don't you see what happens to the rock?"

He saw then that each little fragment of ore, when it had fallen a certain short distance down that shute, began to crumble. He watched hard nuggets of meteoric iron dissolving into fine gray dust, and thought he was going to be sick. He pressed down with his chin to open the receiver in the bottom of his helmet, but the nausea passed. He tried to grin at Ann, and heard her whisper faintly:

"It didn't touch you?"

He shook his head, and kicked weakly to slide another little pile of broken ore into impalpable dust.

"Clever gadget," he gulped at last. "Used to hope I could hit on something like it, for our paragravity separation plants. Some effect that breaks molecular bonds. Grinds ore to individual atoms!"

"Wonderful, I'm sure," Ann said huskily. "I hope you're satisfied!"

"Embarrass me," he muttered. "Saving my life every five minutes. But the company does need this gadget. For milling ore, mining, drilling terraformer shafts. Billions in it. Every shareholder can keep another mistress and grow another chin." He managed to grin. "Thanks again, gorgeous, but I can't stop now."

"Oh, Paul, I—I hate you! Damn Interplanet!"

"Sorry." He felt uncomfortable, but tried not to show it. "P'raps you shouldn't save me any more."

He soared away from her. With an angry little gasp, she followed him toward the lowest of those projecting

186

platforms. It was built against the dark iron wall, with no bright bedplates beneath. He knew it must be terrene, but he waited for Ann to swim ahead and test it with her radium ray.

"Safe," she told him stiffly.

They dropped on the end of it. The seetee footway sloped up near it, and there was a landing where the Invaders must have stood to watch their terrene machines. Two narrow railways crossed it, to vanish in the dark beyond a wide doorway. His light found a little car standing on the rails, as if it had just rolled off the last ore ship, and he moved quickly toward it.

"Here's the way inside," he called to Ann. "All we have to do is follow these terrene tracks, until—"

"Stop!" she gasped. "I—I can't scream any more."

He had already stopped. At the end of that little rail car, his light had found a queer white heap on the dark platform. It had been another spaceman, in regulation armor, but something had sliced it cleanly through at the belt. Frozen moisture from the evaporating body fluids had fallen back over it, in a blanket of glittering frost.

In spite of Ann's faint cry of protest, Anders bent gingerly to brush the frost from the rigid shoulders of the armor, so that he could read the stenciled lettering:

Mandate Property
Size Zero
SS PERSEUS HSG

"Another mutineer." He bent again over the helmet, but the frost inside hid the dead spaceman's face and held the lens immovable. "Cut in two."

He turned cautiously to the car. Its low bed carried a bulky mechanism, cased in dark iron. A number of projecting rods had triangular heads, shaped as if to fit some special tool. The end toward the dead man tapered and divided into two slender prongs, tipped with tiny diamond points. Experimentally, he dropped a stray lump of meteoric iron between the points, and watched the two halves of it roll apart on the platform, split as if by an unseen blade.

He whistled softly.

"A mining tool, I'd say. Prob'ly that same bond-dissolving effect, adapted to slice up meteors and such." He glanced at the mount of frost. "Our mutineering friend didn't know it was loaded."

"Horrible!" She moved quickly toward him. "Paul, won't you come back now? Before this happens to us!"

"Not yet, darlin'. Hood will want a full report on what makes all this tick. With diagrams. But don't take it so hard." He shook his head reprovingly. "S'pose you wait right here till I get back. I'll try to be careful—but don't forget the time."

He wanted to go on, but her face held him. The anxiety so dark in her eyes, the quiver of her silent lips, the stray wisp of dark hair across her forehead that made her look like a lost, frightened child. She breathed suddenly, with a convulsive little shudder. He expected some hysterical outburst of terror and resentment, but she merely made a bleak little nod and started to follow him.

Then something moved.

Chapter XVIII
Coincidence

ANDERS CAUGHT THE MOVEMENT, with a chance sweep of his head lamp. The moving thing was dim in the shadowy distance, out on the floor near the base of the towering stanchions beneath that enormous, empty cradle. Before he could see what it was, it slipped down out of sight, behind a mound of spilled ore.

It was one of the Invaders.

That fear paralyzed him. He stood shuddering and voiceless, turning the furtive shadow he had seen into something taller and more clever than a man, untouchable and terrible.

"Ann!" He got his breath back, and whispered to her hoarsely. She had seen nothing. She didn't understand his terror, but suddenly that cold paralysis was broken. He caught her glove and pulled her flat on the iron platform, too close to that iron-slicer.

"What is it?" she gasped.

"Thought it was one of the Invaders." He laughed feebly, at his own alarm. "Stupid of me, because it's hiding in that terrene ore. Gave me quite a jolt. S'pose it's just a man."

"A man might be bad enough," she warned him softly. "A man like von Falkenberg."

He had to nod, but still he felt relieved. He couldn't even imagine anything to fit the doors and ramps and railings of the seetee Invaders, but he was used to dealing with Martian secret agents.

"Cut off your light," he whispered.

He snapped off his own, and reached for his gun. The black silence gave him a sudden bitter loneliness, and

189

he was glad to feel her glove touch his shoulder. For a moment there was only darkness and the stars beyond the open valve, but then another red point came out, nearer, trembling with transmitted speech.

"Ann?" The voice was an anxious drawl. "Ann O'Banion?"

Her helmet light flashed on instantly.

"Cap'n Rob? It's really you?"

She lifted away from the platform. Anders snapped on his own headlight, and followed her. They dropped to that tall mound of broken iron, where Rob McGee stood waiting. The stubby little asterite waddled eagerly to meet the girl, reaching out his gloves. Anders had a glimpse of his beard-stubbled face, pale and ill and ugly but now smiling joyously.

"Are you all right?" Ann whispered breathlessly. "And Rick—"

"Stand still, McGee," Anders broke in softly. "Don't move your hands."

McGee stood still, while Anders swept by him to disarm him.

"Paul!" Ann gasped. "What are you doing?"

"Arresting a lawbreaker." Anders dropped again near Ann, and tossed McGee's antique testing gun into that huge ore chute, where it went silently into dust. He swung deliberately back to the short asterite.

"Well, McGee?" His voice was clipped and flat. "You were ordered not to land here."

"We were forced to, captain." McGee spoke apologetically. "Von Falkenberg was after us, with the Perseus. Demanding information we didn't have. Threatening to blow us out of space, when we couldn't answer. We came in here to hide."

"Where's your tug?"

McGee pointed with a bulky sleeve, and Anders found the Good-by Jane. Tiny in that cavernous pit, it stood leaning precariously on another mound of rubble, hidden behind that ring of towering stanchions.

"All right." He thrust the glare of his light into McGee's face plate. "Rick Drake aboard?"

"No, sir."

"Then where is he?"

"I don't know." McGee blinked painfully against the light. "You see, I was sick when we got here. Something turned me sick, just before we landed. Rick left me, and went out alone. He came back once, and went out again. That was a long time ago. He's still gone, and I—"

"A long time?" Anders cut in. "How long?"

"I can't tell." McGee squirmed uncomfortably. "Outside, you see, I never need a watch. I just know the time. But this thing felt wrong, when I first saw it. Ever since we got here, I can't tell what time it is—"

"Well, I've a watch," Anders interrupted unsympathetically. "And it says you're lying. I know you haven't been here very long. It's only about fifteen hours ago that we last warned you to keep away, and you were then half a million kilometers behind. What I want to know is how you got here ahead of us, in that rusty little tub."

McGee shrugged.

"Sure you haven't got a seetee reactor?" Anders demanded. "Or some kind of super-drive? Something you looted off this ship last year, when you were steering it away from Freedonia?"

"You're wrong, captain." McGee looked hurt. "This wasn't any sort of ship when we turned it away from Freedonia. It was just a common seetee rock, till that last blowup changed it. That's when it began to feel wrong—"

"How did you get here so fast?"

"We didn't." McGee squinted against the light. "We never saw this machine before, and we still drive the 'ane with a cranky old uranium reactor. I don't know what time it is now, but we didn't even land till the morning of April first—"

"How long ago was that?'

"I can't tell, captain." McGee's face looked sick and

blank. "Except it must have been a long time ago. I can't tell how long. I can't tell anything. Because something about this machine makes me sick—"

"Me, too." Anders grinned sardonically. "But I can tell you that April first is nearly a year ago. 'Cause my watch says today is still March."

"I think your watch is wrong," McGee insisted gently. "Because I do know it was April first when we got here, and a lot of things have happened since. I was sick, and I had to stay aboard. But Rick started back to the valve, to watch for those mutineers, and found them in here ahead of us—"

"What's that?"

"I don't understand it, sir.' McGee shrugged again uncomfortably. "I know they were still outside when we came in here. But somehow they got here first. Rick found them here and there, where they had killed themselves—"

"P'raps von Falkenberg found this thing, and lost those men, sometime before the blowup, Anders interrupted suddenly. "I don't know how he kept our agents from reporting—unless he bribed them with part of the loot! That might explain it. If von Falkenberg did get away with enough of this know-how—"

"But he didn't get away with anything," McGee drawled gravely. "Rick says he died aboard his ship.'

"Huh? What happened to the cruiser?"

McGee's helmet jerked silently toward the huge ore chute.

"No!" Anders gasped. "Though I s'pose that gadget would grind armor plate, at that, as easily as meteors.' He stabbed his light into McGee's eyes again. "How do you know?"

"Rick found a camera." The little asterite gestured vaguely up into the dark. "Lying beside a spaceman who had somehow got himself crushed in an automatic door. The film shows the *Perseus*. Battered nearly to scrap, but Rick could recognize it. He thought it had been fighting you."

"We did fight somebody." Anders nodded dazedly. "But what happened to it?"

McGee nodded toward that gaping chute.

"Rick thought you had driven it in here," he said. "The film shows three men leaving the Perseus with testing equipment. They came in here. The cruiser followed them. It seems crippled in the last shots, though it looked all right when they came off. It went down that chute. I guess von Falkenberg didn't know it was a grinder."

"I—I see," Anders muttered doubtfully. In spite of all those wild inconsistencies of time, McGee's account of the mutineers' fate had a certain troubling ring of truth. He turned uneasily to sweep the dark heaps of ore with his light. He searched the leaning hull of the *Good-by Jane*, and peered at the silent girl, and swung abruptly back to McGee.

"So what became of Rick?"

"I don't know." Worry seamed the small asterite's weather-beaten face. "He was gone a long time before he came back with that camera. We looked at the film, and then he fixed me a pot of tea and got himself a bite to eat before he went back again. I still felt too sick to do anything. I lay waiting for him, and finally went to sleep. I woke up feeling better. I think I'm getting used to—whatever is wrong. I was starting out to look for Rick when I saw your lights."

"Where was he going?"

"Down inside." McGee's shaggy yellow head moved vaguely in the helmet. "Of course he knew about that chute. He thought he could find some safer way, but he's been gone too long now. I don't know how long—"

McGee's soft voice trailed apprehensively away.

Anders stood scowling at the two asterites. McGee's wildly illogical tale had really explained nothing at all, yet he felt that Ann believed it. She said nothing, but he was keenly aware of her watchful hostility. He wasn't sure what to do next, yet he knew that any show of his own confusion could be fatal.

"Int'resting," he murmured cooly. "P'raps even true.

But all the same I'm going to take another look aboard that tug. So please turn around." He gestured with the gun. "I'm borrowing the power leads out of your drive packs, to keep you out of trouble while I'm gone. I'll need your keys, too, McGee. Sorry, Miss O'Banion."

They turned their backs obediently. Neither of them spoke, as he disabled their suits. Ann's bleak silence annoyed him unreasonably.

"Wait here," he rasped sardonically. "I won't be long."

He boarded the tug, and searched it cautiously. He didn't meet Rick Drake. On the table in the little cabin, he did find a three-millimeter camera and a roll of self-developing film. He took time to run the film through the viewer attachment, and saw the crippled hulk of the *Perseus* slip down that dark chute into molecular dust. McGee's story was so far confirmed, but still incredible.

On impulse, with a nagging sense of something overlooked, he rewound the short film to study the first scenes again. They had been shot outside, as the mutineer with the camera left the then undamaged *Perseus* with two armored companions. Bristling with testing guns and other special equipment, the three had cautiously approached the alien craft.

It gave him an uncomfortable feeling to realize that they were all dead now. The cameraman crushed in an automatic door. The little fellow sliced in half by that invisible blade. The giant, in the size five armor, trapped beneath his deadly prize.

What troubled him more sharply, however, was a feeling that he knew the large man and the small one. Anonymous as they were in the air-swollen fabric, there was something in the clumsy-seeming way the giant aimed and fired his testing gun, in the timid way the little man hung behind, that disturbed him with a haunting sense of recognition.

Frowning, he started the film again, watching for their faces. The furtive man in the size zero suit was always too far behind, but once the sunlight had struck into the

194

other's helmet. Anders caught one brief glimpse of the blubbery face inside, and nodded unbelievingly.

The large man looked oddly like Commander Protopopov. The apprehensive little man might have been Luigi Muratori. A curious coincidence, but certainly nothing else; he had left those expensive friends of Interplanet both safe aboard the *Orion*. He shrugged impatiently, dropped the tiny reel in his pocket, and hurried down to the engine room.

In that tiny compartment, he found the same well-worn antiques he had seen when he took off those unconscious spacemen. The same paintless uranium pile, an early Interplanet model older than he was. The same makeshift paragravity drive, looking as if it had been patched together from odds and ends of junk.

Oddly, however, the tuning crystal was different. The perfect eight-gram diamond he remembered had been changed for the same slightly flawed one-gram stone that he had persuaded the port inspectors at Pallasport to seize —which Karen Hood had so unaccountably returned. It really made the little craft unsafe, but he could soon take care of that.

He was reaching for a screwdriver to remove the flawed crystal and immobilize these elusive rock rats, when he began to wonder what they had done with that perfect eight-gram stone. Suddenly, this whole home-made installation looked too elaborately innocent. Had it all been arranged to cover up some kind of seetee super-drive, tuned perhaps with that finer diamond?

He turned to scowl at the controls. The gauges indicated that the battered little reactor was really reacting, at a level just high enough to maintain its own exchanger field and to supply the lights and ventilators. But its full rated output was far too low to have brought this time-battered tub here ahead of the *Orion*.

There was one way to find out what propelled the tug. He closed the drive switch. At the periscope, he oriented himself to steer for the scrap of sky overhead. Then, watching the dials, he pulled the damper rod out to full thrust. He saw his blunder instantly, as the swinging needles wavered.

He slammed the damper in again, before the tiny craft had risen from her ground gear, but still too late. A hot blue arc hissed around the diamond and exploded into acrid smoke. He stumbled backward, strangled and blinded.

A relay clicked, and dim yellow batter lights came on to show him what had happened. He had pulled the damper out too fast. The sudden overload had been too much for that flawed diamond. The short circuit had charred it to useless carbon, and also burned out the exchanger coils in the reactor itself.

"Damned clumsiness!" he muttered. "Didn't mean to do it."

The accident was no disaster, he told himself. He had planned to immobilize the *Good-by Jane*, if not quite so permanently. The ruined diamond and the damaged coils could be replaced from the spares aboard the *Orion*—if he decided to replace them. But he couldn't help wincing from what Ann O'Banion would think.

Outside, in that enormous metal cavern, he found the two asterites standing in their disabled armor where he had left them. Ann shuffled stiffly around to face him, her helmet light trembling with speech.

"Well, Paul?" Her low voice sounded half defiant and half amused. "Find any seetee people?"

"Not yet," he said curtly. "But I grounded the tug." No use trying to explain the accident. "When I'm ready to go, I'll either repair it or take you both aboard the *Orion*."

"What about Rick?" The sharp concern in her tone brought him a twinge of something dangerously near jealousy. "Can't we wait for him to come back?"

"How d' you know he's coming back?" He heard the faint catch of her breath, and instantly regretted the candor of his question, even though he felt fairly sure by now that Rick Drake was dead. Dead, like the mutineers of curiosity. "But we'll be here a while yet," he promised her hastily. "I'm going on down inside. I'll look for him."

"Thanks, Paul," she whispered. "May we go with you?"

"If you like." He looked sharply at McGee. "But if you start getting any ambitious ideas, just remember that I've burned out your pile and drive."

McGee nodded unresentfully, but he couldn't help flinching from the girl's unseen eyes.

"Turn around," he said harshly. "I'll hook up your power packs."

He replaced the leads.

"Thank you, captain," Ann whispered coldly. "Ready?"

"Not quite," he said. "Please wait, while I make sure nothing has happened to the cruiser."

"Why?" Ann's low voice seemed ironic. "Don't you even trust your own loyal men?"

"I do." His tone failed to sound as crisp as he intended. "But I ran that film. Two of those unfortunate mutineers looked oddly like two of my officers. Just coincidence, of course. But still I want to call the cruiser. Please wait here."

Soaring away from them, he thought he saw something cross the starlit rift above. A moving shadow against that mist of distant suns, no larger than a man in armor. He drove toward it, but it was gone before his light could reach it.

He slipped cautiously out between the enormous leaves of that half-closed valve, clutching his testing gun. Nothing physical attacked him there, but the implacable strangeness of that vast and deadly mechanism struck him again with a staggering cold impact, almost as if he had never seen it before.

He was lost for a moment, and he had to orient himself with the glittering tip of a golden spire, creeping like the hand of an enormous clock across the galactic clouds of Sagitarius, before he knew which way to go. Anxiously, then, he flew around the huge curve of that rust-red dome, until he saw the pointed shadow of the cruiser—and thought he saw the white glint of a dirigible suit dropping toward the air lock.

"Anders to *Orion!*" He turned up his helmet light, and narrowed its beam to reach the vessel. "Anders to *Orion!* . . . Calling Commander Protopopov."

The black shadow-ship showed no answering light, for so long that he began to wonder if he had really seen that fleeting figure returning to the lock. Suddenly afraid his own men had gone the way of the mutineers, he dropped warily toward the cover of one of those enormous, arching ribs.

"Anders to *Orion!*" he shouted hoarsely. "Anders calling—"

The cruiser's powerful photophone transmitter glared at him suddenly like a gigantic bloodshot eye from the pointed bow, winking with the vibrations of Protopopov's voiceless demand:

"What do you want?"

"This is Anders." He tried not to sound too curt. "I saw somebody out here in a space suit. S'pose you haven't let anyone off the cruiser?"

"Only Mr. Omura," The Callistonian answered. "He has just returned from a photographic fission."

"What's that?" Anders knew he had to keep cool, yet his voice lifted raggedly. "Don't you remember that I ordered you—"

"I remember," Protopopov broke in harshly. "Unfortunately for you, however, we are no longer dancing for your dirty gold."

"Is this—" Anders had to catch his breath. "Is this mutiny?"

"Mutiny and treason." The red light shuddered with a blubbery chuckle. "Your superior officers will be informed that you lost your head over a rock rat girl spy, and attempted to betray the *Orion* to a Free Space gang."

The dull moronic whisper brightened with invention. "High Commissioner Hood will be told that you were aiding those traitors by stealing military information from the confidential files of the government. He'll be tipped off that you were involved in a rock rat plot to overthrow the Mandate with seetee weapons manufactured on Freedonia."

"Listen, man!" Anders begged desperately. "While you can. If you have any reasonable grievance, I'll consider it. If some other power has got to you, just remember that Interplanet has funds to top every other bid for seetee know-how. I'll come right back aboard, and we'll talk this over."

"Sorry, Anders—"

The sardonic, grating voice broke off abruptly. Anders saw the cruiser's guns moving. He flung himself toward the shelter of that great iron girder, and looked back to see that those long rifles hadn't followed him. They were trained spaceward now, flattened against the black hull as if in readiness for a take-off.

"Wait!" he shouted. "Let me come aboard!"

The red blazing eye made no answer.

"Open up the lock!" Gulping at the dust in his throat, Anders snatched wildly at a dubious straw. "Better let me back aboard, commander, 'cause I've got a film you ought to see. Shows what von Falkenberg got for all his trouble."

The bloodshot eye merely glared.

"Better let me in! Better see this film, before you've gone too far to stop. Shows what became of all those other mutineers. There's even a man who could be you, commander. Sitting dead, now, with a bedplate in his arms!"

Still the light brought no reply.

"You'll come to your senses," he insisted hoarsely. "When you see what happened to the *Perseus*—"

Suddenly, the eye winked at him.

"Sorry, Anders," Protopopov croaked without sympathy. "But nothing has happened to the *Perseus*. Our instruments have just picked it up, out toward Pallasport.

199

Under other circumstances, we might stay to see your pictures. But we want no trouble with von Falkenberg. We're taking off for Callisto."

Anders shivered, and tried to get his breath.

"Let me talk to Mr. Muratori," he gasped. "Or Mr. Omura!"

"Too bad, Anders. But your bourgeois titles are a little out of date. It's Comrade Muratori now. And Comrade Omura. And they're no longer your bootlicking underlings in the Guard. We've all destroyed everything that branded us as slaves of reaction, and pledged a new allegiance to the people's leadership of the Jovian Soviet. We aren't interested in your frantic offers of more Interplanet money. Because, you see, we're all expecting a sudden deflation of the Mandate dollar!"

The red light shuddered again, to that hollow chuckle.

"Aren't you bright enough, my brilliant captain, to observe the trend of history? Can't you see that the rich old empire of Earth is already rotting in its own capitalistic corruption? Don't you know that the Mandate is only a worthless prop? Can't you perceive that your dead reactionary state must fall before the new Soviet democracy and the new power of seetee?"

The tall shadow swayed against the stars.

"You can't leave me marooned!" Anders gasped. "I'm not alone—"

"I know you aren't," the red beam croaked. "But we're leaving you, my so-clever captain, to discuss the coming fall of dollar imperialism with your ambitious friends from Mars. If you really believe von Falkenberg is dead—"

The red light died. The blacked-out cruiser lurched spaceward. The ground gear must have lifted a dozen meters above that dull iron dome before the first shells from the attacking craft arrived.

They fell without warning. They erupted against that rising shadow, battered it back against the huge iron dome, bathed it in a fantastic inferno of smoke and fire and soundless fury.

Anders flattened himself against the cold iron behind that immense arching beam. Above him, the expanding clouds of smoke and vapor made a thin veil across the stars, lurid with the glare of exploding shells and the flash of the *Orion's* answering guns. He felt the metal shuddering, but there was no air to carry sound.

Each second that he was still alive, he knew that no shot had struck anything seetee, but one wild shell must have found his armor with some tiny terrene fragment. He heard the sharp crack of it, but felt no pain. The smoky flicker of that silent battle ceased at last, and he rose cautiously to where he could see the cruiser.

The *Orion* lay battered and helpless on its side, in a kind of shallow crater where that bombardment had caved in the dark iron dome. The long black hull had taken at least three hits. Air escaping from an ugly hole amidships made a thin plume of glittering frost. One gun stood pointing spaceward, frozen where it must have fired a last defiant shot; the other was crushed in its flattened turret underneath.

Warily, he inspected the wreck. The bridge compartment was caved in. A shell had penetrated amidships, exploding inside the reactor room. The *Orion* was obviously crippled beyond repair—immobilized as thoroughly as he had left the *Good-by Jane*.

In hope of salvaging a tuning diamond and exchanger coils to repair the disabled tug, he circled the smoking hulk. The stern section, he found, had received another direct hit. The ground gear was blown away, and the air lock crushed beyond opening.

Anxiously, he inspected the jagged holes in the tough steel plate, but they were all too small for his inflated suit. Terror swept him. Unless he could get inside to find repairs for the tug, his heavy-handed blunder was going to be fatal.

He failed to get inside.

In a frantic search for survivors whose aid might be bargained for again, he began tapping the battered hull with a loose casting from the demolished ground gear, listening with his helmet jammed hard against the steel to pick up vibrations that empty space wouldn't carry. He heard a thin, far-off sigh of leaking air, but no answering tap. If there were any survivors, they were already trying to ease or cheat death with ametine.

He went on around the wreck, tapping and listening to that faint hiss of air, until at last he noticed that it seemed to follow him. He recalled the shell fragment that had grazed his armor, and held up his wrist to look at the air pressure gauge. Only seven pounds . . .

Anoxia. He knew the creeping symptoms. The dullness, the slowed reactions, the insidious sleepiness. He tried to save his life. He left the wreck and guided his armor back around that vast iron dome, toward that empty berth where he had left Rob McGee and Ann O'Banion and the very temporary safety of the crippled *Good-by Jane*.

He had almost reached the wide black mouth of that deep cylindrical pit, when he began to hear the voices. At first they were fainter than that dying whisper of his air and his life leaking out, but when he turned to look toward Pallas he saw a far-off spark of modulated light and heard them clearly.

Or he thought he did, though he was getting sleepy and they still seemed very far away. They drifted eerily on the crashing seas of starlight, queerly almost-human, but yet entirely meaningless. The voices of those unseen contraterrene people, who guarded their queer ship so elusively, and trapped their human visitors so craftily. He wondered why they had wanted a terrene warcraft, but he was already too sleepy to care.

Or perhaps he did care, really, at least for Ann O'Banion. Now she was caught in this monstrous trap, as hopelessly as all those mutineers. Through his own damned blunder. He should have found her a new tuning diamond. . . .

He yawned, and went to sleep.

Chapter XIX
A Matter of Time

ANDERS LAY ON HIS BACK on the highest terrene platform, inside that enormous cylinder. His neck felt stiff and his head throbbed dully, hurt perhaps when he fell there. The pain aroused him only briefly, however; he was still almost asleep.

He thought he was alone.

Without moving his head, he could see a narrow patch of starry space, framed with the half-closed leaves of that great valve. Nearer, straight above, was that queerly narrow footway, starlight shining white on the high, gleaming rail that was untouchable for men.

Drowsily, he tried to picture the beings that had walked that narrow ramp, but even with their voices still ringing in his ears, his dull imagination failed. Perhaps even the word "walk" itself was wrong for them, he thought, because they had always used inclined planes instead of stairs.

He lay very still, watching the ramp and the railing. He felt too heavy to move again, and he had nothing else to do. If he were only quiet enough, if he could wait long enough, some seetee thing might come by. Perhaps he could see why it used no steps, and what made it so thin and so tall.

Or was it there already, something too tenuous for him to see. Was that the answer? Had the Invaders been able to work both terrene matter and seetee, because they themselves were neither? Could intelligence exist in something else than matter? His slow brain fumbled with that problem aimlessly, and gave it up at last. Thinking was too difficult. A gray fog was thickening in his brain.

He lay waiting, staring through that fog, but nothing came along the ramp. The mist thickened until he could hardly see through it. The throbbing in his head was fainter now, too faint to keep him awake much longer. He was afraid he would fall asleep, before the tall Invader came.

But then he saw it.

It was bending over him, a vague blur in the haze. He knew it must be tall and narrow, though he couldn't see it clearly. He knew its touch meant death, but that didn't seem to matter greatly. He didn't want to move his head, and there was nothing he could do.

The thing floated down to the platform, beside him. It began fumbling with his armor. He waited for its foreign stuff to react with his terrene body. When he saw a sudden blaze of light, he thought the end had come.

But the light was not white annihilation. It was only the rosy glow of a helmet lamp. Dimly, it revealed an armored human form beneath it. A faint reflection caught the anxious face of Ann O'Banion. He tried to move.

"Better keep quiet," she said. "You're almost asphyxiated."

"I thought—" he tried to whisper. "Thought you were—"

But no sound came, and he lay back limply. What he had thought was not important now. He heard a faint sound of air again, and suddenly he could breathe. Dreamily, he knew she had removed the air unit from her own suit and attached it to his. He thought she shouldn't be doing that for him. Not when she would soon be dying too, from the consequences of his own clumsy blunder. But he felt too drowsy to try to tell her so. She was no Invader, and he could breathe again. Stretched out on the iron platform, he went back to sleep.

The next thing he knew distinctly, he was lying on a folding berth in the lower hold of the tug. Ann O'Banion stood beside him, looking tired and pale in the yellow dimness of the battery lights, frowning a little as she counted his pulse.

"Thanks, gorgeous." She must have dragged him aboard, and got him out of his damaged armor. He still felt too heavy to move, but he grinned up at her. "Didn't realize you felt this way."

"You had me worried." She released his wrist, with a wan little answering smile, and sat down wearily on an empty water drum beside the bunk. "You've been just lying there so long. And you know you were nearly dead, before I ever found you."

"Good of you to bother looking, everything considered." He lay for a while just watching her face, hollowed and shadowed with strain, yet still tanned and firm and beautiful. He aroused himself to ask, "Where's McGee?"

"Out with Rick," she said. "They've rigged up a cutting arc. Trying to cut through that armor plate, and get inside the wreck of the *Orion*."

"So Rick got back?"

"Days ago."

"Days?" He gaped at her. "How long have I been out?"

"You've had a whiff of ametine." Her low voice turned apologetic. "You see, with the pile dead and Rick needing all the batteries for his cutting arc, there was no power for the ventilators. We've had to save oxygen."

"Ametine?" He blinked through his lingering mental haze. "S'pose it serves me right. Ought to be out with Rick, looking for another diamond."

He tried to sit up, but found no strength.

"Better take it easy," Ann advised him. "Till your pulse comes back to normal."

"But we've got to get repairs," he insisted stubbornly. "I saw what was left of the *Orion*. Quite a job to get inside. They'll need me."

"I know." Her eyes fell, as if he had somehow made her uncomfortable. "But—but your armor's ruined."

"Can't that leak be patched?"

205

"Rick took the power pack, when his went dead," she told him. "Besides—"

Again she hesitated, and he nodded suddenly.

"I see," he muttered. "I'm a prisoner."

"Not exactly. But Rick and Cap'n Rob don't quite trust you."

"Can't entirely blame them." He grinned uneasily. "How are they doing with the salvage operation?"

"Badly, I'm afraid. That steel's too tough for their makeshift tools. Once they gave up the *Orion* altogether, to try another project. Dragged our main photophone light outside, and tried to call Freedonia. No answer."

"Why not?"

"Rick didn't know." Her drawn face had a haunted look. "Of course he had only battery power, but he says the light seemed strong enough." Something made her shiver. "One queer thing," she added huskily, "he had trouble even finding Freedonia. Because this ship has changed direction, since we've been on it!"

"Huh?" He lifted his head, in spite of the dull needle of pain the ametine had left. "Where's it going now?"

"Back the way it came," she said. "Back toward where that big blowup was. Rick wouldn't believe it, till I checked his observations—Cap'n Rob still doesn't know where we are, or what time it is. But we finally got a correct position, and found Freedonia in the 'scope. We kept calling all day and all night, but Mr. Drake never answered. Perhaps something has happened to him—I don't know what's gone wrong. But we were draining the batteries, and we had to give up. The last few days, we've been trying to cut that armor plate again. But still we can't get through."

Anders lay silent for a moment, watching her troubled face.

"Wonder what turned the ship?" he muttered uncomfortably. "S'pose the beings that built it—"

She shook her head. "We still have troubles enough, but Rick says we won't be meeting any seetee people."

"But they're—around." Dread caught his voice. "We've

206

heard their voices. We know they've captured a Guard cruiser. The one that fired on us, and disappeared, and came back to shell the *Orion*."

"I don't know what it was we heard." She shrugged apprehensively. "We can't explain those attacks. But Rick says the things that build the ship are dead. He's certain they died—or killed themselves—long before our galaxy was born."

"What?" He came up on his elbow, and forgot the dull pain in his head. "How could Rick be certain of that?"

"He found an arms factory down inside. Bigger than the arsenal on Pallas V. Full of automatic machinery and the deadliest weapons he ever saw. Mostly guided missiles, with seetee warheads. But there were a few uranium fission bombs."

"An arsenal!" he whispered. "So this wasn't a power plant, after all?"

"Rick says it was, in the beginning. He found empty bedplates down inside, where an enormous reactor must have stood. He says those golden spires were antennae for some kind of power transmitter. But the reactor was torn out, before the end. The transmission equipment all dismantled. Melted down for scrap, he thinks. Made into weapons."

Something hushed her voice.

"That's what became of the seetee people, Rick believes. This plant had been built for peace, but they converted it for war. A little too well. When the fighting was finished, they were too. Rick thinks it must have been some kind of terrene super-bomb that blew their world —or a fragment of it—out of their galaxy, before ours was born."

"Wait a minute!" Anders shook his head. "I know this thing feels old. I s'pose even a few billion years of drifting through the interstellar dark, at the absolute zero, might not have done much to it. But how does Rick date his pregalactic war?"

"With those fission bombs," she said. "There are just a few of them. He thinks they were brought out to defend the power satellite in the early stages of the war, before the machinery was rebuilt to manufacture seetee missiles."

"But how do uranium bombs date anything?"

"By changing to lead. Rick came back for Cap'n Rob's old analytic spectrometer, and used it to test the metal in those bombs. He found just the barest trace of U-235. All the rest had turned to lead."

"Oh!" He nodded dazedly. "I—I see." For a moment he was silent, and then he looked at her sharply. "D' you know how much uranium was left?"

"Less than one atom in ten thousand."

"B'lieve it takes around seven hundred million years for half the atoms in a sample of U-235 to undergo normal radioactive decay." He frowned at her, calculating. "That means this dead machine must have been drifting for something like ten billion years."

"That's—old!" Her dry voice shivered. "Too old. Paul, I'm still afraid. Even since I know they're dead. Because it's this thing that killed them. And it's still deadly. It killed the *Perseus*. Killed the *Orion*. Killed all those mutineers. It will kill the rest of us, too, unless we get away. Just a matter of time."

A matter of time. . . .

The trivial phrase echoed in his mind, grown suddenly meaningful. He caught his breath and sat up shakily on the edge of the bunk, staring blankly past Ann O'Banion. His hands clenched and trembled.

"Paul—" Her voice rose apprehensively. "What is it?"

"That phrase of yours." His haggard bleak face grinned vaguely. "A matter of time. P'raps that's the answer."

"How do you mean?"

"When you come to think of it, every problem we're up against seems to be a matter of time. An interval of time, or order in time. P'raps the first are really the last here on the ship. P'raps it really changes tomorrow into yesterday. P'raps Rick and McGee really didn't get here until April first."

"They say they didn't." An eager anxiety darkened

208

her eyes. "But how can you explain such a thing as that?"

"A matter of time," he muttered again. "And ten billion years is a very long time." He spoke slowly, gropingly, still looking at Ann without really seeing her. "Long enough to prove the ship really came from some other galaxy. 'Cause ours hasn't been here half that long. P'raps time was different where it came from!"

"Could that be?"

"P'raps." He rubbed thoughtfully at the harsh stubble of beard on his jaw. "I remember an old book Rick dug up somewhere, while he was on that research project for the company. An early treatise on seetee, written by a Martian-German professor who had some weird ideas. One of them was that the sign of the nucleus depends on the sign of entropy in the space where an atom is born."

"Which means?"

"The sign of entropy would also be the sign of time." His hollow eyes shone with a sudden excitement. "The old professor thought the contraterrene matter must have been formed in some other part of space, where time was running backward. P'raps he wasn't such a crackpot, after all!"

"But the seetee rocks aren't like this thing," she objected quickly. "They all seem exactly like terrene matter, so long as nothing terrene touches them."

"The professor knew that," he said. "But he thought large masses of either kind of matter would create what he called entropic fields around them, that would carry smaller masses along the same way in time. He thought the seetee rocks we know must be fragments of the Invader that had been caught by the stronger entropic field of Adonis—or p'raps even the field of the whole solar system—and deflected into positive time."

He sat up straighter on the edge of the bunk, breathless now with his triumphant excitement.

"But this satellite ship was too far out from the Invader to be involved in that collision. It has never been near enough to any large terrene mass to be caught and deflected. It's still moving backward in time—with a nega-

209

tive entropic field of its own that captured us when we got close!"

He rose abruptly and then sat down again, still weak in the knees from the drug.

"I think that's the answer!" he whispered huskily. "I think that one fact will be enough to account for everything that's happened to us—and p'raps even a number of things that you might say haven't yet taken place!"

"Everything?" Ann gave him a bewildered look, from her perch on the water drum. "I don't see how."

"Neither do I, quite yet." He grinned uncertainly. "Fact, the notion makes me groggy again. But I really do b'lieve it's going to be the answer. Just a matter of time! Could you find me a pencil and paper?"

"Up in the cabin. In Cap'n Rob's desk. If you feel like climbing the ladder."

His head felt light when he first stood up, but he climbed the ladder. Ann set a chair for him, at the little ink-stained desk built against the bulkhead, and opened a drawer in search of paper.

Something darted out.

"Oh!" She snatched at the object, but it escaped her. "Rick's disk—"

She checked herself, with a flush of confusion, but Anders pursued that fugitive object. It was a circular plate of brightly polished steel as wide as the palm of his hand, with a small hole in the center. It fled from him like something alive, but it was on a leash—a strong cord looped through the hole and tied to a ringbolt in the bulkhead.

He caught the cord and drew the lively disk back toward him, but still it darted skittishly away from his fingers. He towed it back toward the desk, but it shied away from the drawer where it had been confined. He noticed that even the restraining cord stood out from it in a wide loop, not touching the bright metal anywhere.

He maneuvered it back into the drawer, trapped it in a corner, tried to pin it down. A yielding resistance opposed his hands. He couldn't quite touch it, not even when he pushed down with all his strength. Nor did the disk ever come quite against the bottom of the drawer.

"Please put it back!" Ann was pink and breathless with embarrassment. "I didn't mean to show it to you."

He closed the drawer on it and turned to stare at her.

"Untouchable!" he muttered hoarsely. "Where did Rick get hold of that?"

"Oh, Paul!" Agitation shook her voice. "I'm such a fool! Rick didn't want you to know. I can't tell you anything about it."

"Then let me guess." He grinned slowly at her discomfiture. "My guess is paragravity. Permanent negative paragravity! Right, gorgeous?"

Her lips tightened defiantly, but her face turned pink again.

"Right!" His awed eyes fell back to the drawer that imprisoned that elusive disk. "Something we've been looking for, ever since old Maxim-Gore found paragravity in the sunspots. He wrote the equations for a permanent negative field, but we could never make an alloy to hold it."

He swung abruptly back to Ann.

"So that dodging disk is make of some special paragravitic alloy?" he demanded. "I s'pose Rick found the automatic furnaces where it was cast, and analyzed the ingredients with McGee's spectrometer? Learned how to make this alloy? Bedplates good enough to last ten billion years!"

"Please, Paul!" she begged. "I mustn't tell you anything."

"No matter, darlin'," he told her cheerfully. "After what you've shown me." Wonder hushed his voice again. "A surface effect, I could see. Obeys the inverse-square law. Half the distance, four times the repulsion. Means contact just can't happen—even if that disk were pressed close to a seetee surface! Guess those bedplates must be layer-cake affairs. Plates like this locked to the rrene stem, interlocked with seetee counter-plates fasned to the seetee crown?

211

"Right again, darlin'?"

Her eyes fell, but she nodded unhappily.

"And what a bearing surface!" A new excitement lifted his voice. "No contact means no friction. No lubrication needed. 'Splains how those machines can still operate, after all that time. Paragravity fields don't wear out!" He gave her a dazed little nod. "That little disk will make quite a splash—if we ever get home with it."

Ann looked up at him, her confusion suddenly gone.

"Paul—" She spoke his name in a breathless way, but something made her pause.

" 'Smatter, gorgeous?"

"Rick didn't intend for you to see that." She spoke very softly, watching him with wide, dark eyes. "Now that you know so much, I don't think he'll let you go back to use what you've learned to make seetee bombs for Interplanet. Now I think you'll have to go to work for Drake and McGee."

He looked for a long time into her intense bright face, and the faint grin faded slowly from his lips.

"Might do that," he whispered at last. "That is, if we ever get back alive and you really want to let me in." He nodded soberly. "Fact is, right now I'm not so keen about making any kind of bombs for anybody. Not since I know what happened to that seetee civilization. B'lieve I'll sign up, darlin', if you really want me."

She stood tall and near, not breathing, lovely even in her pale weariness. Her dark hair had a faint clean scent. Her hollowed face was slightly smiling, her tired eyes half closed and her lips a little parted.

"I do, Paul!" Her brown throat pulsed. "I really do."

He wanted very much to kiss her then, but he checked himself because it suddenly seemed unfair.

"Thanks, gorgeous." He grinned instead. "But don't let's be too hasty. We're still marooned here, remember. If we do get away alive, I'd jump at a chance to work with Drake and McGee—we could build a new kind of civilization on that little disk! But I'll always be an Earth-

212

man, darlin'. After all that's happened, your friends might not want me around."

The gray pinch of trouble caught her face again.

"Rick will be hard enough to convince that you're really on our side," she agreed soberly. "He's in a bad mood, anyhow. Afraid something has happened to his father, back there on Freedonia. Discouraged because that armor plate won't cut. Worried about all those queer things that made you think we were mixed up in some kind of plot. Upset by the way the ship turned back, without us even knowing when—"

"P'raps it didn't," Anders said. "And now, since we're finding out the facts, I think all those suspicious circumstances are going to have a different look."

She brightened. "I'd nearly forgotten your time theory. Do you really think you can explain those ametined spacemen, so that Rick and Cap'n Rob can't be accused of anything? And those queer voices that called Freedonia? And that enemy cruiser that fought the *Orion?* Without involving us?"

"B'lieve I can," he said. "If you'll just find me a piece of paper."

Chapter XX
The Whirlpool

ANN FOUND PAPER FOR HIM in another drawer, and he bent over the desk to draw his simple diagram. Straight arrows pointing upward, to represent the normal motion of Pallas and Obania and Freedonia in time and space. One shorter arrow, for the orbit of the seetee rock that Drake and McGee had steered away from Freedonia. Another arrow, slanting downward to the point of that one, for the path of the seetee ship, backward through time. He numbered the days of the month along the edge of the sheet, and sketched in curved lines to show the movements of the *Perseus* and the *Good-by Jane* and his own *Orion*.

"Seems to make sense." He looked up at last, triumphantly. "The ship may be ten billion years old, in its own minus time, but it will never be much older. 'Cause that's the end of it!"

He set the pencil down on his diagram, where the slanted arrow met the short one.

"On the evening of March 23rd. When that biggest blowup lit up space. That's when it hit that seetee rock and ceased to exist—except for the one stray fragment that von Falkenberg photographed as it went by. Or p'raps I should say that's when it will cease to exist speaking from our present point of view." His stubbled jaws hardened. "Rick and McGee had better get the *Jane* repaired before we're carried that far back."

"I don't quite see—" Alarm choked her voice. "You mean the ship is really carrying us back toward that collision, since it turned around?"

"Right, darlin'." He nodded grimly. " 'Cept it didn't turn around. We did the turning, as we landed. Seems that everyone who lands here is carried right along, in the field of the ship. And of course in this inverted time, the one who gets here first becomes the last arrival—as McGee was warning Rick, in that call he still hasn't made."

She frowned at the diagram, and looked up bewilderedly.

"We were the first, on the *Orion*." He paused to trace their route on the diagram. "First by our own time—but last by the time of the ship. We weren't here when the *Jane* arrived next day, 'cause tomorrow in our time is yesterday here. Von Falkenberg and his mutineers got here later still, in time to kill themselves before Rick and McGee arrived." He looked up at her. "See how it works?"

"I—I guess so." She nodded suddenly. "It's just like changing from one train to another going the same way on a parallel track! The farther you go on one before you change, the farther you have to come back on the other. And the more time it takes."

"Right, darlin'." He nodded, somewhat bleakly. "Right now, this train we're on is rolling toward a head on collision. Hope Rick and McGee manage to get us back on the other track before we meet that seetee rock." He traced a line on the diagram, and straightened abruptly. "But they can do it! Fact is, this shows they've already done it—if you don't mind another shift of tenses. Seems to clear up everything. So cheer up, gorgeous!"

"I'm afraid I still can't see much to cheer up about." She pushed the dark hair back from her worn face, with a slow, troubled gesture. "Those unconscious spacemen? That enemy ship? Those weird voices?" She shook her head at his diagram. "What has time to do with them?"

"Quite a bit. Though the fact sort of throws you at first." His voice turned faintly rueful. "Y' see, those frightful voices were our own."

"Ours?"

"But we heard them in reverse, the way you hear the voices on a phonograph record run backward. No wonder they sounded almost human!"

"The enemy cruiser—" A wild amazement widened her eyes. "That wasn't—"

"The *Orion*." He nodded, with a wry little grin. "It was coming back in time when we met it, by then in the hands of Protopopov and his mutineers. We followed the normal procedure of asking questions first and then shooting when we failed to get a satisfactory answer. So did the mutineers. But, for each of us, the order of events was inverted. The shells came first. Even when the questions arrived, nobody understood them."

"I—I think I see." She caught her breath. "And that's why Mr. Drake didn't answer, when we tried to call Freedonia?"

"That's why. After all, if you remember, we were there."

She gaped. "But—of course! That first queer call from out here!" She frowned again. "But I still don't quite understand about that other cruiser. How could it have been the *Orion* when it was trying to ram us? And what made it disappear?"

"That must have been the turning point," he said. "The moment the entropic field caught us. We were watching ourselves moving on from that point, but of course it looked as if we were coming back. The lurch we felt was no collision, but just the turn in time."

"But there must have been another cruiser!" She stared at him. "Those unconscious spacemen—could they have come from the *Orion?*"

"I think they did," he said. "Protopopov and his comrades had destroyed their Guard identification and started to Callisto before the *Orion* lost that battle with itself. I think the survivors opened an ametine bomb, when they found themselves trapped in the wreck. I think the commander and Muratori and twenty-six others are still alive there, waiting for Rick and McGee to rescue them and load them on the *Jane—*"

216

She made a baffled shrug.

"But it was days and days ago that you took those men off the *Jane* and turned them over to von Falkenberg."

"I know." He nodded cheerfully. "Seems our mutineering friends got caught in a sort of whirlpool in causation, between the two time tracks. Once around wasn't enough. They woke up on the *Perseus*, and told von Falkenberg about the ship, and helped him pull off a second mutiny. Don't know whether he bought them for Mars, or they bought him for the Soviet. Or p'raps they meant to salvage a load of seetee munitions and equipment for auction to the highest bidder. Anyhow, they followed the *Jane* back here. They had put three men off to explore the ship and secure a sample bedplate, when they saw themselves coming. Seems they made the same blunder, all over again. Seems the *Perseus* was crippled in a battle with itself. Slipped in here to hide, and fell through that ore-grinder."

"Those men we found?" she whispered hoarsely. "Those dead men?"

"The looting party," he said. "The film Rick found shows them coming off the *Perseus*, before it was damaged. Thought I recognized Protopopov and Muratori. Prob'ly Omura with the camera. Von Falkenberg must have been trying to be more cautious than I was, when he sent them off and stayed about, but he failed to anticipate that last misunderstanding with himself!"

"So they're still alive out there? Yet dead in here?"

"Very dead." He grinned bleakly. "Even though they failed to find those seetee weapons. The cameraman caught himself in a door. Muratori cut himself in two. Protopopov got his sample bedplate, and had nowhere to go with it."

She shivered. "I never liked them, but that seems a ghastly way to die!"

"More or less what they were asking for." His hard grin died. "When you consider what they were up to. The Mandate may seem a pretty shaky foundation for interplanetary peace, but it's the best we've got. Trying to

217

break it up with seetee bombs isn't exactly a forward movement in time."

"Maybe you're right." She looked nervously toward the ladder well. "But I still don't feel at home here. The ship's so terribly old, Paul. So terribly dead! Time it hit something! If we can only get away before it does. I'm going out to talk to Rick and Cap'n Rob."

He waited for her, uneasily retracing the curves on his diagram that showed the tangled routes of the vessels trapped in that deadly eddy of time and consequence, trying not to think of the men it had caught, Muratori beneath his mound of frost, Protopopov with that key to illimitable power wrapped in his frozen arms.

The time she was gone seemed endless, but he heard the clang of the valves at last, and climbed down to meet her at the air lock.

"They got inside the wreck!" Her voice reached him through her helmet, faint but triumphant. "That armor plate was too tough for their tools, but it sliced like cheese when they decided to try that queer ore-cutter. They found everything we need to fix the *Jane*."

"Wonderful, darlin'!" He helped unlock the helmet and watched her emerge from the ungainly chrysalis of her armor. "D'you know how much time we have left?"

"Not much, I'm afraid." Her bright elation faded. "Cap'n Rob still can't tell the time or where we are, and it's hard to find out anything by observation, with our chronometers probably running backwards. But Rick has just taken another sight with the instruments, and he says we're only about a million kilometers from where that collision happened—I mean, where it's going to happen."

"Which gives us about five hours to repair the Jane and load those sleeping mutineers and get back to the kind of time where that blowup has already occurred." He grinned suddenly at her white-lipped alarm. "But we can do it, darlin'. 'Cause we've already done it!"

"Rick says we can." She smiled back at him uncertainly. "At first he laughed at the minus-time theory, but now he thinks it's true. And—Paul!" Something caught her breath. "I talked to him and Cap'n Rob about you. And they've both agreed we need you in the firm."

Suddenly, it no longer seemed unfair to take her in his arms.

"In a hurry, Paul?"

He hadn't seen Rick Drake struggling out of his own armor in the dark lock behind her, and that quizzical inquiry startled him. He turned somewhat sheepishly to meet the tired, red-stubbled giant.

"Congratulations!" Rick shifted an armful of salvaged equipment, to give him a hearty handshake. "Quite a relief, when Ann told me how you'd unravelled this nightmare. Glad to have you on our side. Always sort of liked you, Paul. Even when I thought—" He flushed and turned incoherent. "That is, I mean—"

"When you thought I wanted Karen?" Rick's red face turned redder, and Anders grinned. "P'raps I did, once. She's all right, too. But when she got back your tuning diamond and quit her Interplanet job, she wasn't doing it for me."

"I didn't know," Rick whispered. "She didn't say she'd quit."

"Going home on the *Planetania*." Anders nodded. "Fact is, I think she was already getting fed up with the company's business methods, the way I was, though she was nearly too stubborn to admit it. Hood didn't know what had got into her."

"You say she's going back to Earth?"

"P'raps you can stop her," Anders said. "Why don't you sign her up for us? Drake and McGee ought to prosper now, 'cause we've got more to offer mankind than Interplanet ever did. We're going to need somebody in Pallasport, and seems to me the firm could use her pretty head. Why don't you call her, before the *Planetania* takes off?"

"Thanks, Paul." Rick gulped. "I—I'll do that."

Anders turned quickly back to the tall girl in blue.

"We're going to build a lot of things on that bedplate," he told her softly. "Think I'm lucky to be let in the firm."

He caught her hand, and his voice dropped lower. "Darn lucky, darlin'! Used to think you and I were opposites, but p'raps after all we weren't so very far apart."

Rob McGee came back aboard, with a salvaged tuning diamond—the same perfect eight-gram crystal that had puzzled Anders before. He replaced the burned-out stone. Working side by side, Rick and Anders repaired the damaged field coils. The dim lights brightened. The ventilators purred. The *Good-by Jane* was suddenly alive again.

"Ready, Cap'n Rob!" Rick shouted up the ladder well. "Take us out of here."

McGee's sense of space and time was still confused, however, and he let Ann take the controls. She lifted the tiny craft out of that dark place of death, and set it down again on the terrene dome, beside the wreck. Working desperately beneath the pale starlight, they rigged a fabric tube to the hole Rick and McGee had cut in the *Orion's* battered hull.

Eight pounds of air distended it to form a rigid tunnel from ship to ship, but that pressure was not enough to unlock the automatic bulkhead doors. Rick had to slice new openings with that invisible blade, before they could reach the undamaged after compartments.

The first glimpse of the survivors turned Anders ill. The cruiser lay heeled far over, and the men had come to rest in grotesque attitudes against the tilted wreckage. Most of them were naked to the waist, as that last grim battle for oxygen had left them, soiled with smoke and blood and vomit. A few wore sodden bandages. Lifeless faces were fixed in expressions of agony and peace and silent mirth.

Though they had tried to strip themselves of whatever might convict them of treason to the Mandate, Anders could still recognize the blubbery bulk of Protopopov, the dark leer of little Muratori, the sallow smile of Omura. Deep in the saving sleep of ametine, they looked as dead as they soon would be.

220

"Paul!" Rick's worried voice made a startling hollow boom in the fabric tunnel. "I've just taken another sight on the sun and Pallas. We're getting dangerously near the collision point. We haven't got two hours left."

"But we must take these men." Staring at them, Anders shivered. "Not to save their lives—I know they're all coming straight back to kill themselves. But still we've got to take them. 'Cause we *took* them!"

And at last the sleepers were loaded, dragged out through the reactor room and the fabric pipe, and laid to sleep, side by side, in the narrow holds of the tug. Rick sealed the valves and cast off the pipe. With Ann at the periscope, the *Good-by Jane* fled from the empty wreck and the seetee ship.

The deck lurched suddenly.

"I've got it!" Rob McGee nodded his shaggy yellow head, beaming triumphantly. "I've got the feel of time again!"

"Which means we're back where we belong," Anders whispered. "What time is it?"

"Thirty-one minutes after nineteen hundred, March 23rd."

"So we had all of fifteen minutes to spare. Enough, I s'pose." The Earthman grinned uncertainly. "Now don't forget to call Ann and Rick."

"But they're right here—"

"Ann is also back on Obania, getting together a load of supplies for Mr. Drake. And Rick's also at Pallasport, still at work for Interplanet. Both badly discouraged about the proposition of a seetee bedplate. You mustn't say too much, but they both need cheering up. Got to get them ready for what they have to do. Tell Rick to get his space bag packed, and kiss his girl good-by."

"The ship—"

Ann spoke from the periscope, breathlessly.

"It has turned around again—or looks as if it had. Now it's going back again, the same way it came. And I see— *us!*" Something shuddered in her voice. "The *Jane* dropping back beside the wreck. The fabric tube inflating it-self—as if we meant to put those men back where we found them!"

"Don't look at it," Anders urged her gently. "We know enough about what's happening there. From our viewpoint now, the film's running backward. The ship has just been miraculously put together again out of the flame and debris of that collision. It has just begun an insane voyage through intergalactic space and billions of empty years, that will end when its dead builders come alive to take it apart.

"But let it go. 'Magine the rest of its secrets are safe, since it's already trapped von Falkenberg and all those other enterprizing spies. B'lieve we've got all we need. Whatever we build on that bedplate will be our own, and I don't think we need too much that b'longed to *them*."

"I know we don't!" Ann said. "And I'm glad it's gone. Even after Rick had found out how old it was, I couldn't help thinking about those seetee people. Imagining the way they died—or killed themselves and all their world —with those dreadful weapons—"

Her troubled voice trailed away, but she clung to the periscope with a sick fascination until Anders nodded for McGee to take the controls.

"I was seeing ghosts, myself." He caught her trem-bling arm and drew her away from the hooded instru-ment. "Thin, tall ghosts, on those narrow ramps that it was death for us to walk. But they didn't hurt us, darlin'. Fact is, I think we should have thanked them, for setting us straight in time. B'lieve they brought us one last chance not to go the way they did, s'long as we don't build bombs on that bedplate."